HERRINGWOOD MESSIAH

Dedicated to [YOUR NAME HERE]
Thank you for [WHATEVER YOU THINK YOU DID]

ONE

The church today was a far cry from what it was six months ago when Eddie returned from the Underworld. God—Helen, for friends—had gifted the humble building to him. At the time, he didn't care much about the state it was in. The gnawed chicken bones on the floor, the faint smell of vomit, the clearly recognizable smell of Jolene's moonshine all added their charm. That was what Eddie thought, anyway, and it lasted right up until a minute later when he realized he was in a relationship with a woman who probably expected better and definitely deserved it. His new job drawing concept models at the local Century Motors branch gave him the means to give Rosalie what he agreed she deserved, while at the same time making a better home for himself. There were no more chicken bones on the floor now.

Eddie came out of the master bedroom, which used to be Helen's private quarters. At half past eleven in the morning, he woke up painfully early to make sure it was perfect. It had to be. Everything had to be perfect today. Not that he was suddenly a stickler for perfection, but today was an important day. Important enough that going to the Underworld to kill the Devil and rescue the girl was merely a fleeting thought in his head now. At the time, Eddie was worried that Rosalie may have been so overwhelmed by the whole experience that she became his girlfriend out of sheer confusion, and he continued to worry that she would one day come to her senses. He figured that he was punching way above his weight when it came to dating a girl like her. And it had to be said that if you saw the two walking down the street, you probably couldn't help but wonder if Rosalie lost a bet.

Since Eddie was well aware of this fact, too, he only afforded himself just enough money to show Rosalie a good time and keep the Vindicator's thirst quenched so he could drive her to those good times in style. The rest of the money he made went into remodeling the church, but sometimes Eddie worried he would run out of money before things were done. He probably would have, had Rooney not been playing *Fallen Kingdom* with a master carpenter in the neighboring town of May Valley. When Eddie went to see him, they immediately hit it off, and Jonah Craig said he'd do it for a little less. He didn't disappoint at all, and neither did the other workers Eddie hired, so now the church was completely done.

The master bedroom, to start with, was fine, and Eddie went on to check the rest of the building. The chancel and part of the nave had become a spacious living room. Also perfect. Mostly. There was still space for a dinner table, which Jonah had yet to deliver, but Eddie wasn't worried.

Off to one side, he had an open kitchen put in. While he would have been content with eating at the Rising Wind Diner every day, he figured a kitchen would come in handy at some point. Probably. Maybe. It was spotless. As was the guest room to the right of the entrance.

Eddie's initial plan had been to break through the wall of the church and put in a big garage door so he could park the Vindicator right in his house, but Rosalie had talked him out of it. According to her, exhaust fumes and oil stains in the living room weren't "cool" or "awesome," and with the number of strays he dragged in, a guest room would be the better option. He left Rosalie in charge of it, and it turned out fine.

Amongst the strays she referred to were three goths, for whom he had converted the basement into a hangout. They used to hang out in the cemetery with Lilith, but when she went back to Hell to be the next Devil, the goths seemed kind of rudderless, and he felt somewhat responsible for that. The basement probably looked fine as well.

To the left of the entrance was an office. Or rather, everybody just kept calling it an office because nobody wanted to admit it was a room.

If Eddie was going to give the goths a room, it was a simple fact that he would have a place set aside for his best friend since forever. Rooney needed a place to hang when his Wi-Fi was down, which turned out to be always. The whole reason nobody admitted to it being a room, even though there was a bed in there, was so they wouldn't have to talk about living together.

The door to the... *office* opened, and Rooney came out to get a soda.

"Still staring around, are you?" he asked and wandered to the kitchen. "Or are you chickening out?"

"Of course I'm not chickening out. It's not like I have to fight ostriches."

"Really? You just went there?" Rooney grabbed a soda from the fridge. "I'll have you know I didn't chicken out of that and fuck you very much."

"Fuck you too, sweetie."

Eddie smiled. He'd be lost without the guy. Like, literally. Lost *and* dead.

"Woodwork's a little crooked," Rooney casually said, nodding at the door to the staircase that led either to the bell tower, back door, or the basement, depending on your choices in life. In response, Eddie jerked his head around hard enough to hurt his neck and grunted with some disdain.

"Made you look."

"Ha ha, very funny, asshole." Eddie rubbed his neck. "Jonah did a bang-up job with the wood. Drafts should be at a minimum."

But however confident he was in Jonah's work, his eyes still lingered on the doorframe. If there was anything wrong with it after all, he had no idea how to fix it in time. There really couldn't be anything wrong with it.

Oh god, was there something wrong with the frame?

"Jeez, dude. Relax," Rooney said. "I doubt the state of your church slash house is going to influence Rosie's answer. You two were made for each other. If she hasn't run away screaming in the last six months, some discoloration on the beams isn't going to change that."

Eddie looked up at the beams and sighed. "Dammit, Rooney. Stop that! I'm about to ask her the big question, alright? What if--"

He caught a glimpse of the cemetery through the window.

"The goths!"

He went out the back and headed to the shady corner because even though they had a basement to hang in now, goths do as goths do, and the three of them were leaning against the wall. Lupus saw him come first, but because he was committed to being a wolf, he didn't say anything. Scar did.

"Hey, what's up, Ed?"

"Hey guys," Eddie said and immediately apologized to Asphyxia. "Sorry, it's just a figure of speech."

"I know, dear," she answered theatrically and winked. "You

made my operation possible; you get a pass."

"Awesome. So, hey, check this out. Could you hang in the basement for a bit? I need the cemetery for a while."

Scar looked confused. "What do you need a cemetery for?"

Eddie leaned in and, with a hushed voice, said, "I'm going to ask Rosalie the big question."

"In a cemetery?!" Asphyxia burst, surprising herself with that reaction. She took a moment to compose herself, cleared her throat, and said, "I'll be in the basement."

Lupus followed her, and Scar patted Eddie on the shoulder. "Good luck, man."

Eddie saw far too little of Rosalie these days. He had his job and the remodeling, and she was balancing her job at city hall with helping out her father at the police station so he could take the occasional day off. Something that didn't happen often when the entire police force consisted of a whole two people.

He checked the time. Wouldn't be long before Rosalie would arrive, so he really didn't have time to get invested in anything else. Still, she wouldn't be here so soon that he didn't have to stand around like a dumbass with his hands in his pockets.

Like some creepy weirdo that hung around cemeteries for no reason.

"Well, damn..." he muttered to himself and lit a cigarette. Laughing, he leaned against the wall his gothic friends usually occupied.

"What's so funny, Sterling?"

He looked at Rosalie as she walked into the cemetery and took a moment to watch her move. Sometimes he tried to find a flaw in her because logic dictated there had to be at least one. Nobody this perfect would willingly spend their precious time with the likes of him. Maybe she was an angel sent by Helen because she felt sorry for him, and if so, he was okay with that.

"I'm goth now, Watson."

"Nice to see you're branching out. That rock 'n' roll schtick was getting old," she joked and came in for a kiss. "What did you summon me for, dark prince?"

"Romance. Come."

Eddie pulled her along to the last row of graves, and Rosalie hoped with all her heart that he wasn't implying they were going to have sex on one of them. She considered herself very open-minded, but this just seemed a tad--

She froze as she saw the headstone Eddie stopped at.

Rosalie Watson - Daughter, friend.

She broke a few awkward moments of icy silence by snapping at him.

"I don't know what your plans are, Edward Sterling, but if this is your idea of romance, you might have me confused with Asphyxia."

"What?! No! What are you thinking?"

"I haven't been back here since..." She stared at her own grave. "Am I still in there?"

She preferred not to think about the logistics too much. They arrived in the Underworld as souls, but she never felt disembodied. When they left the Underworld, she didn't return as a ghost of any kind.

"Well, I'm not going to dig for it, if that's what you're asking," Eddie said, "but I assume we are. At least we're next to each other."

Eddie nodded at the hole his body was tossed in. A wooden cross that was already showing signs of decay stated his name, and that was it; nothing particularly dignified about it. Helen, Lilith, and Rooney buried him quick and cheap since he wasn't supposed to be gone for long.

"Please explain to me how this is even remotely romantic," Rosalie demanded.

"We had our first date here."

She squinted at him. "I don't think I was here for that."

Eddie let out a short chuckle. He was the only one who considered it a first date, but he stuck to his guns on it. When a demon came and killed Rosalie by mistake, Eddie got the blame for it. He obviously couldn't be at the funeral, considering her father, the Chief of Police, was there, so he had to settle for saying his goodbyes in the evening when everybody was gone.

"Wasn't an ideal date, no. The day of your funeral, I came here and sat with you for a while. I played--"

"Oh!" Rosalie's eyes widened. "'Safety Dance'! That was you?"

"You heard that?!"

Rosalie slowly shook her head and stared at her grave.

"No... Maybe," she spoke softly. "It's like a memory, but not my own, and veiled in fog. Is that how it's supposed to go, you think?"

"I don't think it's supposed to go at all. We weren't exactly following the rules."

Eddie reached into his pocket and fiddled around with something in there. Rosalie wasn't really expecting anything, but she had a strong feeling as to what he was fiddling with.

"We've been together for six months now," Eddie said, trying hard not to stutter and unsure if he should be looking directly at her. "To me, it feels like much longer, obviously. I'm not even sure how long we've known each other, but I think I know you well enough to be able to ask you this..."

From his pocket, he produced a blue velvet box and held it out for Rosalie. She swallowed uncomfortably, her eyes darting back and forth between the box and Eddie.

"Oh, Eddie... I, ehm... Don't think--"

Then Eddie flicked the box open to reveal a set of keys.

"Do you wanna move in with me?"

Rosalie let out a long, relieved sigh and clutched her chest. "Oh, thank God."

"What, you thought I was proposing?" he answered with an amused smirk.

Rosalie laughed away the nerves and nodded. Then the nerves came right back when Eddie's face went all serious, and he reached into his other pocket.

"Well..."

But before he could push the joke any further, he couldn't help laughing. "Don't worry. It's been only six months; I'm gonna take a whole lot longer than that to propose. I'm not a rockstar, for Christ's sake."

"In that case, yes. Yes, Eddie Sterling, I will move in with you."

She held him tight and kissed his neck, which made him twitch because it tickled, so his only defense now was to do the same thing to her. The moment started to snowball up to the point that Rosalie had to stop it and say, "I'm not going to have sex on my own grave."

Eddie, being a man, hadn't considered that as a reason not to have sex, but since it turned out to be one, he involuntarily glanced at his own grave.

"No!" Rosalie told him and gave him a push to snap him out of it.

"Alright. Okay. Shit." Eddie scratched behind his ear and put his other hand on his hip. "How about the bedroom?"

"How about Rooney?"

"Ehm... I kinda wanted you to myself--"

Rosalie covered her face and shook her head. "Jesus, Eddie. I'm not talking about a three-way! What does Rooney think about me moving in?"

Eddie shrugged. As much as he loved the guy, Rooney could either deal with it or go set up his own Wi-Fi somewhere else. Besides, he already knew Rooney could deal with it because he was the first one Eddie talked to when he decided to ask Rosalie.

"He was pretty stoked on the idea. If he wasn't my best friend, I'd feel threatened by him."

Rosalie took Eddie's hand and pulled him along to the church.

He wasn't quite sure if the sex thing was still on, but he just went along and hoped for the best.

As it turned out, Rosalie did want to involve Rooney in their activities, but the activities weren't very bedroom-based. Rooney had been waiting for them to come back in and stuck his head around the corner of his door to check if the footsteps he heard were indeed theirs.

"And?" he asked, about as excited as if it was his own girlfriend moving in.

"Yes," Rosalie answered with a big smile.

Rooney nodded. "Alright, I'll move out tomorrow."

Eddie frowned. This wasn't the plan. He loved Rosalie, for sure, but he also loved Rooney. There was no reason they couldn't coexist. "What?!"

"Yeah, I thought about it some more," Rooney said matter-of-factly. "You two don't need me around. I know you, Ed. You didn't leave the confessional in for the hell of it. There is going to come a moment that I will catch you two in there, and it'll just be awkward all the time."

Rosalie snorted. "Robert Rooney, you're not going anywhere. You and Eddie were a thing long before I came around; far be it from me to break you up. You're staying."

"You're pretty cool about it, Rosie." Rooney nodded approvingly. "Our favorite idiot is lucky to have you."

"Your favorite idiot is right here," Eddie muttered.

Rosalie ignored him. "You'll just need to be a lot louder so we can hear you coming."

"And we should be less loud," Eddie muttered, "so he doesn't hear us--"

"No," Rosalie stopped him. "Just... no."

She pulled Eddie toward the front door, and Rooney took this as his cue to get back to whatever he was doing. Eddie, however, started to tug back and looked in the direction of the bedroom.

"Sex now?"

"Dad now."

Eddie froze. Not that he disliked her father; quite the contrary. He had a lot of respect for the man, but he was never sure the feeling was mutual, which may have had something to do with him indirectly being the reason Rosalie got killed. Or, as if that wasn't enough, there was the time Eddie broke into the psychiatrist's office for Asphyxia, an issue that was basically left unresolved. That, and Eddie's frequent visits to the drunk tank in a life before Rosalie, was enough reason to keep contact with Vernon Watson to the bare minimum.

"Oh, grow a pair!"

"The one pair is fine, thank you."

"Then work with those. You'll have to be around my father every so often. Kinda comes with the girl."

Eddie knew, but he still pursed his lips. "Don't make me go with you to tell him I'm taking away his daughter again. He hates me enough as it is."

"Dad doesn't hate you. He just... likes you less."

"Less than what? Cheeseburgers?" Eddie looked back at the bedroom one more time. "Can't we just go in there and forget about it?"

Rosalie tugged him back into motion. "If you're worried about my father now, you should see him when I just stop going home and he comes looking for me."

She had a point, Eddie thought. She always had a point. Being "liked less" for merely dating the Chief of Police's daughter would probably be preferable to being "wanted" for kidnapping the Chief of Police's daughter. Terrible waste of a good excuse to go to the bedroom, though.

"I'll meet you at the car," he said. "Gonna grab my coat."

Rosalie squinted at him. "Coats are usually by the front door."

She really wanted to give him the benefit of the doubt, but it wasn't unreasonable to assume he would flee out the backdoor and pretend to be lost just to get out of seeing her father.

Eddie nodded. "Yes. In a normal house. Say what you will, but we are not normal."

She had to agree with him there.

"So, my coat is under the bed."

"Why is it under the bed?"

"Because I dropped it next to the bed last night after taking Orpheus out for exercise. And when I cleaned the place up this morning, I kicked it under the bed."

"I have several questions," Rosalie stated. "May I?"

"Please, go ahead."

"Who is Orpheus? What the hell are you doing up before noon? And, since when do you clean up?"

Eddie processed her questions before answering and nodded when he had all the words in order.

"The car. *The Vindicator*. I've named him Orpheus." Seemed rather obvious to Eddie, but he knew Rosalie wasn't into cars like he was. He went on, "I got up early to make sure the church was perfect because I was going to ask you to move in."

"Babe, you came to get me out of literal Hell. You think some discoloration on the beams is going to influence my decisions?"

Eddie looked up.

"Made you look," Rosalie giggled and gave him a kiss. "See you at the car. Don't keep a girl waiting."

He gave her a thumbs-up and rushed to the bedroom. His leather jacket was right where he left it, and he took it with him without putting it on. He didn't exactly need the jacket in this weather, but it was the male equivalent of a purse. His house keys, car keys, and usually his cigarettes were in it. When he came out of the bedroom, Asphyxia came up from the basement and stopped him.

"How did it go?" she whispered.

"She said yes," Eddie answered proudly. "So that means you're gonna have to stop accidentally trying to catch me in the shower."

"I never-- I wasn't trying--"

"I'm sure you weren't. I'm just saying you'll have to start knocking before you burst in here. All of you." Eddie put on his jacket at that point, mostly to signal Asphyxia he was heading out. "Next thing you know, you'll be walking in on us doing it on the couch."

Asphyxia nodded, but the twinkle in her eyes suggested there would be no knocking ever. Eddie pretended not to see it and headed for the door.

Two

Lilith's black leather boots thumped through the fine art deco hallway. She always enjoyed the sound—it made her feel important. A lot of employees came through here, but none of their shoes quite sounded the way hers did. Some of theirs squeaked. But the looks she got when passing those employees bothered her sometimes.

Literally the only reason she got this job was because she was her father's daughter. While it wasn't true nepotism, since only legitimate offspring of the Devil could run the Underworld, she still felt like people thought Daddy's girl had taken over.

Some of the changes she implemented weren't popular either, but the use of sinergy—the energy refined from sin washed off souls in Purgatory—had been downright wasteful under her father. It was her responsibility to generate enough sinergy to power the Afterlife, and with Heaven regularly adding new districts to accommodate every half-assed religion people came up with, they needed to be more efficient. Thankfully, even with humanity's declining interest in divine worship, or perhaps because of it, there were still enough deals to be made. While Lilith strived to keep her deals fairer than her father did, she still managed to generate a steady influx of souls. Along with the standard arrivals, of course. Everybody went through here, saints and sinners; how long you stayed depended on which one of the two you were. A Samaritan who spent her life bottle-feeding orphaned puppies was going to be out of here far sooner than, say, Jeffrey Dahmer. Serial killers are kind of obvious, but a Samaritan? Dog person. She kicked kittens.

But once the sin was washed off, everybody got a ticket for the Number 9 and a top-of-the-line, comfortable journey to Heaven. Even the Samaritan.

Numbering was a bit odd, though. There was only one train, and nobody knew why it had the number nine. Souls didn't care, though. For them, it was the only way to get eternal peace. Or eternal parties, depending on your choice of Heaven.

However, when Lilith went through a door and entered the Purgatory district, she was in the company of souls that were far from that point in their journeys. And, after a brisk walk, she found herself in the company of the smartest soul this side of Heaven: the esteemed Dr. Ignacio.

The good doctor's number had already come up long ago, and a ticket lay ready and waiting for him. But since his arrival in the Underworld and subsequent forced employment under Lilith's father, he had been able to increase his knowledge infinitely further than he could ever have imagined. The tools and information available to him here made him choose to stay and absorb every morsel of wisdom he could until his brain would literally become too big for his head. He already had a fair idea of how to deal with that anyway.

When Lilith found him, he was standing in front of a large

window, intently looking down at something with his arms behind his back.

"I must say, doctor, I find it a little disagreeable to have my presence requested at R&D only to find you are not actually in R&D."

"I apologize, Ms. Lilith," Ignacio said without really looking at her. "Your father sometimes wouldn't even come at all, so I expected you to at least take your time."

"There's a new Devil in town, doc. I might be busy, but I think listening to my employees works better than setting them on fire."

Ignacio chuckled. "You might be onto something there, Ms. Lilith."

"Just Lilith is fine." She looked down into the circular room Ignacio was so interested in. "What are we looking at?"

All she saw was a naked young man behind a desk with a telephone on it, which he was watching as intently as Ignacio was watching him. Didn't seem very terrible at all.

Ignacio brought a walkie-talkie up to his mouth and said, "Dr. Fian, go ahead."

A few seconds later, the phone on the desk rang, and the young man grabbed it without hesitation.

So far, so good, Lilith thought. But she was mistaken. The moment he brought the phone up to his head, sparks flew, his body flashed bright enough to show his skeleton inside, and his smoking remains fell out of the chair.

The brightness of the electricity surging through him made Lilith jerk back. "Whoa!"

"Nice, yes? I rigged it up--" Ignacio said but interrupted himself by raising his hand.

With the smoke still rising out of his ears, the young man got up and got back in the seat to watch the telephone like a hawk with a sniper rifle.

"Jeez, what's his problem?"

"Telemarketer," Ignacio said. "Or, to be precise… phone-scammer, but those are just a variant of the same strain. We've finally found a use for them."

"Really? Imagine the sinergy we could get out of them. Maybe we can start taking weekends off!"

"I'm sorry, ma'am. Telemarketers and their ilk are irredeemable, but we have found a way to generate some sincome from them."

Lilith raised an intrigued eyebrow.

"I have put them to work. We're in the telemarketing business now," Ignacio said with a hint of pride.

Lilith kept her eyebrow raised. A very efficient way of posing a question, she had found.

"Hm, yes," Ignacio continued. "There's no shortage of companies that keep believing telemarketing is effective, so now we're offering the most voracious and persistent telemarketers in exchange for their souls, or the CEO's souls, rather. Granted, most companies don't have a lot of soul left, but I've checked with Accounting, and we can turn a profit."

"And Legal?"

"They don't foresee any problems as of yet, but they do require you to sign off on it before we can take it out of the beta stage."

Lilith crossed her arms and considered it. Not a bad idea at all. Otherwise, they would just have to waste time and energy herding all those souls into the incinerator. She'd seen it before: the first few would go in willingly, but as soon as the rest found out what was going on, they'd have a riot on their hands.

"As usual, Dr. Ignacio, you prove why you're our brightest mind."

"Oh, I wouldn't go so far--"

"Take the compliment, doctor. You didn't have me come out here for shits and giggles."

Finally, Ignacio managed to direct his complete attention to Lilith. "That's not why I called for you." He started walking. "I've learned something during my weekly visit with Mr. Domino--"

"Wait, weekly visit? How? He won't even crack the door for me. I only ever get to talk to him through that stupid intercom he had installed."

Dr. Ignacio nodded apologetically. "He might have some issues with Devils in the House of Fates. Your father really messed things up in there."

"I am not my father!"

"I know, Ms. Lilith. And he will, too, given enough time."

Lilith grumbled to herself. This was exactly what she was trying to avoid: people likening her to her father as if she were the same kind of evil. She scoffed. Her brand of evil was far better. Nicer, she would say.

"Nevertheless," Ignacio continued. "Mr. Domino informed me that there is a lot of activity around the church in Herringwood. Fate-wise."

Lilith shrugged. "There's a lot of Fate activity everywhere."

"Yes, and if it concerned any place other than Herringwood, he would not have mentioned it, I'm sure. But since you and Ms. Helen are above averagely interested in Mr. Sterling and his friends, we thought you might want to know."

That was true. Helen more than Lilith, but they both did consider the Herringwood bunch their friends.

"What kind of activity?"

"Nothing very pressing as of yet, but it does seem that the Current Day Saints are hanging around there now."

"Pf!" Lilith knew of them. She'd done a lot of reading up since she started her job here. "Those jokers? They think Eddie is Jesus now?"

She laughed. The idea! She'd rarely come across a more unlikely Jesus than Eddie.

"He did technically return from the dead, ma'am."

Lilith stopped laughing. This was indeed the sort of thing that could cause these kinds of misunderstandings. Nevertheless, she was 99% sure Eddie wasn't actually Jesus Christ, and the fact that the CDS was barking up his tree sort of confirmed it.

"If we can't even find Jesus, how do they hope to?"

"They don't know we can't find him," Ignacio answered. "And to be honest, for the last thousand years, we haven't really been looking very hard anymore either. That soul's kind of a write-off at this point."

When they arrived back in the hallway, their paths split. Ignacio needed to get back to R&D and Lilith to her office.

"I'll call Domino and tell him to keep an eye on things," she said. "And for future reference, doctor: a phone call would have sufficed."

Ignacio nodded. He knew. Perhaps he did want to show off a little bit to impress the new boss. He put his hands in the pockets of his lab coat and watched Lilith head for the elevators. Ignacio knew a lot of things in several degrees of certainty, and amongst those things was the reasonable certainty that she'd make an excellent Devil.

Asshole.

Somewhere, far away, a voice was telling Eddie he was an asshole. However, his subconscious often confronted him about a wide variety of things, so Eddie didn't pay much attention to it and made a point of staying asleep. Maybe he would have taken a bigger interest if Chief Watson hadn't insisted on driving the night before.

After screwing with Eddie for a bit, the Chief invited them for dinner to celebrate. Had Eddie been the one to drive, he wouldn't have drunk at all. Considering he drove almost everywhere these days, what used to be a little was now too much.

His subconscious was persistent today, though, and for the first time ever, it resorted to shaking him about. This was a very new experience for him, so it was time to wake up and figure out how a subconscious was able to do that.

When he opened his eyes, it took him a few moments to piece the situation together. The drawer he had cleared out for Rosalie was open, and the bag they picked up at her house after last night's dinner sat on the floor. Next to the bed was where things got interesting. Rosalie stood there in an unmistakable "you fucked up" pose, and the reason for that pose was dangling off her finger.

"Wake up, asshole. What the Hell is this?"

Eddie rubbed his eyes and took a better look. "A rather attractive pair of lacy white panties, which I hope you are going to show off for me."

"These aren't mine, loverboy."

Quite a shame, Eddie thought. They'd look great on her tanned skin. But that thought was stomped into oblivion when Rosalie took both sides between her fingers and spread them out for him to read the message somebody had scribbled on them with a sharpie.

You were great. Should do it again. -Helen

"Oh..." And that's all Eddie had for now.

"Not *oh*. *Oh* isn't gonna cut it. I want an explanation!"

Eddie shifted his gaze upward and met Rosalie's. She was definitely not pleased and he could probably have chosen something better to say.

"Where did you find those?"

"Stuck in the back of the drawer you cleared for *my* underwear!"

Eddie got up and wriggled into his jeans. Normally he didn't have any sort of problem being naked around his girlfriend but in this situation, it seemed inappropriate. He tried salvaging it with a joke. "Heh, the irony, right?"

Rosalie tossed the panties in his face and scowled. Eddie caught them as they fell down, looking stupid.

"Need to get more jokes out of your system before you explain why I found God's underwear in your drawer?"

Eddie scratched his head. He wasn't entirely sure why either.

"Remember when we woke up after the going-away party?"

"Waking up is usually the only thing anyone remembers about any party involving Jolene's moonshine and Helen's infinite-pour trick."

"Yeah, well, I also remember you waking up without pants, which I rather enjoyed. But when we went looking for your jeans, I found these on the altar."

He waved the panties at her and realized too late how inappropriate it looked.

"And you didn't think to tell me?"

"I was going to, but then Scar woke up in a puddle of what we all hope was his own vomit, and Asphyxia came to get me because they thought Rooney died, then I just forgot."

Rosalie threw her hands up. "How do you forget a pair of God's panties?"

"By waking up with a half-naked you, goddammit! Do you have any idea what that did to the me of six months ago? Hell, it still does that to the me of right now."

Rosalie put her hands on her hips and smirked at him. With a sigh, she said, "It's bad enough I have to live with the fact that my boyfriend slept with the one woman I know I can't compete with, and now I also have to find out you kept her panties! Is this what I can expect? A relationship full of affairs?"

Eddie shrugged. "Well, if you plan to have affairs, maybe. I'd prefer if you didn't but I've wanted you for so long that at this point I'm open to discussion." He raised his finger to stop her from replying, and added, "I'm pretty good at being drunk, and even with Jolene's moonshine in play, I'm sure I'd have some recollection of sleeping with God. And while we're on the topic of uncertainties, I'm also not so sure Helen could compete with you, so... there!"

Rosalie tried to remember anything of that night, but she'd been as blacked out as everybody else. The only ones who might possibly know what went on that night were Helen and Lilith. Well... Helen definitely remembered, because panties.

"There's no point arguing about this," she finally said. "We'll forget about this because everybody involved was so blackout drunk it might as well not have happened, but you will explain to me why you've kept a pair of used panties for six months. Is there a kink you neglected to mention? Do I need to put a lock on my underwear drawer?"

It sounded a lot like he was being let off the hook, so Eddie was more than willing to answer all her questions.

"No kinks that I'm aware of, but I'm keeping my options open. Just like you can do with your drawer. I might want to pick out something for you to wear sometime."

"Babe, no offense, but there's a difference between dressing sexy and dressing pornographic, and previous experiences teach us that you don't know that difference." She nodded at the panties still in his hand. "Well?"

"I guess I just forgot I pocketed them. They're really thin, you know. Like a cobweb on a bow."

He rubbed the fabric to demonstrate; a move no man should ever make in front of the woman who caught him with said panties.

"Err, yeah... Anyway... I guess they must have gotten tangled up with my own stuff to wind up in the drawer."

Without even thinking about it, he stuffed Helen's panties in his pocket. Again. He was genuinely surprised to see Rosalie's displeased smirk.

"Really?" she snapped.

"Well, what do you want me to do?"

"With a used pair of panties that somebody wrote on?"

"I get the impression you want me to throw them away."

"I want you to throw them away," she stated.

Eddie would have, too. He didn't really have a use for worn panties, usually. But it seemed wrong to throw these away.

"These are God's. They're, like, a relic."

Rosalie didn't buy it. "A relic, really?"

Eddie nodded, though he knew she'd throw a perfectly logical argument at him. Right about... now.

"I bet you wouldn't just be stuffing the Shroud of Turin down your pants like that."

This surprised Eddie. Between them, Rosalie was usually the smart one. Granted, her facilities might have been a bit clouded due to seeing her boyfriend stuff another woman's panties in his pocket, but if *he* knew the counterpoint he was about to make, surely she would, too.

"Considering what we know about the Shroud, it would make more sense to just jam that down my pants instead of a garment we know for a fact comes from a deity."

Rosalie flipped him off with a smile. "Don't make a habit of being smart."

Eddie wasn't worried. "So we're good?"

"We're good. But you don't get to bitch if I ever get my shot."

Eddie puckered his lips. A question burned in his mind but he wasn't sure he wanted to hear the answer to it. Before his mind could send his mouth the memo, he heard himself say, "Who's your, ehm, shot?"

Rosalie just crossed her arms, probably not accidentally pushing up her breasts, and shot him a coy smile.

"No, seriously," Eddie insisted. "It's Jason Momoa, isn't it?"

"Too easy."

"So I'm right."

Rosalie didn't feel like looking at his smug face anymore and chose to torture it right off him. "You are *so* right, baby, ooh! I would definitely let him put those muscular, tattooed arms around me and squeeze until I'm just a quivering, spineless, *wet* mess--"

Eddie stuck his fingers in his ears. "La-la-la! La-la-please stop talking!"

She leaned in and kissed him on the cheek to signal she had stopped talking, but when he took his fingers out of his ears, she whispered, "Don't ever think you can psych me out, sweetheart."

Her warm breath on his ear, her deliciously smug chuckle, everything made him want to grab her and pull her onto the bed. And she knew it. If she was any less conscientious she could own him like a pet, probably. Thankfully for Eddie, who would happily let her, Rosalie was nothing but kind. Yet no sex was to happen. There was a more urgent matter to deal with.

"Put on some more clothes and meet me in the living room," she said before leaving. "There's cake."

THREE

The Bible states that jealousy is a sin. Eddie didn't read the Bible and was indeed very jealous of the big slice of cake Rosalie had set out on the table with a candle on it. He would have really liked a slice of his own, but according to Watson birthday traditions, nobody got any cake until the birthday-person in question had theirs. Eddie thought this was a stupid tradition. He would have ignored it completely if Rosalie wasn't in control of the cake-cutting knife and guarded the cake like a sphinx. All he could do now was hasten the arrival of the guest of honor, so he got up and went to bang on the door of the office.

"Rooney! Put your pants on and get your slow ass out here, pronto!"

"I'm wearing pants already!"

"Really? You're at home. The Hell is wrong with you?"

"Momentary lapse of reason."

Eddie was about to order Rooney out of the office when

somebody started enthusiastically using the cast iron knocker he'd left on the door because it looked cool, instead of installing a proper doorbell that didn't hurt your fingers if you used it wrong.

"Now what?"

He opened the door and saw two men he didn't recognize at all, but judging by how they were dressed the same, they were clearly here to fleece him for money in the name of some company he didn't care for. He decided to cut this off before they could start it because there was cake in his future.

"I've got all the accordions I need, thanks."

He proceeded to shut the door, but the first guy put his foot between it. A callous move, considering they were working with a heavy oak church door. A fact Eddie was very much aware of, so he looked at the man with a vicious smile and swung the door shut as hard as he could. But it didn't shut. Instead, it hit the man's shoe and the wood creaked under the pressure.

"Hm, yes." Eddie looked down. "Surplus store army boot. That kind of inventiveness earns you two minutes."

"Hello, I'm Brother Yaeger and this is Elder Rigby. We would like to talk to you about the Lord Jesus Christ."

Eddie sighed. "Ugh... Rosie, get the Mormon-stick!"

"What's a Mormon-stick?" she called back.

"Anything sharp will do!"

Yaeger didn't seem too pleased, but his older colleague stepped forward.

"Sir," he started to explain, "we are not Mormons."

"Yeah, Church of Jesus Christ of Latter-Day Saints. That's a lot more words than just 'Mormon', so you're Mormons."

"No, forgive me, we're neither of those."

Eddie examined the men. They sure looked like Mormons. White blouse, black tie, black pants. Except for the army boots, but with the amount of broken feet they must have been bringing home, this development was to be expected.

"We're Current Day Saints," Rigby continued.

"Sounds a little arrogant..."

"We don't think we are actual saints. We used to be, err... Mormons, but our group broke away for a more hands-on approach."

Rosalie also came to the door and held out a large carving knife for Eddie. "Is this the Mormon-stick?"

"Oh, thank you. Yeah, this will do nicely. But these guys aren't Mormons."

"They look like it, though."

"I know, right?" Eddie agreed. "But look, they've got army boots. And a story to go with it. I kinda wanna hear where it goes."

"Okay. Keep the knife in case you change your mind," Rosalie sighed. "But wrap it up when Robbie comes out."

Rosalie turned around and went back to keep an eye on the cake. Eddie might have been busy now, but she didn't know the goths' attitude toward birthday cake, so she decided to be safe instead of sorry.

"Continue," Eddie said, and as a joke only he found amusing, wiggled the knife around. "Better make it good."

The older Saint was torn between bringing their story to the people and not getting cut by the people, but the younger took over.

"The Current Day Saints believe that if we wish to get to Kolob, we should make an effort to actually go there."

"What's a Kolob?"

"A planet. Our promised land."

"Cool," Eddie stated with an actual hint of sincerity.

Yaeger took this as his cue to get enthusiastic about it. "Yes. In a nutshell, the Latter Day Saints believe they go there when they die, but our leader, the great Mr. Hall, says it's out there and believes we can go there now--"

Eddie held his hand up. "I am entertained, but there's a bunch of scientists who've never heard of Kolob. They're kinda picky about their planets. Killed off Pluto because it wasn't pulling its weight. I don't have high hopes for your... *planet.*"

"Yes, that's why we're looking for our Lord Jesus Christ. He will be our pilot."

Eddie looked confused. "Wasn't Pilot the one who nailed him to the cross?"

Yaeger had to put in a serious effort to make sure his face didn't yell "dumbass!" without actually saying it.

"Not Pilate," he said, straining to remain polite. "I mean the person who drives an airplane. Or, in our case, a spaceship."

Eddie sputtered up a laugh. The spaceship piloting skills of a two-thousand-year-old carpenter aside, there was the more pressing matter of localizing him. "Good luck with that. Even God herself can't find him."

"God is not a woman!"

Eddie turned the knife in his hand so the sunlight reflected in Yaeger's face. "This is not an argument you want to start with me."

Yaeger wasn't impressed and instead became angry. "I think I can win any argument about God from a man in a Judas Priest t-shirt."

Rigby started tugging on Yaeger's arm. "We've bothered this gentleman long enough, Brother Yaeger."

"Gentleman my left foot," Yaeger hissed as they slinked away.

Eddie made sure they heard his chuckle before he shut the door and then went back to Rooney's office.

"Get the fuck out here! Mommy and Daddy need to talk to you!"

Rather proud of himself, Eddie paraded into the kitchen to put the knife back and caught Rosalie's look.

"What?"

"Mommy and Daddy?" she laughed.

"Practice run. And it worked, look."

Rooney emerged from the office and approached with

trepidation. Like a deer inspecting a pond, he came into the living room and carefully examined his surroundings. Something was up, and, like the deer, his instincts told him to stay alert.

"Why is there cake?"

"Dude, seriously?"

"You should understand my apprehension toward cake, as a gamer."

"How's your apprehension toward birthdays, numbnuts?"

"Birthdays?" Rooney thought for a few moments. "I know it's not your birthday... I'm pretty sure it's not Rosie's either, unless you plan to eat cake alone, pretending you're able to wish her a happy birthday personally--"

"Dude!"

Rosalie put an arm around Eddie. "Aw, that's so... sad. I wish I could believe he was joking."

"How do you know everybody's birthday but your own, you asshat!" Eddie burst. "It's you! Today is your birthday. Happy fucking birthday, now eat your cake because she won't let me have any until you do."

Suddenly, Rooney found himself in a position of great power, and because he was human, he immediately went and abused it.

"Eh. Don't feel like cake, thanks."

And like any human under the yoke of power abuse, Eddie rebelled. He slowly approached Rooney, pointing to something off to the side.

"Right there, next to the couch, beyond your power-drunk cone of vision, is an awesome birthday gift of a level of appropriateness and thoughtfulness the likes you have never seen and never will see from me again. It's all yours because, up to a minute ago, you were my best friend. We can get out of this hole, you and me, be best friends again. Friends who share gifts. *If I get cake!*"

Rooney looked down his nose at Eddie and grinned. Royally, he turned to Rosalie.

"Let him eat cake," he said and started on his own slice while Rosalie brought some for herself and Eddie.

"I'm offended," she said, handing the plate over. "If you were half as determined about me, we could have been dating years ago."

Eddie prodded the cake. It was fluffy and moist. It was good cake. "I'm going to change the subject now."

Rosalie winked. "Good idea."

"Why do you insist on ignoring your own birthday?" Eddie said, nudging Rooney.

"I had nothing to do with being born, and then I had nothing to do with going around the sun several times over. Birthdays are not that much of an event to me."

"Alright then, you nihilistic dick," Eddie stated firmly, "we're not celebrating your birthday. This'll be, err... we'll celebrate you as a person. Your cheerful disposition and countless years of me having to live with that shit."

Rooney patted him on the shoulder. "I'll take it." He stuffed some cake into his mouth and barely waited to continue speaking, "Talking about taking things—you mentioned gifts?"

With a full mouth, Eddie held up his plate. "Busy."

Some whipped cream flew from his mouth, and he started to chuckle, doing his best to not start sputtering. This, of course, caused a chain reaction in Rooney, who got tears in his eyes from trying not to laugh and launch the chewed-up remains of cake.

Rosalie put her plate down and grabbed the box Eddie had strategically hidden right next to the couch.

"Helen give me strength. I'm living with cavemen."

"Happy birthday, nerd," Eddie said.

"Wow, big box." Rooney weighed it in his hands and asked the question that accompanied every gift ever. "What is it?"

A wholly pointless question, since he could have saved himself time, energy, and oxygen by just opening it, instead of looking at Eddie who formally wasn't allowed to answer. As per gift-giving protocol, Eddie gave the only answer he could: "Open it."

So Rooney did, as this was now the last option he had to get his question answered.

"Whoa..."

On top of a fine brown leather jacket was a handwritten note from Mayor Everett.

Pops says hi. Enjoy. -Henry

He looked from Eddie to Rosalie.

"It was his idea," she said.

Rooney took the jacket out of the box and examined it extensively before looking up at Eddie.

"What... Why?"

"It's your birthday, dipshit. Seemed like a good time to get you a gift."

Rooney smirked. "No, I get that. But an ostrich leather jacket? This must have cost--"

"We don't talk about what gifts cost. And this isn't just regular old ostrich leather either." Eddie tapped the note. "That's alpha bird leather, dude."

"You mean--"

"That's Pops."

Rooney touched the jacket to see if it felt any different now than a minute ago. It didn't, but he chose to believe it did and looked at Eddie, who knew what he was thinking.

"I went to Mayor Everett's farm to see if he could maybe get me a good deal on a jacket. Turns out, Pops died. Constantly being angry takes it out of you, I guess. Old bird had a heart attack, can you believe that?"

Rooney could not. He re-examined the jacket and noticed this new information did actually make him feel something. Felt a lot like sympathy, even though he and Pops weren't exactly the best of friends. After Rooney went to Mayor Everett's farm to get ostrich feathers and the bird made a fool of him, he warned Pops he'd be wearing him for a jacket. But he was a formidable bird, and a heart attack seemed undignified. Pops deserved something more... awesome. Rooney decided he'd wear the jacket with pride.

"Try it on," Rosalie said.

Rooney hesitated. He didn't want to find out it didn't fit, though never wearing it at all obviously wasn't an option either, so he did and it felt good.

"How do I look?"

"You kinda look like me," Eddie said.

"Now you've ruined it."

Rosalie got up. "Alright, I'm gonna grab a shower before we go out."

She walked away, and both Eddie and Rooney watched her sway to the bathroom. Eddie elbowed Rooney.

"Dude. Don't ogle my girlfriend like that."

"It's my birthday. I can ogle whatever I want. Who was at the door anyway?"

"Nice deflection."

Rooney nodded by way of thanks.

"Two guys looking for Jesus so he can fly a spaceship they want to build to uh... some planet."

"Kolob."

"That one."

"I've heard about these guys. Current Day Saints, right? They're a real religion now."

Eddie chuckled. "Anybody can do religion these days, huh?"

"Tell that to the Pastafarians."

"Literally the only religion Helen would appreciate. Anyway, get yourself some outside pants because we're going out unless you insist on wearing sweats."

Rooney nodded and trotted back to his office. Eddie leaned back and debated whether or not to seize the opportunity and have more cake. He decided against it because he didn't want to be full when they sat down at the Rising Wind.

Now that he didn't need to stalk cake, he suddenly had a lot of time on his hands and wasn't sure how to spend it. Oddly, as much as Eddie just sat around, very little of his time was actually wasted.

The staircase door opened with its recognizable creak. Most of the doors in the church had a creak but not one was the same. Very handy.

He turned and saw Asphyxia creep out. Appropriately dressed in black, the slender girl would have made a great gothic ninja if the excessive amount of buckles on her didn't jangle with every careful step. She stopped in her tracks when she realized she had been discovered. Motionless, she stood there for a few moments as if facing a T-Rex from the early 90s.

"Hey," Eddie said.

"Hey," she answered.

She relaxed some and held up the neatly folded towel she was carrying.

"Ehm... Heard the water run," she explained, "thought you might need a towel."

Eddie nodded. He guessed as much. "I always bring a towel."

He wasn't even joking. A wise man once told him to do so, which was why he even had one in the trunk of the Vindicator.

"I'm also not in the shower."

Asphyxia nodded and looked at the towel in her hand. "Cool, cool..."

"Rosie's in the shower."

Asphyxia looked up without moving her head. Eddie grinned, because he recognized the mischievous twinkle in her eyes. It was the same as in his own eyes when he was about to see Rosalie naked.

"No. Bad Phyxie," he said. "As much as I hate for you to miss it, you don't get to see Rosie showering either."

"Fine." She balled her fists and marched back to the staircase. "I'll go and lurk in the graveyard again."

"Somebody's gotta keep the dead in line. Before you know it, they start rising."

"Let's hope one of them got buried naked then," she replied snippily and left again.

Eddie chose not to dwell on that. The reason for the goths always hanging in the cemetery—other than adhering to a good cliché—was still unclear to him, and if it had anything to do with seeing naked dead people, he didn't want to know about it either. Whatever the reason, he hoped it wouldn't distract them from attending Rooney's party.

FOUR

Yaeger sat down and slammed the passenger door shut. Angrily, he looked at the church.

"Well, that was a bust."

Rigby glanced over at him and reluctantly agreed. "Yeah, it doesn't bode well for our expectations. But let's not despair just yet. Mr. Hall sent us here for a reason; Sterling might surprise us just yet."

"How?" Yaeger exclaimed. "I really don't see how the Lord would wear a t-shirt glorifying the man who betrayed him."

"It's called hiding in plain sight. The fact that you and I have trouble believing he is the Christ proves that the t-shirt is working. It's quite smart, if you think about it."

Yaeger looked at Rigby in disbelief.

"I'm beginning to understand why we've had no success in finding Jesus Christ. Apparently you're all too blinded by faith to see reason."

"Alright," Rigby said and calmly turned to Yaeger, which surprised the latter. He expected Rigby to get agitated at being accused of his faith getting in the way, but now it seemed to be cause for a reasonable argument.

So Rigby did. "Have you ever listened to Judas Priest?"

"Of course not!"

"Why not?"

"*Judas* Priest. Seems obvious to me."

"God's hooks, Yaeger. You accuse me of seeing no reason, yet you are so narrow-minded I'm surprised any coherent thoughts manage to slip through the gap." Rigby nodded at Yaeger's phone in his breast pocket. "Listen to them some time. Try 'Painkiller.' Some good Christians even believe it is about Jesus Christ."

"You listen to that crap?"

"You would run crying to your mother if you knew what I listened to. And I would tell your mother off for not raising you to broaden your horizons."

"You leave my mother out of this!"

Rigby grinned. He struck a nerve. "Case in point. I assumed your mother raised you wrong, but judging by your response, she is a good woman. I spoke out of ignorance, just like you did."

Yaeger held his mouth shut and pouted at the church. He hated when Rigby made a good point, and it was even worse when he did it with that fatherly tone. Fact of the matter was that they weren't going anywhere, so he might as well make the best of the situation and try Rigby's approach.

"Why are we here anyway? The carpenter we were watching had far more potential."

Rigby nodded. "Yes. But one of our Brothers in Las Vegas took pictures of a woman."

"So did I," Yeager argued. "Surely you'll remember the auburn haired woman entering the carpentry shop. Her hindquarters even looked like God's work. Why would we jump at some dirty pictures a random guy in Vegas--”

“You will not sully the memory of Brother Muller, young man!” Rigby snapped. “His hunches were the stuff of legend. Whenever Brother Muller had a hunch, we listened. The CDS is worse off without him.”

Yaeger bit his lip. He knew Muller and Rigby had been close, and the man’s death still weighed on him.

“I’m sorry. You never told me how he died.”

“A sudden freak sinkhole opened up and their car fell in. Muller and Gardner died on impact... We owe it to them to investigate.”

Yaeger wondered how a sinkhole deep enough to kill two men in a car could open up in downtown Las Vegas, but he didn’t get a chance to ask. The church demanded their attention.

“Rigby. Movement.”

“I see them.”

They watched Sterling, his friend, and the girl enter the car.

“Did you notice something about Sterling’s friend?” Rigby asked, the same way a teacher did when he wanted the kids to learn something from finding the answer.

Yaeger knew what he was asking. “The brand new-looking jacket?”

“Yup. Which implies?”

“I wish you wouldn’t take that condescending tone with me.” Despite that, Yaeger knew what it implied, though it required quite a flex of the imagination. “Clothing the poor?”

Rigby just nodded and reached for the start button, but Yaeger stopped him.

“You’re going to follow them?”

“Of course. Did you want to stay and watch an empty church?”

“No, but, I mean... We’re in a big, black SUV. If we chase a white coupe, they’ll spot us on symbolism alone.”

“They won’t spot us.”

Rigby started the car but waited until the distance between them and the Vindicator was good enough for his tastes.

"They're not expecting to be followed," he said. "They won't notice us; if they do, we break it off and catch them back at the church."

Yaeger rolled down the window. "Or we just follow the infernal noise that vulgar machine is making."

The tail took them in the direction of the diner they passed when they first arrived in Herringwood, and it bothered Yaeger. One of the big drawbacks of spying on people from a car was that they rarely got a chance for a good meal, and the thought of decent food made his stomach rumble. He quietly hoped they'd just keep driving on to May Valley, but fate seemed to enjoy making life hard for him.

Wistfully, he watched how Sterling parked in front of the diner and how Rigby just kept going.

"What do we do now?"

"There," Rigby said to nobody in particular. He braked suddenly and smoothly backed the SUV into a dirt road until they were mostly obscured by hand-planted conifers that looked even more out of place than they did.

"We've got a reasonable view of the diner here. Grab the binoculars and get comfortable."

Yaeger did and wondered which was worse: staring at an empty church or watching people eat while he was hungry.

Eddie parked the Vindicator in his regular spot, right outside from the booth at the Rising Wind diner where he always sat.

"Alright! Let's get this shindig started."

As they got out, Rooney seemed far less enthused than Eddie and chose his words carefully to make it known why.

"I appreciate you going through the trouble of taking me out to a birthday dinner, but we eat at Gina's every other day."

"Problem?"

"No, but... I figured you'd take me somewhere special for a

special occasion."

Eddie snickered and looked at Rosalie.

"He's got a point, though," she said.

"Oh, you're both divas. It's just to get a good base layer for the real party."

"Why do we need a base layer?" Rooney asked, a little worried.

"Because we're going old school, dude. Gina's is just the pre-party. How long has it been that you and I got a little crazy? Between remodeling the church and all the sex I needed to have with Rosie--"

She slapped him on the back of his head.

"--and all the romantic evenings on the couch I needed to have with Rosie, we haven't spent a lot of time together."

"All true, but you didn't answer my question."

"Main party's at Jolene's. We're blacking out tonight, like we used to all the time."

Rooney snickered. "Like you used to. I just grayed out, at best, so I could drag your limp carcass home."

"That's how good a friend I am, dude. I'll put my liver at risk just so you can get to drag me home once again."

As he said that, he noticed something in the treeline marking the start of Solomon's Woods. A hunched-over figure in a ratty trenchcoat tried to hide its face under what appeared to be a wide-rimmed mountie hat that had seen better days. Rooney saw him, too.

"I don't mind if you make friends with more hobos, but could we eat first?"

Eddie was definitely planning to make friends with this hobo but Rooney raised another good point. Not on an empty stomach.

As much as they ate here, this was the first time that a few people yelled "surprise!" completely out of sync. Poorly planned, that.

Rooney was pleasantly surprised anyway. Amongst the

people—most of whom were actually just random guests roped into this by Gina—he noticed Laura. They weren't necessarily birthday-going friends, but it seemed Eddie remembered his interest in her. It was Laura's presence that made him decide to get into a window cleaner's basket, against his better judgment. Unfortunately, Rooney spent all his courage-surplus on going up in the basket, and didn't have any left to actually ask her out, so nothing ever came from it. Maybe he'd be able to balance talking-to-a-girl drunk and don't-sexually-harass-a-girl drunk later to see what came of that.

Eddie was in the middle of apologizing-to-a-girl sober. He greeted the Rising Wind's owner and Employee of the Month for Infinity, Gina, who immediately had questions for him.

"I thought you were calling ahead so we'd be ready for the surprising and the yelling."

"I do realize now that I forgot to do that. You want us to go out and come back in again?"

Gina shook her head. On the list of silly things he said, this didn't even break the top fifty.

"Alright, hon... I made sure no one sat in your booth, and I've got a bunch of Chicken Legs firing up right now. Have a seat. Nice jacket, Robbie. You two look like brothers."

Eddie laughed as Rooney threw his hands up and sighed. He gestured for Rooney and Rosalie to go ahead and take a seat. Before he joined them, he had one more thing to ask of Gina. "Can I get one portion to go?"

"You're not leaving already!"

"It's not for me," he said. "Have you seen the hobo by the trees?"

"Hon, how could I not? Gives me the creeps, that one. I don't like to refuse people service, I don't, but I do hope he doesn't try to come in." She leaned on the counter and stared down Eddie. "Which he will, if you go out there and feed him."

"No, he won't."

"Yes, he will. If you feed them, they just keep coming back for more."

Normally, he would agree with that, but in this case, he thought the counterintuitive option was the best one. "I have a plan that will achieve just the opposite."

"Oh great," Gina sighed. "You've got a plan."

"Don't worry about it," Eddie said and took a seat with his friends, where Rooney was in the process of unwrapping the gift Laura gave him. Eddie was mostly curious to find out if it was better than his gift, and judging by how wide Rooney's eyes got, this came very close. Closely inspecting a figurine of a warped and twisted humanoid, Rooney muttered some praise as he inspected the detailing on its wings.

"Whoa," he finally said, "the Harbinger. I've fought him."

He looked up at Laura. "This is too much, I can't--"

"It's nothing," Laura countered. "My father knows a guy who knows a guy. Give me your *Fallen Kingdom* tag, and we'll call it even when you help me beat the Harbinger."

Eddie studied both of them. Even though he had the girlfriend to end all girlfriends, that didn't mean he lost his ability to see when a girl was interested. He was never sure that Laura and Rooney were a match, but now that this Harbinger guy sat there on the table, it became clear they had more common ground than he assumed.

"Hey, maybe you can take Laura to the fantasy fair next time. You know I love you dude, but I'm not gonna elf up like some trophy boyfriend every time you wanna go out."

Rooney blushed. He thought that was a great idea, but he'd never have brought it up. Mostly because Laura was already dating Christa, who had just drawn up a coupon on a napkin for "one free ride in my windowwashing~~basset~~ basket" and threw it on the table before putting an arm around Laura.

"Uhm..." Rooney started to stammer, "I think Christa has an

opinion about it, too. Heh."

Laura gave Christa a peck on the cheek. "She won't mind. Neither will Mitch."

"Mitch?!"

"Hm hm," Laura answered as casually as ordering the soup of the day. "Eddie won't mind either, right?"

"Eddie?" This time it was Rosalie who sounded surprised, though Eddie could hear a healthy amount of indignation in there as well.

"Yes, Eddie," he said. "Not recently, obviously. You might remember there was a lengthy period where I wasn't your boyfriend. I tried to fill that hole in my existence with all other girls except for Christa."

"Oh, you tried," Christa corrected him, "but I was also more interested in Rosie."

Rosalie laughed. Everybody was interested in her, which made it that much more impressive she didn't have an attitude to match it.

Gina planted several plates on the table and looked around, a little disappointed she'd have to make two trips to get everybody served. She wasn't one to pat herself on the back—aside from her employee of the month for infinity gag—but she got quite some satisfaction from bringing a complete order in one go. However, she could blame the white paper bag she was also somehow holding. She put it in front of Eddie instead of a plate.

"Thanks," he said. "I do get a plate, too, right?"

"Yeah, but I'm gonna do you last because of this bag."

"Oh, good. That gives me some time to deal with it then."

He grabbed the bag and got up again.

"Where are you going?" Rosalie asked, rightfully worried. Every time Eddie did something out of the ordinary, like walking away from a Chicken Leg dinner, there were usually out-of-the-ordinary events that followed to put everything back in balance.

"Quick delivery," he answered and went off before anyone could ask anything else.

"He's got a plan," Gina reassured Rosalie, thus achieving the opposite.

With some trepidation, she watched as her boyfriend and his plan practically skipped by the window. She lost sight of him before he got where he was going, which was the treeline. In any other situation, Eddie would have stayed away from disheveled characters like the one he was approaching, but the first moment he laid eyes on the hobo, he saw right through the poor disguise. It wasn't a hobo, and he had no ill intent. The figure had stuffed his body into the old trenchcoat, but it barely managed to contain him, and it was painfully obvious that he was trying to make himself smaller so the coat would reach the ground and hide his... base.

"Hello, Chickenman," he said apologetically from under the big hat.

"Hey, George. What's with the outfit?"

"So people won't get scared when they see me..."

Eddie snickered. It was always nice to find a smoke demon, and the Devil's personal—if somewhat simple—assistant, had self-awareness. But the disguise wasn't helping as much as George thought.

"I don't think you're supposed to be out here, and that's probably why."

George nodded. "But I wanted to smell the chickens."

"Yeah, I kinda figured." Eddie held up the bag. "I can do you one better."

George gasped. Excessively. This might have been because he didn't know how to gasp, as it wasn't generally a thing he had to do. Usually, the people who met him gasped, and that was the last thing they did. He looked from the bag to Eddie, unsure if he was allowed to take it. Only when Eddie nodded and jiggled the bag did he do so.

"Does Lilith know you're here?"

George nodded yes, but his mouth said no.

"How are you here then?"

"Uhh..." Apparently, George wasn't quite sure either, as the answer conflicted with what he just said. "Lillie says it's okay."

Eddie squinted and George took this to mean he needed to explain more.

"Lillie says I'm not a slave, so then she made it so I could go where I wanted."

"But not topside then."

"Not here." George shook his head. "Because I scare people."

"I think I get it," Eddie said, rubbing his chin. "Tell you what, buddy. Next time you feel like Chicken Legs, you tell Lilith so she can call me, and I'll bring some to the tunnel."

George was amazed at Eddie's solution. A lot of things still amazed him, so it wasn't that high a bar to clear, but not many amazing things made him as happy as this. So happy, in fact, that he forgot to keep himself small. He raised up to hug Eddie, revealing the billowing black smoke he was made of. Eddie briefly accepted the hug and then pushed George back.

"Careful, big guy. If anyone sees you--"

"I'm sorry." George shrunk again and gripped the bag with both hands. "I go now."

"Alright. Enjoy the Chicken Legs."

George wanted to answer affirmatively, but he already had one in his mouth. Eddie just grinned and went back to the diner.

Just as he was about to pull the door open, he heard a familiar sound that reminded him of his own car, but with fewer wheels, and it made him feel good. He turned around with a grin to see Jonah Craig pull into the spot next to the Vindicator, and it looked like the beginning of an awesome movie.

The air around the two upturned thunderhead exhausts still

trembled. Either from the heat or out of sheer fear of what would happen if the custom-built chopper would start up again. Jonah extended the kickstand and got off the bike in one smooth move.

"Yeah, I thought I heard the White Horse."

"Obviously. It's the best bike I ever rode, but it isn't subtle."

Nothing about the bike was subtle, except maybe for the plain white teardrop gas tank sporting a Westgate logo. But whatever the tank offered in normality, the extended chrome fork and the easy rider seat negated fanatically. And it looked so good it made Eddie think of taking motorcycle lessons.

He held the door open for Jonah and followed him in. Jonah looked around.

"Didn't bring your goth friends?"

"No, Asphyxia thinks Gina hates her because of something she did for me a while back. Wasn't pretty. Why?"

"Thriftshop Betty's been asking if Scar is alright. She hasn't seen him in a while."

Eddie thumbed randomly over his shoulder. "The goths will be at the main party later; you can tell him there."

"You can tell him for me. I just dropped by to apologize to Rooney for not coming. I've got a date."

Eddie prodded Jonah. "Good for you. Same girl?"

Jonah nodded.

"When do we get to meet her?"

"It's still fresh. At this point, the choice between meeting new people and getting sticky with each other is pretty straightforward."

This time Eddie nodded. If this had been anybody other than Rooney's birthday, he'd definitely prioritize being sticky with Rosalie.

"Well, grab a seat and..."

His words trailed off as he looked at the table and saw how Christa had strategically squeezed up against Rosalie so Laura could sit on her other side. She laughed and then put her arms around both girls.

"Looks like we're eating at the counter, if you ask me," Jonah quipped.

Eddie smirked at him. "Nature abhors a vacuum, and my absence appears to have created a disturbance in the Force."

"Alright, *Luke*."

"That's Mr. Skywalker to you. I'm gonna get my order and…"

"And what?"

"Hell if I know. But if anything happens, I wanna be close when it does."

He rapped his knuckles on the counter to get Gina's attention. Unnecessarily, as she had his order ready to go, as well as a plate for Jonah. She was just that good.

FIVE

During his stint as mayor back in the '80s, Stan Faust did what he could to make Herringwood relevant. While some attempts were successful, like the tax exemption that brought Century Motors to town, others were less so. When looking at a map for reasons known only to him, Mayor Faust noticed that there were at least three Palm Springs in America. Though unsure if it was Palm Springses, or Palm Springsii, he was pretty confident he could trick less observant tourists and piggyback on the success of the original ones and renamed the Herringwood Trailer Park.

Unfortunately, there was no palm tree in sight, unless one counted the palm-shaped air freshener in an abandoned RV, which did a horrible job at masking the stench from the backed-up waste water tank. As for the springs part, that could either have been the old well with a dead hedgehog in it, or the communal shower. Also with complimentary dead hedgehog.

Thanks to the unwelcoming natives, with whom Mayor Faust

never discussed turning their community into a tourist trap, the whole plan was torpedoed before it gained any momentum. The tourists left, but the name stayed. Some residents left, most of them stayed, and one of them was the hostess of Rooney's birthday party-slash-binge.

While the idea of slumming it at a trailer park might have been a lousy idea for a birthday party to some, Eddie was pretty excited about it as they approached Palm Springs. Rooney seemed to be less so and checked the rearview mirror to see what Rosalie was doing. Like everybody alone in a backseat, she was staring out the window, not expecting to be included in any front-seat conversations. All Rooney had to do was find the right volume to whisper over the music without drawing her attention.

"So, ehm..." he tried, "you really want to do the party at Jolene's?"

Unaware of what Rooney was trying to do, Eddie answered at regular speaking volume.

"Yeah. I thought about doing it at the church, but I'm not Helen. Jolene's not legally allowed to sell her moonshine anymore, so I can't get any, and if we want to get old-school blackout drunk, we're gonna have to be her guests."

Rooney quickly checked the mirror again. Rosalie wasn't paying any explicit attention, but he could see a slight smile.

"Yeah, sure, but ehm..." Now he had to try and say what he wanted without saying it, but he really didn't know how. Still, it was his duty as best friend to at least try and save Eddie from doing something stupid. He hoped some extra emphasis would do the trick. "At *Jolene's*?"

"Dude, if you didn't wanna go, you could have told me sooner."

At this point, Rosalie stopped politely pretending she wasn't listening and leaned forward.

"He's trying to subtly make it clear I might have a problem with that because of all the Jolene-sex you had."

"Oh," Eddie answered, quite unfazed. "Didn't really work out, did it?"

"Nah." Rosalie sat back.

Eddie flashed Rooney a shit-eating grin. "Anything else, birthday boy?"

"Yes. Fuck you." Rooney thought for a moment. "Uhm, yeah. That's it."

He caught Rosalie's gaze in the rearview mirror. She laughed and leaned forward. "Aw, you thought we were just doing it all day? We talk, too, sometimes."

"Of course, I know that," Rooney answered. "But whenever I talk to him, nothing sensible comes out, so forgive me for thinking Jolene never came up."

Rosalie briefly looked at Eddie. "She was pretty much the first one who came up, wasn't she?"

Eddie nodded. "A prostitute seemed like a safe place to start."

"So you discussed your complete love lives?" Rooney asked incredulously.

"Was his idea, actually," Rosalie said. "Though he didn't take it as well as I did."

Rooney glanced at Eddie, who caught the look.

"I didn't go ape; don't look at me like that. I mean, look at her. I might be easily fooled into thinking shady-looking guys are handing out free Vindicators, but I'm not naive enough to think a woman like her is gonna be single for very long."

Rooney laughed and leaned back. "Good for you two. I don't know much about relationships, but I hear communication is key. Like with Jesse, am I right?"

Eddie saw Rosalie's better-explain-that eyebrow come up in the mirror as he turned to glare at Rooney.

"Jesse?" Rosalie inquired urgently.

"Ah... I kinda forgot about Jesse."

"And why did you choose to forget about Jesse?"

"I didn't choose to forget!" Eddie argued. "We met online, and decided to see if we'd hit it off for real, too. It was a fun evening, but he really wasn't my type."

Rosalie snorted. "He?"

"Hence the communication," Rooney said. "You'd think something like gender would come up at some point."

"We exchanged pictures; he was very good at cross-dressing, okay? You shouldn't be so high and mighty, Rooney. How sure are you that elf you always play *Fallen Kingdom* with isn't actually a troll--"

"Don't change the subject, Sterling," Rosalie warned him. "We're talking about Jesse, whether you like it or not."

Eddie shrugged. "There's not much to talk about, other than that he looked rather fetching in a plaid skirt."

"Did you have--"

"No. And that's why Jesse never came up. I don't even talk to him anymore. Oh, look, we're here."

Rosalie looked out, expecting Eddie was just trying to change the subject again but they were actually at their destination.

"Stop here," she said, so Eddie did. He was nothing if not accommodating.

Rooney let her out, and because Eddie remained seated, she went around and opened his door. With a nudge of the head, she made him get out and held up her hand. "Keys."

"Why?"

"Because I'm not coming."

"Why?"

"Because Mitch is, which means he'll be hungover tomorrow, which means Dad will be alone at the station tomorrow, which means I'm going to help him out."

Eddie got out of the car. "You're a real cop now?"

"No, just helping out for now. Considering it, though. We discussed it during dinner with Dad."

"I was drinking during dinner with Dad."

"Well, write it down somewhere because I'm sure you'll have forgotten by tomorrow morning."

Eddie pouted. "Okay, but I don't wanna trade you for Mitch. You're far more fun when we reach the look-I'm-naked point of drunkenness."

"While we're on the subject," Rosalie said, pinning him against the car. "Don't get to the let's-fuck-Jolene point. I will find out, and I will cut you, and I will cut your car."

She finished her warning with a kiss. Not just any kiss. The kind of kiss that made sleeping with other women irrelevant.

"You have a point," Eddie finally said. "Several points, actually. If you don't mind, I would like to go over that last one again."

Rosalie pushed him aside and got in the car. "Be home safe by tomorrow, and we'll talk about it."

She didn't need to wait for him to promise he would and drove off. Eddie put his arm around Rooney, watching her go until the car was out of sight. He usually didn't let other people drive the Vindicator, but there was something incredible about this. The woman of his dreams, driving the car of his dreams—and, it has to be said, driving it like a muscle car needed to be driven. Loud and sexy. Eddie may have been biased on this, but it was a little arousing.

"That's what I wish for you, dude," he said. "I don't know what I did to deserve her, but I hope you find a girl like her."

"You went to Hell and brought her back. That'll do it."

Eddie turned them both around, and they started walking to Jolene's trailer.

"Sounds pretty cool when you say it like that, but the fact of the matter is that she was in the middle of busting out by the time I found her. I just gave her a ride home."

"From Hell."

"From the Underworld's garage."

"Over the Highway to Hell."

Eddie nodded. "Yeah, I am pretty awesome."

Rooney let out a relieved sigh. "There you are. All this sincere stuff was making me nervous."

"Well, Jolene's got something against nerves," Eddie said, stepping onto the patio of number 73. The Christmas lights bordering the patio were on and tacky, as were the lights in the trailer, but there didn't seem to be anybody there. Aside from partygoers, obviously. Christa and Laura were here since they'd gone ahead, and Scar greeted Rooney on behalf of the gothic delegation.

"What kept you, guy? We've been taking it slow, so we'd be conscious to wish you a happy birthday."

"Thank you," Rooney answered. "Don't hold back on my account now."

Scar and everybody else certainly wasn't planning to, but it seemed to Eddie that they would need Jolene to help them get drunk, and the hostess was nowhere to be found.

"But you had a drink already. Where's Jo?" he asked.

"Inside. With a guy."

Eddie frowned. He really didn't mind if she took on clients—after all, a girl's gotta eat—but the guest of honor was here now. He turned to Rooney.

"I guess we give her ten minutes?"

Rooney nodded. He didn't mind. From experience, he knew the drunk part of the evening was longer than the sober part, so they had some leeway. Eddie lit a cigarette, and at the clink of his gasoline lighter, the trailer door opened.

"Ten minutes?" Like a redneck queen, Jolene emerged from her trailer. "Sugar, you know damn well ten minutes ain't enough. I was just changing."

Eddie examined her. She didn't exactly look changed. Cowboy boots, then a whole lot of nothing until the so-short-why-bother jeans shorts, and a plaid blouse tied around her bosom.

"Thank god lookin's free, right?" she said with a wink. She pulled her thick auburn hair into a ponytail, and then someone else appeared from the trailer.

"Hey, Ed."

Eddie had to do a double-take because Jonah was the last person he expected here.

"Wait, Jolene is your date?"

Jonah nodded and Jolene got a big ol' grin on her face. "I'm guessin' you two have some things y'all wanna discuss without me present. I'll go and get you some drinks."

They both watched her walk away. Then Jonah turned back to Eddie.

"So, you two know each other?"

Eddie nodded uncomfortably. "Err, yeah. Jo and I, we, ehm... Look, in the interest of our friendship, I'm gonna need to tell you now--"

"Yeah, you *know*-know her."

"Man, I knew the Hell out of her--"

"Yeah, we're talking about my girlfriend now."

Eddie raised his hands. Now he knew where the line was. But there were other questions that still needed an answer.

"Just out of curiosity, I promise; does she still... work?"

Jonah nodded.

"And you don't mind she's pay-for-play?"

"I'm not gonna watch her work, no, but that's all it is: work. It's actually not the first time I've dated a hooker," Jonah chuckled. Then he leaned in. "And I get it for free."

Eddie thought about it for a moment and tried to put himself in Jonah's shoes. Seemed fair enough, though. Jolene was already a working girl when they met. If Jonah had a problem with that, they shouldn't have started dating.

"Good for you, man. She's a good woman. I mean... privately.

Not professionally. Well, she's professional, too. Jesus, please stop me talking."

Jonah just stood there amused and let Eddie ramble but finally took pity on him.

"Wanna talk about Judas Priest instead?"

Eddie nodded.

"I finally took the time to listen to *Ram It Down*, and it's awesome--" Jonah stopped and looked at the person approaching. "Is there a problem, officer?"

Jolene returned with two jugs full of 'shine and pushed them into Jonah's arms. "What did I tell you about showin' up here in uniform, Mitch?"

"I'm sorry. I was running late, and I didn't wanna go home to change first."

Jolene smirked and pointed at Mitch while she turned to Jonah. "Pour him a big one."

There were a few things worth knowing about Jolene's moonshine. She brewed it herself, obviously. Otherwise, it would have been called Raphael's moonshine, or Donatello's. Michelangelo, famously, preferred pizza.

Nobody really knew the recipe, and nobody cared to, but it had enough kick to fell the best of 'em. In a pinch, it could be used as horse tranquilizer. Moreover, it was illegal. Most things about Jolene were illegal, considering prostitution wasn't allowed in the state either. Chief Watson had decided that she was actually providing a valuable service to the community, so as long as she kept running her business properly, he would look the other way. But as far as the moonshine went, he did bring her in a few times.

When Henry Everett became mayor, things changed. Overall, everybody gracefully assumed that he used the moonshine to clean the rust off the hinges on his barn, but he was also one of the few human beings alive today who could take a straight shot of 'shine and remain standing. And nobody assumed this was common knowledge because he accidentally licked it off the hinges. Whatever the reason, be it rust remover, good drinking, or possibly an alternative fuel source, Mayor Everett had kindly asked Chief Watson to also look the other way on this. Chief Watson agreed, provided she didn't sell it anymore because, unlike her other service, this stuff had the potential to do some serious damage.

So, that's how it was possible, not much later in the evening, there was a mostly uniformed off-duty police officer trying to explain what he thought was quantum physics to a hedge at a prostitute's trailer.

Eddie was also having a conversation, but luckily for him, Rooney proved to be a much better speaker than the hedge. Relatively, anyway. The first jug of moonshine was empty, after all.

"You know, Ed. You know..." Rooney stammered.

Eddie nodded at his friend. "I know Ed."

Rooney nodded and looked at Jonah sitting on a crate beside them.

"I know Eddie, too," he said.

"You know," Rooney tried again, but he still had to think hard about what he wanted Eddie to know. Mere moments ago, an idea had been in his head, but it was already starting to drown in alcohol—never a good place for ideas.

"You know... You're kinda like Jesus."

Jonah chuckled, but Eddie and his booze-addled brain agreed without hesitation. Though he still wanted to know how Rooney finally came to this obvious conclusion.

"Cuz-- Because you fucking came back from the dead, you know?"

"I know."

"And you hang with hookers."

"I'm not drunk enough to let you talk about Rosie like that."

"No, dude! Rosie is an angel... dude. Which is kinda Jesus-y, too. I'm talking about Jolone. Lene. Jolene." Rooney paused and checked with Jonah to confirm her name was actually Jolene. After a nod, Rooney paused again, just because he forgot he was talking. Then, as if someone slapped him, he started up again and tugged his jacket. "You clothe the poor, and you feed the hungry."

"You didn't eat that much..."

"The hobo, dude! Jeez. Don't drink so much... hic... man."

"At the diner?"

Rooney nodded.

"That wasn't really a hobo..." Eddie chuckled. "But he was hungry, I guess."

Rooney tapped Jonah on the arm. "Look, I found Jesus."

"Did you now?"

Eddie spread his arms. More to say "it's me!" than to do the crucifixion pose it actually looked like, but nobody was sober enough to do anything about it. Rooney poured the three of them a fresh mug, which Eddie downed before unsteadily pointing a finger at Jonah.

"It's me, man. I'm the Jesus. I'm a religion now! Wanna be my second apostopeple?"

Before Jonah could respectfully decline, Eddie slapped Rooney on the shoulder. "You my first ap... apops... follower. Don't worry, dude."

He sort of got up and leaned on Rooney's shoulder because he thought he was going to whisper something in his ear. Instead, he yelled. "Laura, dude. Talk to her. You're drunk enough to talk to her." He righted himself as best he could and started to wobble away. "Fukkit. I'm the man. I'll talk to her for ya, buddy..." Eddie stopped to burp and then wobbled on. "You my main apozzel, yo... Lemme fix this shit! Laura! I don't want to have sex, but Rooney does."

Rooney chuckled and watched gleefully how Eddie tried to arrange a date for him. With Jolene. According to both Eddie and

Rooney, it was going very well.

Rooney stared into his tin mug, and after a while, Jonah thought he needed to break the awkward silence.

"You've got a thing for Laura?"

"You heard that?"

"Yes. That wasn't whispering what ol' Jeezy there did."

Rooney moved a little closer to the man and got a surreptitious smile on his lips. "He's not really Jesus."

"You don't say."

"No, I say. He's my best friend, like, ever! And he does Jesus-things. He's my best friend, like--"

"You mentioned that."

"Did I also mention he just goes to Hell when he feels like it to get people?"

Jonah grinned. "He does?"

Rooney snapped his fingers. Or, he thought he did, anyway. "Like that! Ain't no *thang*. He got me this jacket, it's ostralian leather-- No. The birds. Not the country. Ostralia is a country, right?"

"Yeah, but not everybody believes so. You mean ostriches."

"Birds who live in Ostralia. That's what they made my jacket out of."

Rooney had a lot more to say, and he would have done so if his attention hadn't been drawn by the sharp snap of a hand on skin. He wasn't quite sure what happened, or where he was, but he thought he recognized Jolene's voice when she said, "You're not drinking out of my boot, Sterling! You'll ruin them!"

She got up and pulled Eddie to the trailer.

"No-no-no-no. I'm not allowed to have sex with you."

"Good, 'cause I ain't open for business. We're gonna get you a big boy mug and then you're going to stay right the hell away from my boots."

Eddie quickly reviewed everything he vaguely remembered

discussing with Rosalie, and as far as he could tell, staying away from Jolene's boots seemed like a safe option. Moments later, he emerged from the trailer with a boot-shaped glass full of high-octane booze.

There would be more to say about the evening, like Eddie's drunken retelling of his adventures in the Underworld to the carpenter he now considered a very close friend, or Rooney attempting to ask Laura out. Sadly, she never answered because he was talking to the neighbor's dog, who had wandered over to see if any food was being dropped on the ground. When there wasn't, and the only good thing turned out to be a human asking it for a date, the dog trotted off again. While flattered, even the dog knew no good could come of dating a human. Or consuming moonshine.

Suffice it to say that, as with every party catered by Jolene, none of the guests would remember much the next day but still know they had a seriously good time.

SIX

The sun was out, and light poured in through the arched windows. Otherwise unnoticeable particles of dust now danced merrily in the rays, but all was quiet in the church. Dust isn't very noisy, even when it's dancing. The Zen-like silence was disrupted by the creaking of the stairway door. Before entering, Scar stuck his head around the corner to check if the coast was clear. Not for any nefarious reasons; he just wanted to make a sandwich but didn't want to risk walking in on anyone doing anything that required blushing and explaining it wasn't what it looked like. When he determined safe passage was possible, he headed for the kitchen. He was barely a few steps in when he heard something familiar... Not really his thing but he recognized it as the opening to Thin Lizzy's version of "Rosalie" repeating itself.

"Eddie?"

Scar squinted as he listened for the source. Eddie had to be here somewhere, or at least, his phone. Rosalie was calling him. Just as he started zeroing in on the sound, it stopped, and the closest thing that could hide either a phone or a body, or both, was the confessional. He opened the door, and Eddie poured out.

Scar took a step back. "Hey, guy…"

Eddie did not respond and just lay there.

"Are you dead?"

"…Yes."

"Okay. Do you mind if I make myself a BLT?"

Eddie opened his eyes and looked up at Scar. "Do I look like the kind of guy who has either L or T?"

"You kinda look like a guy who severely misjudged his capacity for alcohol." Scar scrunched his nose. "Smell like one, too."

With some effort, Eddie raised his hand and flipped off Scar, who took that hand and pulled him up. Eddie groaned and leaned against the confessional.

"Bet you wish you were dead," Scar remarked.

"I'm not entirely sure I'm alive yet."

"Cool, I've never met a zombie before."

At the other side of the church, Rooney emerged from the office, not looking any better, and headed for the kitchen.

"Now you've met two," Eddie said and checked his phone. Some part of him seemed to have registered a call coming in earlier, but no parts were very interested in making the effort to answer at that time. As he focused his vision on the screen, he saw he missed a call from Rosalie and intended to call her back right away, but just before his finger touched the call button, Rooney asked if he wanted coffee.

Eddie zombie-shuffled to the kitchen to tell Rooney he did. He could have said it from where he was standing, but that meant raising his voice, which was really not an option right now. Scar joined them as well because he still fostered some hope for a BLT, against his better judgment. The chance of there being lettuce or tomato anywhere in the church was minimal and hinged entirely on whether or not Rosalie had time to do groceries.

"Anybody have any idea what happened yesterday?" Eddie tried.

"Dude, you should know better than to ask that," Rooney answered. "Even if by some miracle either of us would know anything, it would probably not be something we want to think about sober."

Eddie nodded. There was probably an interesting reason why he was only wearing jeans. He'd lost some nice shirts like that but somehow never his phone. He wouldn't have minded if he did, though, because it started ringing again. Loudly. Rosalie's picture appeared on the screen. He left the general kitchen area since his presence didn't seem required while Scar and Rooney dodged each other, trying to make their respective consumptions. He cleared his throat and answered as smooth as he could muster.

"Hey, babe."

"Ooh, good job trying to sound like you're okay. How are you really feeling? Hungover?"

Eddie thought he was doing pretty well, actually—all things considered, anyway. He was definitely hungover, but with how plastered he got last night, it could have been worse. Imbibing like he used to without notable repercussions required regular practice, and since he had gotten with Rosalie, he'd calmed down, but he hadn't lost it completely yet.

"I'll manage... Did you know I fell asleep in the confessional?"

"Yes."

"And you just left me there."

"Hm, yeah. I was on my way out," Rosalie said matter-of-factly. "I was surprised you actually made it all the way home, but I didn't have time to drag you to bed this morning, and you didn't give the impression you were gonna walk on your own."

"Ehm, I'm not sure what happened yesterday, but it involved me losing my boots and shirt, so... I may have--"

"You haven't. They're in the bedroom."

"Really?" Eddie sauntered over to have a look. Indeed, his boots were lying in a corner, and his shirt dangled haphazardly off a knob on the dresser. "How did they get here?"

"You made an attempt to come to bed, but I didn't let you."

"God... I didn't do things that require a hashtag, did I?"

Rosalie laughed delightfully. "You didn't get the chance. The alcohol wafting off you made my eyes water, so I sent you to the couch."

"Never made it."

"You could have. You passed it on the way to the confessional."

Eddie shrugged involuntarily. "I prefer the relative safety of closed doors."

"Speaking of closed doors," Rosalie masterfully changed the subject, "have you been outside yet?"

"You kidding me? Where the sun is?"

Rosalie wasn't really surprised. "Could you do me a little favor?"

"Absolutely."

"Okay, go to the front."

Eddie jogged to the front door and stepped out. There didn't seem to be anything out of the ordinary here.

"Over the door," Rosalie said, already guessing that Eddie was looking elsewhere.

Eddie took a few more steps out and looked up. "Ah."

"Hm hm. Deal with that, would you, please?"

"Yup..."

"Alright, talk to you later."

Rosalie hung up, and Eddie looked at his handiwork. This was impressive, to say the least, considering he'd done this while he was fully sloshed last night. Before he dealt with it, he had to show Rooney first. If only for laughs, but hopefully, it jogged some memories as well. He went back inside to get his cup of coffee and call Rooney. Perhaps Scar as well, but he seemed to have retreated again.

"Is Scar coming back?"

Rooney had himself propped up against the kitchen counter and shook his head. "He left with a Nutella sandwich."

"Okay." Eddie poured a mug. "You have to come see this."

Yaeger was very annoyed with what he saw. There was no way on God's green Earth that the Lord Jesus Christ would put up a crudely made banner on the front of a church with the words *Thou shalt not be an asshole* in big, bold letters.

Subsequently, the call Rigby was making now annoyed him as well, for roughly the same reasons. Rigby was talking to the Old Man about their suspicions of Sterling being the Lord based on the wildest assumptions. Worst of all, it was basically Yaeger's own fault that the call was being made, as he'd harped on Rigby to elicit a miracle from Sterling.

Initially, they had no idea how to do that, as a man who had been in hiding for the past two thousand years would probably not break cover to change water into wine. Still, based on that initial idea, Rigby made the call. After arguing with Mr. Hall's assistant to put him through, he finally got hold of the man himself. And now Mr. Hall was also annoyed for being interrupted in something he didn't feel the need to explain, though Rigby thought he heard a woman's voice in the background.

Sam Hall's annoyance only increased because Rigby proceeded to argue with the orders he'd only just asked for.

"But, sir," he said, "you can't be serious."

"I'm dead serious, Brother Rigby," Mr. Hall answered in his distinctive Texas drawl. "Your boy had a good idea, and we ain't getting any younger."

"You seem to be underestimating the gravity of--"

"*You* seem to be underestimating how little patience I have left for you questioning the order I gave you *after you asked for orders*! Either deal with it or don't call me."

Rigby glanced at Yaeger and felt the need to lean away as if that made any difference.

"Sir, respectfully--"

"Respectfully, my ass. Do it and report the results back to me directly."

Though Mr. Hall abruptly ended the call, Rigby held the phone to his ear for a while longer. He regretted calling.

Yaeger wondered if he should speak yet. The call was clearly over and the fact that Rigby was now the one doing the sighing told him what they had to do. Carefully, he tried to get a reaction from Rigby.

"So, ehm... What did the Old-- What did Mr. Hall say?"

Rigby finally lowered the phone, but needed to stare at the church for a few moments before answering.

"He said 'do it.'"

Yaeger nodded solemnly and reached for the glove box, but Rigby pushed his hand down.

"I'm saying we don't."

"But the Old Man said--"

"He did. And I don't agree."

Yaeger frowned. Not so much because they were right back where they were before the call, but because not following orders had repercussions.

"Salt Creek's gonna be very upset. We could get exiled, and we'll never see Kolob."

Rigby seemed very resigned to the matter and calmly explained himself.

"I've long since made peace with that. Even if we were to find the Lord right this minute, I will still have shuffled off this mortal coil long before we ever got in sight of Kolob. I only ever was in this for those who come after me, and they won't get to go if we introduce ourselves to the Lord guns blazing."

Yaeger didn't agree at all. "First of all, you're implying that Sterling *is* the Lord, which means that you are actively sabotaging our chances by not following the order to shoot someone close to him so he'll have to resurrect them. And secondly, if you get *me* exiled, I will never get to see Kolob."

"You won't either way!" Rigby snapped.

Yaeger looked at him in shock.

"Kolob isn't amongst the planets we know of," Rigby continued. "Just getting somewhere to even start looking for it is going to take longer than you will live. Worry about that instead of getting exiled, because I'm your senior and I've just ordered you to belay the previous order."

That didn't satisfy Yaeger. Rigby might have had the authority to order him, but not to overrule the Old Man.

"Jesus probably knows a way to get there faster and I want to be there for it."

Rigby let out a condescending sigh. "Of course. I'm sure he'll be happy to oblige if we shoot all his friends. Which one did you have in mind? The girl? Or maybe the fat gothic one makes an easier target."

Yaeger pursed his lips and glared at the church. He hated when Rigby had a point. Then again...

"Movement."

Rigby nodded. "I see them."

Sterling and his friend looked a little worse for wear. Yaeger assumed there would be a party after their dinner at the Rising Wind, but when Sterling's car stopped at the trailer park, Rigby kept on driving. There was no place for them to park and hide to see what was going on, and snooping around a trailer park seemed like asking for trouble.

Clearly they didn't miss much, judging by the two in front of the church. Apart from how that banner got up there. If these guys were so hungover, it must have been quite a spectacle to see them put it up.

"I get the impression they're close," Yaeger said. "What does the file say about the other guy?"

"I don't know, I don't care. We're not shooting anyone."

"You just don't want to admit you're too old to figure out how to open a PDF on your phone, do you?"

Rigby stared extra hard at the church because Yaeger was right. When he first received the file, Yaeger helped him open it, but whatever magical button presses were made never registered with Rigby. Initially he just kept the file open permanently but, at some point, his phone decided enough was enough and closed it while he wasn't looking.

Thankfully he had a good memory and was able to recall most of what he read, but not all of it, so if there was anything about Sterling's companion, it was in one of the blank memories.

"No, I'll admit it," Rigby said. "I don't know how to work all those new devices. I'm very good at *Snake*, though. It's all about sticking to the edges, a Hamiltonian cycle, if you will. The reason I don't care about the contents of the file is because *we are not shooting anyone.*"

Yaeger turned to him. "What happened to that faith of yours? Do Muller's legendary hunches suddenly mean nothing anymore? Where's your loyalty to the Old Man?"

Angrily Rigby grabbed the steering wheel to prevent himself from physically lashing out at his colleague.

"I am loyal to Mr. Hall! He is a great man and he knows far more than either of us. Whatever the reason for him to casually condone murder must be a temporary thing and it will blow over!"

"Oh man, it's impressive how you try to justify yourself."

"Keep that up with me and I'm going to impress you by how I boot you out of this car. I am unable to comprehend how Mr. Hall could give us that order, and unwilling to believe he meant it. I do not want to be in the middle of committing a heinous crime and miss the call that tells us there was a mistake. We wait, and if you can't deal with that, you can go sit under any tree you like until I say you can come back in…"

Rigby's attention was drawn by a familiar noise. It was the sound of an engine and, moments later, a motorcycle pulled up to the church.

"Is that…?"

Yaeger didn't have to look long. Even without the sawdust in the man's hair, and the scruffy beard that might have been a five o' clock shadow a week ago, he easily recognized Jonah Craig.

"The carpenter we were staking out before we were sent here."

When they saw him drop by the diner, they assumed it was coincidence, but now their previous suspect was showing up at the church of their current suspect.

"What's he doing here?" Rigby wondered out loud.

"I don't know. Carpentry?"

Rigby took a moment out of intensely scrutinizing the church to scowl at Yaeger.

"Well, what do you want me to say," the latter defended himself. "I'm seeing the same thing as you and that's all I have to work with. Although…"

Rigby saw the gears in Yaeger's head turning and didn't like it at all.

"No."

"Yes," Yaeger answered. "Look how it's all coming together. Salt Creek is clearly on to something. The guy we were staking out is showing up at the guy from Muller's hunch."

"That is still no reason--"

"Isn't it? If we overlook yesterday's party situation, and factor in that this other guy is too poor to afford a place of his own, Sterling did in fact clothe the poor. And he fed the hungry. If the hobo he gave a meal to was a friend, he would have invited him in. This was a random act of kindness, like the Lord would do."

Rigby shook his head and rubbed his nose. "When we get back to Salt Creek, I'm going to inform them that you are unstable. I don't care what they do with you, but I don't want to share a car with somebody who is looking for any excuse to kill."

Yaeger crossed his arms and pouted. The three men at the church were clearly discussing things that might have been important, but they weren't remotely close enough to hear anything.

"I wish we could hear what they were talking about. Maybe that would give us something to work with."

Rigby grunted but Yaeger had a point, so he crawled between the seats to get to the back. "Let me see if I can get the parabolic mic working. That old thing mostly gives static, but you never know. It's a good thing Mr. Hall has a military background. Anybody else probably wouldn't have thought to put a survival kit in all the cars... Well, I guess it's more of a spy kit. But if the police ever pull us over and find the rope and shovel, there will be questions..."

He heard the passenger door open and knew he walked right into it with open eyes.

"God's hooks. Yaeger!"

SEVEN

Rooney was initially skeptical about the coolness of what Eddie wanted to show him and would have preferred to deal with the marching band in his head first. However, Eddie seemed somewhat excited about it, and that meant he would eventually start talking loudly, so it became a priority to keep him from doing so.

Now that Rooney was looking up at the banner, he was actually impressed as well.

"Nice penmanship. Good serif-work, considering you were pissed up," Rooney said.

"Isn't it 'brushmanship' in this case?"

"Whatever it is, it's nice."

Eddie nodded and put his hands on his hips. "I don't remember doing it."

"Me neither. It's good advice, though."

"I know, right? If they'd just put that in the Bible, we'd have world peace by now."

Rooney scoffed. He didn't have that much confidence in the human race. Eddie briefly looked at him. "Did we even do this?"

It seemed unlikely, considering that they were drunk to the point of incapacitation last night. There was no way they managed to put up the First and Only Commandment without critically injuring themselves. Eddie had so many questions and nobody to answer them. Whose sheet was this in the first place? How did he paint it without drunkenly covering himself in tar black? How did he do that shading, because--

The rumble of Jonah's motorcycle derailed his train of thought. "Maybe he's got answers."

Jonah stepped off the bike and grinned when he saw the hungover and slightly confused pair.

"Oh good, you're still alive."

"Relatively speaking," Eddie answered.

"I just stopped by to see if you two made it home safe. Why are you checking your pockets?"

Eddie took his hands out of his pockets and shrugged. "I thought maybe Jolene sent you because I accidentally took her panties again."

"Again?" Jonah asked, confused, but Eddie waved it off. It wasn't important enough to dwell on, and panties had a habit of getting him in trouble lately.

"I've extensive experience with Jo's moonshine, so I can safely say that neither Rooney nor myself will be remembering anything. Do you?"

"Hm, yeah. Somewhere after you drank a boot full of 'shine, you thought it was very important to write down the commandments for your 'religion', and you used Jo's sheets."

"I guess I should apologize then."

"I think she's okay with it," Jonah laughed. "She gave you the paint. Quite magical to watch a man who could barely walk paint as if possessed by the ghost of Rembrandt."

Eddie looked at the banner again. It was good, but he didn't consider it his best work, let alone something Rembrandt's soul would have painted.

"Meh. I'm good at being drunk and I draw pretty pictures for a living, so... Not as magical as how it got up here."

"I wasn't here for that. But I didn't expect you'd actually manage, so I figured I'd check on you."

"You're a good man, Jonah Craig," Eddie stated. "But I need to get it down before Rosie gets home. Rooney and I are going to check if we have a ladder."

Jonah looked at Rooney, who'd been very quiet during the exchange, and it was clear why.

"I'll help you. It doesn't look like Rooney feels like laddering."

Rooney raised his coffee mug in appreciation. To Eddie, it was all the same, as long as that banner came down.

"You're not getting off that easy," Eddie said. "I blame you for this as well, so you're waiting here because you have to hold the ladder. If we have one."

Rooney managed half of a shrug and stood firmly in place to let them do whatever they needed to. He squinted against the sunlight as he looked up at the banner. It was probably best to get it down either way. No doubt somebody was going to take an unreasonable amount of offense to this, and the man approaching from his right didn't give him the impression he was wrong about that.

"Excuse me, sir. Do you have the time to talk about our Lord Jesus Christ?"

Rooney sighed and turned to face the man for a proper telling-off.

"Sorry, I only have time to tell you to piss--"

Yaeger raised the gun and fired twice. Rooney clutched his chest as if that was going to help with the two holes, and fell backward onto the street.

"God's hooks! What did you do?" Rigby called out in utter horror. He couldn't get out of the car in time to stop Yaeger from doing this incomprehensibly stupid deed; all he could do now was grab him by the arm and pull him back to the SUV.

Shocked, Yaeger stared at the results of following orders. It looked so much easier when they did it on the news, and the hand holding the snub-nose .38 didn't feel like his own anymore. Neither did his thoughts. The human in him was appalled at the body in the street reaching out to him, yet it was drowned out by a voice that insisted he did a good thing.

Rooney fought hard to keep breathing, to give whatever could save him the time to kick into gear, but it felt like a very long time, and he was losing faith that he would make it. The shooter and his accomplice retreated to their car, and Rooney ran out of energy to keep his head up. With the last of his strength, he lowered it slowly so he wouldn't also hurt himself hitting it on the pavement.

The church door flew open, and Eddie burst out with Jonah in tow. It didn't take long for them to figure out what that noise was.

"Rooney!" Eddie yelled, panicked, and fell to his knees next to him. "Goddammit! What the fuck?"

He put his hands on the bloody holes in his best friend in a reflex, not knowing what he had to do or how to help. Rooney was already barely able to acknowledge him anymore.

"Jesus..." he managed to utter, which wasn't really something Eddie could work with even if he hadn't been in a stressed frenzy.

All the yelling and shooting drew the goths from the cemetery, and Asphyxia gasped at the sight of Rooney in a puddle of blood.

"Oh my god! What happened?"

Eddie half turned around, holding Rooney in his arms. "What does it look like? Rooney got shot! Why are none of you motherfuckers calling 911?"

Asphyxia grabbed her phone, and Eddie held Rooney's head in his bloody hands, carefully putting him back down. He'd heard somewhere he shouldn't move victims around, though he couldn't quite grasp how lying still would fix those holes.

"Hold on, buddy, goddammit. We're gonna get you through this, alright?"

Rooney actually worked up a bloody chuckle and shook his head ever so slightly.

"Yes, dude! Listen, sirens! You're gonna make it, dude."

True to tradition, when Eddie said something Rooney vehemently knew to be wrong, he tried to argue, but there was nothing left in him anymore. All he could do was curl the corner of his mouth as a quiet goodbye. Eddie thought he could feel the life leaving and quickly whispered, "Ask for Lilith."

Snarling as if possessed, Eddie stood up and looked around. There had to be some clue or evidence to lead him to whoever did this. It didn't take him long to notice the SUV, and he started to make a move to approach them, but Jonah grabbed his shoulder.

"They've got guns," he cautioned.

"God's got my back." Eddie slapped his hand away. "At the very least, they saw something. At the very most, I'm ripping off some heads."

By the time he realized he still wasn't wearing a shirt, he was already wiping his hands on his chest and walking to the car.

Rigby got in the car after roughly shoving Yaeger back in and snatching the gun from his hands.

"Holy Mother Mary, what were you thinking?"

Ghoulishly casual, Yaeger shrugged and answered, "Now Sterling will have to perform a miracle to save him."

Rigby gestured at the unfolding scene. "Listen! Does that sound like a holy man to you?"

Yaeger held his breath to catch any words being said, and though he could mostly only hear his own wild heartbeat, he heard enough of Eddie's frantic anger to establish the general mood.

"He doesn't speak like a saint, no... But--"

"Oh, dear Yaeger, if you plan on making more insipid excuses I will be saying some very unsaintly things of my own. Do you have any idea what you've done?"

"I followed orders, is what I did!"

"You've turned us into felons!" Rigby couldn't help himself and swiped at Yaeger, getting a good hit in on his arm. "And God help you if that man does inexplicably turn out to be the Lord, because--"

"Drive."

"Don't interrupt--"

Yaeger pointed out the window. "Drive-drive-drive!"

As if things weren't bad enough, Rigby saw one of the scariest things he had seen in all his time on the road. Barefoot and bare-chested, with bloodied hands and likewise smears on his torso, Eddie strode toward them.

And Rigby did nothing.

"He's coming this way," Yaeger whined. "Do something, Brother Rigby."

"Me? You shot his friend. Why don't *you* get out and apologize?"

"Does that look like a man who will accept an apology?"

Rigby grunted disdainfully and started the car. "Christ would forgive you."

"Christ would have healed his friend, too. This guy looks like he's on the other team," Yaeger exclaimed. He was on the verge of a breakdown, already sure that Rigby would toss him out of the car at the last minute and leave him to be torn apart by this savage.

Nearly in tears, he tried one more plea. "Please, Elder Rigby. I am begging you to drive."

"Yeah, yeah."

Rigby pushed the pedal down hard just before Eddie reached them, racing the SUV backward and spinning it into a J-turn. Yaeger looked back and saw that Eddie stopped, watching them as they sped away.

"Well, he's not raising anyone from the dead," Rigby sneered, keeping one eye on the road and the other at Eddie in the rearview mirror. "What the H-E-double-hockey-sticks were you thinking, hm?"

Yaeger pressed himself into his seat and let out a sigh of relief when he was sure Eddie wouldn't perform a miracle of a more nefarious kind. Suddenly, the adrenaline that had gotten him into this mess decided he could deal with the fallout on his own. With the post-shooting clarity dawning on him, despair started to take hold.

Rigby could see the color drain from his face.

"Yeah, shooting someone isn't as cool as the movies make it out to be, is it?"

Yaeger struck a cross. "Lord forgive me..."

"Oh, now you ask for forgiveness," Rigby scoffed. "It's bad enough that we would expect Christ to do tricks like a trained dog, but you just had to one-up it by adding violence to the mix."

"I was following orders."

"Shut up, you sound like the Nuremberg Trials."

Yaeger opened his mouth to argue against being called a Nazi, but Rigby didn't give him the chance.

"Worst of all, you were going against orders, and you refused to acknowledge it. We have a command structure for a reason. I made a judgment call, and by the looks of it, it was the right call. If you had just listened, we wouldn't have to drive to the police station right now."

In another impulsive reflex, Yaeger lunged at the wheel and pulled it, steering the car off the road. Rigby managed to slam the brakes just in time to stop them from driving into a tree.

"Heavens help me, Yaeger!" Rigby burst. "Is carnage your new way of life now?"

Shocked with himself, Yaeger raised his hands and stared at Rigby. "I'm sorry. Please don't take me to the police."

"Us. I'm taking us. You have made me an accessory."

Yaeger's mouth fell open. He never even considered this would get Rigby in trouble as well. They might not have seen eye to eye on everything, but turning him into a criminal was never the intention. His mind raced for a solution, and like the tentacles of an anemone, his thoughts flailed at whatever they could get until something stuck, however absurd it seemed. He just had to sell it right.

"Four days!" he exclaimed.

"What?"

"Give me four days! Did the Lord not raise Lazarus after four days?"

Rigby glanced at him before focusing on the road again. He thought Yaeger's idea was clutching at straws, but then again, they weren't there for those resurrections. This straw Yaeger was clutching at did have something intriguing about it.

Rubbing his chin, Rigby said, "Yeah, but if Jesus had been there, he would have healed Lazarus even before he died. He was just making a point by showing up late."

"But what if he wasn't?" Yaeger really thought he had something here. Like a biblical Sherlock Holmes he went on. "What if he needed a certain time to power up?"

"I do not believe the Lord Christ is a videogame character," Rigby scoffed. "You seem to forget about the others he raised."

Yaeger could see he was onto something, even though Rigby wasn't willing to admit interest.

"Four days is all I ask. If nothing has happened by then, I will go to the police station and take all the blame."

A risky gamble since he knew Rigby would make sure he held up his end of the bargain. Plus, he was gambling on a foul-talking, bloodied psychopath most often found in Judas Priest t-shirts to be their Lord Jesus Christ. He couldn't help but feel a little panicked again. Yeah, he was probably going to jail...

However, this turn the car took rather suddenly was uncharacteristic of Rigby's driving style.

"Where, uhm..."

"Even in the unlikely case that nobody saw our license plate when we hauled off with screeching tires, it's not going to take long for the police to find a big, black SUV. If we want to see any resurrections after four days, we'll need to ditch this car."

Yaeger could hug Rigby right now but knew better. He was still on thin ice, and the sun was coming out.

"If I'm not mistaken, there's a scrapyard around here somewhere, and I'm hoping the owner is the sort of person who doesn't ask too many questions."

Yaeger let out a long, relieved sigh. "Thank you, brother."

"Don't thank me yet, young man," Rigby said sternly. "We're going on the lam for four days. There are no comfortable seats or air-conditioned hotel rooms in your future."

Considering the other option, Yaeger was okay with that, but he still got a little extra comfortable in his seat before having to relinquish it to a hungry car compactor.

EIGHT

Chasing a car barefoot wasn't a good idea, even to Eddie. As he walked back, he became acutely aware of the road under his feet and took care not to step on a loose pebble or an errant shard of glass. He would have simply taken it on his way to the SUV, but not going back. That would be like tripping and breaking your neck after returning from war.

The ambulance had arrived, and more importantly, so had Rosalie and her father. She was actually the one to receive the call from the 911 responder and more or less prepared to see horrible things, yet she didn't expect this.

Looking the way he did, Eddie certainly ticked a few boxes on Asphyxia's fetish list, but Rosalie covered her mouth. Eddie raised his hands to make it known he couldn't hug her without getting her bloody, but it just made him look like a monster that just ravaged a virgin.

"Hug her for me, please," he said to Vernon.

Automatically, Rosalie turned to her father, who took her in his arms.

"What happened to you?" Vernon asked.

"Oh, it's not my blood." Before explaining any further, he focused on the goths. "Get your asses in the basement!"

Scar took offense to his tone. "Calm down, guy--"

Eddie wasn't able to suffer arguing and erupted in unprovoked anger.

"Get in the fucking basement! Pretend it's the fucking Batcave for all I care, you vampire-looking motherfuckers."

"Are you calling me a vampire, rockstar wannabe?" Scar answered angrily.

Eddie took a step in his direction and pointed at him. "I will call you whatever it takes to get you the fuck into the fucking basement before you get shot as well."

Scar glared at Eddie, but Asphyxia knew he was just lashing out because he knew they could take it, so she tugged him along.

"Jonah, take them around back. Make sure there are no other bad guys."

"Ed--"

Before Jonah could even start a sentence, Eddie was up in his face. "I'm trying to fucking keep the lot of you alive because there are motherfuckers gunning for my friends. If you all could just stop arguing with me for a moment and-- Hey! Hey!"

This time, the paramedics invoked Eddie's wrath by doing what they were supposed to do. Up until now, they'd been trying to resuscitate Rooney—probably more for the bystanders' sake than Rooney's—but now they were about to load him into the ambulance, and Eddie was having none of it.

"Where are you taking my friend?"

He grabbed the paramedic, who turned around and quickly looked at the police officer next to him. Vernon nudged Eddie away from the man.

It took the paramedic just a glance to determine Eddie was in shock, but Eddie wouldn't hear of it.

"I said I'm fine!" Eddie barked at the man. To the trained medical eye, he clearly wasn't, but that eye was in a man who didn't feel like losing it, so that was that. The cops could deal with him and so Vernon did.

"They're taking Rooney to the morgue to look for anything that might help in apprehending the shooter."

"Oh. Okay..."

Suddenly Eddie noticed his hands. He looked at Rosalie as if he'd discovered an extra finger and held his hand up to show her.

"They shot Rooney." Eddie stared at his hands again. "He was, like, my friend, man." He flinched when the ambulance doors closed and they drove off.

"'kay, bye..."

Rosalie saw him come apart at the seams and called out, "Catch him!"

Eddie's legs gave up, and he began to topple over, with Vernon catching him just in time. "Gotcha, son. Let's get you inside."

Rosalie supported him on the other side, and they walked him in. After setting him down on the couch, Vernon tried to get some information from him, though he didn't expect much with Eddie in this state.

"Can you tell me what happened, exactly?"

Eddie shook his head. "I was inside when it happened. I heard two shots, but that's it."

"You heard gunshots, and you *went outside*?" Rosalie hissed. "Normal people run away from gunshots!"

"Well, I'm not normal people, am I?" Eddie yelled. "I knew Rooney was still outside because we were looking at the banner. If *you* hadn't brought it up, we'd--"

"Oh, you did not just say that, Sterling!"

Vernon thought it better to put a stop to this before it got worse.

"Calm down, both of you. You're both shocked. This is not a time to argue." He gave them a stern, fatherly look. "I saw the banner. What kind of crazy nonsense are you up to this time?"

"We got drunk for Rooney's birthday and somehow managed to put it up..." Eddie rested his face in his hands. "I guess some religious nutter took offense to it. You know how those extremists get."

Aside from seeing it on the news, Chief Watson didn't really know. Herringwood wasn't exactly brimming with nutters, present company excluded. Still, he simply nodded and went back to a more practical line of questioning.

"Is there anything you can tell me that might help? Did you see the shooter? License plates?"

Eddie shook his head. "They raced off when I tried to confront them. Didn't really catch the plates. I'm sorry."

"CDS011," Jonah said, coming from the stairway at just the right time. "Black Cadillac Escalade. 2012, maybe '14; I'm not great with the current generation of cars. You're looking for two guys, white blouse, black tie. One's older, I guess early sixties, but that's an estimate. The other's probably around his late twenties, early thirties."

Jonah scratched his beard. Maybe it was time for a shave again.

The others just stared at him, and it had nothing to do with his beard. Finally, Eddie said something, and it was quite concise.

"How?"

Jonah seemed to slump a little, becoming almost apologetic. "This might be my fault."

Eddie got up. "Say what?"

"I didn't send them!" Jonah defensively held up his hands, seeing the look on Eddie's face. "But they might have been looking for me."

"Why are murderers looking for you at my house, Jonah?"

"They were hanging out in front of my shop for a while. I

reported them to the May Valley sheriff, and they left shortly after. I didn't expect them to move their shit over here. I didn't peg them for murderers either. They're a bit goofy, but I never heard of them killing people."

The gears in Eddie's head started turning, working on a plan to get some sweet, sweet revenge.

"You seem to know a lot about them," he said, just before Vernon could do the same. "Who are these guys?"

"I've run into them from time to time. They're looking for Jesus."

"The Mormons!" Eddie exclaimed. "Rosie, they were at the door!"

Now Rosalie was glad she'd brought Eddie the Mormon-stick when she did, even though it was against her better judgment at the time.

"They're actually not Mormons," Jonah said. "They're an offshoot. A lot of the same principles, but the Latter Day Saints have made it very clear they are not affiliated."

Eddie suddenly leaned on his knees and panted. Rosalie kneeled by him. "Are you okay?"

"Just getting a little woozy from all this..." He dramatically fanned himself. "All this excitement. I need to shower. Look at me; I'm covered in my friend's blood. Oh my God, I'm losing it. I don't know what to do..."

Rosalie turned to her father. "Dad, can we continue this tomorrow? I think the stress is finally getting to him."

Vernon looked at Eddie and nodded. This seemed like a panic attack he didn't want to deal with, so he got up, and Rosalie walked him to the door. When she came back, Jonah had taken Vernon's place and tried to calm Eddie down, but it didn't seem to help. Rosalie had the perfect solution to this problem: slapping Eddie on the head.

"Dad's gone. You can quit your soap opera."

Instantly, Eddie popped up. "Alright then, I'm gonna grab a shower."

"No, you're not. What are you up to?"

"I have a plan."

"Aw, dammit."

Jonah looked back and forth, thoroughly confused. "Err, look, I've only known you two for six months, and I'm happy to be considered a close enough friend that you feel you can argue in front of me, but I've not yet experienced one of Ed's 'plans.' Plans are good, right?"

Generally, they were, so Rosalie nodded halfheartedly. The problem here was that normal problems had normal solutions that didn't require a Sterling-level plan, but precisely because they'd only known each other for six months, Rosalie wasn't sure they should expand on this particular plan.

Eddie didn't share the same reservations because it was his plan, and therefore automatically a good plan. As far as he was concerned, anyway.

"It's simple," he started. Rosalie tried to get his attention with the don't-do-it look she had honed quite quickly, but Eddie just went right on, and all she could do was hope Jonah thought it was a weird joke.

"You know where to find them," Eddie explained. "Rooney knows what they look like, and I know how to give a guy a, let's say, stern talking to. No motherfucker shoots my friends and walks away from it."

"I have questions," Jonah said, unsure if he was allowed to laugh at Eddie right now.

"Knock yourself out."

"It's a nice plan; let's get that out of the way first. I can see how that would be a plan. It just kinda hinges on a few assumptions that might be, for all intents and purposes, incorrect."

Jonah looked from Eddie to Rosalie, hoping to determine the

general attitude so far, but Rosalie was halfway to burying her face in her palm, and Eddie was waiting intently for Jonah to continue, so... mixed messages.

"Yeah, so, I don't actually know how to find them. They found me. We could work around that but then there's the significant issue of Rooney being, uhm, dead."

"Not as much of an issue as you might think," Eddie stated, and turned around. "I'm gonna grab a quick shower and fix that right away."

He trotted off, and Rosalie turned to Jonah. He stared back at her, his mouth starting to form "what?" but no sounds came out. She sighed and took a few steps to the kitchen.

"Want a beer with those questions?"

"Absolutely."

Rosalie grabbed two beers and as she handed one to Jonah, the staircase door opened. Asphyxia took a look around the living room and frowned when she saw Jonah and Rosalie.

"Oh, err... I thought Eddie might, ehm, need a hug right now?"

"Back into the basement!" Rosalie ordered. "This is not the time, and if anyone is giving *my boyfriend* hugs in the shower, it will be me."

"Fine, go hug him then. I'll watch that instead."

"Get!"

"Shit." Asphyxia closed the door.

In the meantime, Jonah was just getting more perplexed at the complete casualness during a time like this.

"What's wrong with everybody? Rooney just got shot dead in the street, and the shooter is still at large."

Rosalie sat down and sighed. "Look, Robbie is... It's kinda hard to explain without sounding crazy."

"Try me, because you're all looking pretty crazy to me already."

Rosalie took a sip and, for a moment, Jonah was mesmerized by her. Then she started talking.

"Rob isn't dead. It's more of a witness protection kind of thing."

"Witness protection. Right."

"Yeah. In Boston. The shooter is, ehm... one of the witness protection guys-- agents."

In truth, Rosalie hated the Boston excuse. They'd used it on her father when she appeared on his doorstep after having been dead. It was easier for him to swallow than the idea that God, the Devil, and the Afterlife were real. Or perhaps just easier to ignore and focus on his daughter being back with him.

Due to its effectiveness then, Rosalie was using it again now. It just didn't work this time.

"Rosalie, I like you and I like Eddie because I like people who are a little weird." Jonah pointed at her with the bottle. "But I don't like liars. If there's something you don't want to tell me, just say so, but don't lie to me. Those guys weren't government agents. I know them, I know the CDS."

Angry about being caught in an admittedly flimsy lie, Rosalie groaned. "Fine. You want the truth? Rooney's dead, and Eddie is getting ready to bring him back."

"I didn't expect that."

"Not a lot of people do."

"Yeah, but no. I didn't expect Eddie to have a Jesus complex."

Rosalie grimaced. "No. He has all kinds of complexes, I'm sure, but Jesus isn't one of them. He's actually physically going to the Underworld and probably annoy the Devil until she just gives him back Robbie to get rid of him."

Jonah let a sip of beer roll over his tongue and took in the taste while he pondered her words. It sounded quite a lot like Eddie. He was probably capable of annoying the Devil into a snowstorm, but one does not simply walk into the Underworld. That struck him as quite a kink in the cable.

"The Afterlife isn't exactly accessible for the, you know, living."

Rosalie raised an eyebrow. "Oh, I didn't peg you as religious."

"Momma was a good god-fearing woman. Don't change the subject."

"I wasn't trying..." But then Rosalie realized she probably was and shrugged. So far, Jonah had been nice enough not to dismiss them as insane right away, and she had already said more than she planned anyhow.

"Look, a while back, Eddie killed himself to get me out of the Underworld--"

"I've already got a bunch of questions."

"Shoot."

"Poor choice of words there," Jonah joked. "What were *you* doing in the Underworld?"

"Eddie pissed the Devil off, and he sent a demon that accidentally killed me."

"Right. Right. Those demons, huh? And Eddie just went ahead and killed himself because...?"

"Because God told him to."

"Obviously." Jonah did a formidable job of making it seem like this was all very normal to him, even though Rosalie already expected him to laugh in her face.

"So God just came down from the heavens and said--" Jonah asked carefully.

Rosalie shook her head. "No, she lived here. Remember the nun who used to live in this church?"

"I thought it was abandoned, actually."

"It wasn't. Helen was pretending to be a nun here and she helped Eddie on his way." Rosalie studied Jonah. "You're taking this surprisingly well."

Jonah finished his beer and took his sweet time putting it on the table.

"If anything," he started thoughtfully, "this makes for a nice story. I've met a lot of people in my time and heard of as many different beliefs. If this--"

He didn't get to finish his sentence because Eddie burst from the bedroom in full gear and grabbed the manliest knife he could find in the kitchen.

"Okay, time to go," he said. "I'll be right back."

Rosalie practically launched herself from the couch and ran to the kitchen.

"Edward Sterling!" she yelled, stopping the knife just short of his wrist. "I am not going to clean up the mess if you bleed all over my kitchen floor!"

"It's okay. I'll get it when I come back."

With one of the moves her father taught her when she was younger, Rosalie grabbed Eddie's wrist and twisted until he had to let go of the knife. Eddie whinged, but she didn't let go until she firmly held the knife in her own hand.

"You're not killing yourself," she said as if she was talking to an unruly child who wanted ice cream. And because he had just been bested like an unruly child, Eddie reacted like one: angrily and inappropriately.

"Why? Because your soul is the only one worth saving?"

He regretted his words even before Rosalie's palm made painful contact with his cheek.

"Be happy I'm not using the knife," she hissed.

"Very happy. But... Rooney?"

"Just call Lilith, you dumbass."

Eddie looked at her like she just turned water into wine. Like an IT specialist, he went straight to reprogramming the system instead of checking if the computer was plugged in. A simple phone call was the safer and more obvious option.

"That's why we're a team," he said and kissed her forehead. "Jonah! Do you mind staying here in case the shooter comes back?"

"You're asking if I mind getting shot, which, yes, I mind. Where are you going?"

"Make a call."

"You have a phone, right? I see you holding a phone."

Eddie slipped his phone back in his pocket. "It's a special call. If I use my own phone, something horrible screams at me. I need to use the phone at the crossroads."

Jonah made a throw-away gesture. "Make your call."

Eddie ran out, and Rosalie put the knife back in the block. The engine of the Vindicator started up like rolling thunder and, shortly after, disappeared into the distance. Rosalie looked at Jonah.

"I'm sorry. You don't have to stay."

"No, I'm actually curious to see how this plays out."

"You and me both."

There was very little chance a simple phone call would be the end of this, but she could hope.

NINE

When the Vindicator went under the highway overpass that most people generally used to visualize the county line, the quaint Herringwood scenery was replaced with increasing emptiness. Grass along the road went from green to brownish, then to sad patches and sand.

Usually, Eddie would merrily belt along with whatever song came up in his playlist, and he did have Metallica's "Fuel" driving him along at the moment, but he didn't sing. He didn't know that much about the Afterlife and Fate, but according to the little he knew, Rooney's death was fated. Unless someone unqualified had pushed Domino out of the House of Fates again, the shooting was supposed to happen, which would make it hard to convince Lilith to give back Rooney.

Unconsciously, Eddie grunted. If Lilith didn't want to cooperate, he already had half a plan to make her job very hard.

The last payphone in Herringwood became visible at the

crossroads that marked the actual county line. Eddie slowed down until he came to a full shop on the side of the road next to it.

This was just one of those places that never changed. The dead tree still stood there against all odds, the disused tunnel wasn't suddenly in use again, and the sand had probably been here since before he was born. The only change he noticed was that someone had scratched the word "bell bottom" into the base of the payphone. Though he couldn't help a little chuckle, this marked today's quota for bad puns.

Time to get serious, but even though he'd done this before, the buttons felt resistant under his fingers, as if even they knew they shouldn't be pressed.

666-1318.

The answer was almost instantaneous but Eddie remained quiet because he remembered the menu.

"For reservations, press one. If you wish to sell your soul, press two. If you have questions about the sale of your soul, press three. To contact a relative or loved one, press four--"

Eddie pressed four and wound up in a part of the menu that was new to him, which meant he immediately felt the urge to screw with the automated service.

"You have pressed four. Please clearly state the name and birthplace of the person you wish to contact."

All he needed to say was "Rob Rooney." But that would have been too simple; plus, this was a nice opportunity to get some questions answered.

"Robert Johnson of Hazlehurst, please."

He wasn't sure what good this would do him, but it would be nice to find out if the Devil actually taught him to play guitar.

The automated operator burst his bubble, though. "We are very sorry but *Robert Johnson* can't come to the phone right now. Would you like to leave a message?"

Eddie scoffed. "Pf. I guess. Tell him his ride is waiting at the crossroads."

The automated operator neither confirmed nor denied and simply cut the connection.

"I should stop screwing with the menu..."

He dialed again, and not a moment later, the system started rattling off the options again. Eddie didn't wait until it got to number four; instead, he just pressed the button.

"Rob Rooney of Herringwood, please."

After a few moments, the system came with an answer and it wasn't one Eddie enjoyed.

"We regret to inform you that there is no *Rob Rooney of Herringwood* in our system. Thank you for choosing Hecatelecom Automated Phone Services. You will now be disconnected."

"The fuck?"

Annoyed, he dialed a third time, but instead of choosing option four again, he pressed two. He wasn't planning to sell his soul—though that was one of the aces up his sleeve—but it was the only way he knew how to get a live operator on the line.

"Eddie Sterling, Herringwood," he said when prompted and waited when the system told him to "please hold."

It was to be expected when dealing with the Underworld. They probably just had him on hold to screw with him. An automated phone menu was just one of many possible hells.

Thankfully, he wasn't on hold for quite that long before a familiar voice answered.

"Mr. Sterling, this is Debbie--"

"Wait, like, Customer Services Debbie?"

"Yes, sir. Management now, though," Debbie said proudly. "Thanks to you, actually. The previous boss got really angry with my manager for making you his problem, so he set him on fire."

"Oh. You're welcome, then."

Debbie let out her delightful giggle. "I do hope you're in a better mood this time."

"Hm, I'm not making any promises, but I didn't call to yell at you."

"Oh, good. Because I have bad news—you can't sell your soul."

"Eh? Why not? I did it before... by accident."

Debbie hummed a confirmation. "That's exactly why you've been blacklisted. We prefer to no longer do business with you."

Eddie wondered if this was maybe the time to start yelling at her again since that netted far better results the previous time they spoke. Then again, Debbie was nothing but friendly, and she was only passing on a message from some suit in Legal.

"Actually, I don't want to sell my soul," he said. "You should put in an option for speaking to a live operator."

"Sir, that would defeat the whole purpose of the automated system."

"The system has failed anyway. I need to talk to my friend, but your computer says he isn't in the system."

"Let me check," Debbie answered. "Name, please?"

Eddie gave Rooney's name again, and Debbie put on the waiting Muzak while she had a look of her own.

He felt a little proud of himself for being instrumental in Debbie's promotion. Granted, not on purpose, but still. In fact, if she came back on the line and didn't have a satisfactory answer, he would yell at her a little bit. He earned it, after all.

Debbie came back on the line. "Your friend really isn't in the system, sir."

"I told you, the system has failed." Eddie did his best to remain calm. "Listen, could you put me through to Lilith, please?"

"No, sir. I can't."

"You mean you won't."

"Yes, sir."

Eddie groaned and pinched the receiver between his ear and his shoulder so he could light a cigarette.

"Listen, Deb," he said while exhaling, "can I call you Deb?"

"I'd rather you didn't--"

"Deb, I saw my friend gunned down in the street. He is dead. Since your system has clearly shit the bed, Lilith probably doesn't know, and I need to tell her."

"I can't--"

"Debbie! Sweetheart. Don't make me come down there. You know I will."

Debbie was well aware she was dealing with someone who could back up any threat he made and thought about it for a few seconds. Putting any simple human through to the boss was grounds enough for getting fired. Literally. But this was something that personally affected the boss, and keeping that from her would probably also not be appreciated very much. Finally, she gambled on the new boss being less violent than the old boss.

"Fine. Please hold."

She redirected his call, and the Muzak popped back on. It took him a while to recognize Sabbath's "Heaven And Hell," and he made it all the way to what would have been the acoustic outro, but it sounded just a bit daft as a Muzak version through the phone. Thankfully, that was also the moment that Lilith finally answered.

"Lilith speaking. Who's this?"

"The man who almost made it to the end of a six-minute song waiting for you to answer."

"Eddie! It's nice to hear your voice. How are you?"

Eddie groaned. "Shitty. Rooney died."

Lilith gasped.

"Why is everybody down there surprised? Don't you people specifically deal with this?"

"I have people that deal with this *for me*, yes," Lilith answered. "I don't sit around and have orgies all day, you know. I'm busy. And even if I did, do you have any idea how much work goes into planning a nice, convivial orgy?"

"I will let you tell me all about it when you invite me to one, but if you don't mind, I wanna talk business right now."

"I'm not letting you sell your soul."

"And I don't want to. I need you to find out what the Hell is going on down there because your people are fucking everything up. I know what I saw, and I saw Rooney die in my arms. He's got to be there because he's dead as disco."

Lilith chuckled. "Still doing alright, disco."

"Yeah, tell it to Twisted Sister. Just send him back, will you?"

"No. How do you think it's gonna look if I just send back souls left and right? I'm already getting the stink eye from some people for not keeping George on a leash."

Eddie grunted. "So that's what this is? You won't help me because you need to save face? Well, thanks a lot, goddammit! You've really taken to being the Devil."

Lilith remained quiet for a few moments to compose herself. Eddie struck a nerve with her, but she knew it was just the anger talking. He would probably regret being mean later.

"Eddie, bud, listen..." she said and gave him a moment to respond, which he most definitely did.

"Don't 'bud, listen' me, girl. If it wasn't for me, you'd still be hanging out in the cemetery with your Batman-wannabe friends, all emo about how daddy was mean to you--"

"If you keep talking like this, I'm gonna hang up, you dick."

"Oh, honey, you fucking well know that's the worst you could do. I went down there once; I'm not gonna have a problem doing it twice." Eddie got increasingly cocky, as would anyone who was giving the Devil an earful. He had her on the ropes, and it started to look like a checkmate.

"You know you can only come here if you're dead or invited," Lilith said. "I'm not that worried."

Eddie leaned on the payphone and looked at the angry grille of the Vindicator. "I've got 425 horses that say you should be very worried, Red."

"Yeah, you've got all the power and no clue where to point it," Lilith scoffed and allowed herself an unprofessional jab. "For Rosalie's sake, I hope that only applies to the car."

Eddie didn't care for that kind of talk from someone who was keeping him from bringing his best friend back to life, and he snapped.

"You know what? Fuck off! And when you're done fucking off, fuck off some more. In fact, keep fucking off until you get back to where you are now, and then fuck off again!"

He slammed the receiver down and was torn between emotions. He felt some pride over that offensive ouroboros of verbal assault, but more sadness over unleashing it on someone he previously considered a friend, especially under these shitty circumstances.

And it was all going to get worse as well. There was a reason they called the Devil the Prince of Lies. Or Princess, currently. Eddie had no choice but to go to the Underworld and get Rooney himself.

For Gina, today was just another day. A diner full of customers, two of them actually from overseas, and regulars flirting with her at the counter. She flirted right back because that's how you get the good tips.

What had also become a familiar sight and sound was the Vindicator pulling into a parking spot. Gina could have tossed her Famous Chicken Legs in the pan—or made Cookie do it, anyway—right at the sound of the rumbling V8, but like all of her customers, Eddie enjoyed her "what can I do you for?" too much to forego it, so she politely waited until he came in and told her what he wanted.

"Alright, hon," she then answered and turned to the open kitchen. "Cookie--"

"Yardbird with a heart attack, yeah, yeah. I heard the car."

Eddie grinned. "To go, please."

"Oh?" Gina turned back to him. "Not staying?"

Eddie shook his head. "Got an issue to deal with. No time."

"And what issue would be so important that you haven't got time for my Legs?"

Eddie puckered his lips. This seemed like a great opportunity to do some innuendos about her legs, but he bravely resisted the urge.

"It's kinda hard to explain," he said instead, "but it will solve your hobo problem."

"I have a hobo problem?"

"The guy by the trees you said was giving you the creeps?"

Gina shrugged and proceeded to polish her spotless counter. "That guy? I fail to see how you feeding him a second time will motivate him to go away."

"Yeah, but I don't, so leave it to me."

"As you like, hon."

Since the Vindicator could be heard coming from afar, Eddie didn't have to wait long for his order. Cookie put out a bag of Chicken Legs and rang the bell. Out of habit, Gina made Eddie wait just a little bit longer because anticipation made them taste even better. It just wasn't necessary for Eddie since he loved unanticipated Chicken Legs just as much.

She handed him his order. "Good luck with your thing, hon."

"Thanks."

He jogged back to the car and drove it just a bit farther down the road. He would have preferred to drive it up to the tree line, but it looked like the terrain would get him stuck. Hopefully, nobody would notice a smoke demon floating along the wrinkled, grassy terrain to the car.

Leaving the door open, Eddie went up to the trees, jiggling the bag and whistling like he lost his dog.

"George! Come and get the Chickens."

Something loudly sniffed the air, and when the smell of Gina's Famous Chicken Legs hit his olfactory parts, George appeared. The ratty trenchcoat wrapped around him unnaturally, and the mountie hat fell off when he caught it on a branch.

Eddie quickly looked around to check if anybody was seeing this.

George's catlike pupils floated in a sea of dead white but still came to life at the sight of the bag.

"For me?"

"I thought I told you to go back to Lilith."

"I'm sorry…" George tapped his fingertips together nervously. "I wanted to smell the chickens again before I go."

Luckily for George, although slightly confusing, Eddie was very happy about that.

"Don't worry about it, buddy." Eddie held up the bag. "These are all yours if you take me to the Underworld right now."

"Oooh."

He reached for the bag, but Eddie didn't hand it over.

"No, buddy. You have to get in the car first. I need to visit Lillie."

"Lillie!"

"Yes. Can't do it without your help."

George briefly thought about it. If he helped Eddie get to the Underworld, he would probably have a hard time going back to smell more chickens, but then again, he would actually have chickens if he did. The choice was pretty easy.

Whatever force held George's body in its current shape let go. The coat fell down limply, and a cloud of black smoke rolled across the ground into the car, where it reformed. Eddie quickly jogged after him and sat down. Slamming the door, he handed the bag over.

Happy as a kid in a candy store, George started munching on the Chicken Legs. Although he had a mouth that could swallow a person whole, he took the tiniest of bites at a time to make this last longer.

"Don't get any on my seats."

George grunted something, but he was too busy dissecting

chickens. The physics of it just didn't make any sense. Sticky bits of chicken should be falling right through the smoke George was made of, but then Eddie remembered staring down the unholy vortex that time George almost ate him. Somewhere in the Underworld, there were probably chewed-up chunks raining down, and unlike the demon janitor who had to clean it up, Eddie was in a relatively good mood. He had the car that could withstand the trip and the guide that could light his way. There was nothing stopping him from rolling up on the Devil and demanding his best friend back.

TEN

Maybe there was just one thing that could stop Eddie from confronting the Devil, and she was waiting for him at the payphone. Rosalie had her arms crossed and stared along the road as if she was trying to burn a hole in the horizon. She leaned against the phone, and the only thing missing from this picture was a rolling pin to beat some ass with. Though Rosalie was probably thinking about a spiked mace.

Behind her, Jonah was unsure if he should start a conversation to kill some time. He gave her a ride here, but beyond that, his part was done. When Eddie appeared on the horizon, he took a few extra steps back—not necessarily for privacy, but because he didn't want to get any blood on him.

Though the car seemed to roll into a stop, there was an air of hesitation around it, but if Eddie ran now, he could only keep running. Seemed like a bad choice, so he eventually got out and put on his best surprised-to-see-you face.

"Hey, baby. Wha--"

"Oh, Hell no. Instead of smooth-talking your way out of this, try explaining why I just got a call *from the fucking Devil!*"

"You talked to Lilith? What did she say? Is she sending Rooney back?"

"Not quite, no," Rosalie snarled. "She did tell me she suspected you were planning on going to Hell. I'm gonna give you a chance to lie about it if that makes you feel better, but after that, I will indignantly point at the demon in the passenger seat."

Eddie puckered his lips in preparation to say something; however, one look at the car and its occupant told him there was no lying his way out of this. Perhaps there was some brilliant misdirection he could come up with, given enough time, but he'd be lying to Rosalie, which wasn't something he wanted to start doing. The first lie would be hard, but then it would just get easier and easier, until all he did was tell lies.

"Yeah, I am going to the Underworld. Just quickly popping in, though. Grab Rooney's soul, and right back out again."

Rosalie grabbed him and shook him. "You didn't think that was something you should tell me, asshole?"

"Why? Did you wanna come?"

"God, no!" Rosalie said, genuinely repulsed. "I still have nightmares about that place sometimes, Eddie. It's hard enough for me to stand here so close to... I don't ever wanna go back there again."

She glanced at the tunnel. Eddie immediately regretted not just calling her so she didn't have to come all the way here. All he could do now was try to make it better, and he put his arms around her. Sadly, that was the only good thing he tried. The rest of it...

"It's gonna be unavoidable at some point, I think."

Rosalie pushed away from him.

"I love how sensitive you are," she scoffed. "But until that unavoidable time comes, I'm staying right on our plane of existence, and so should you!"

"Yeah, but... somebody's gotta go and get Rooney back, and since it's clearly not gonna be you--"

"Condescension isn't making me more understanding, *sweetheart*."

Eddie threw his hands up and turned around. Then he turned back to her because talking with his back turned was difficult and impolite.

"I've got the car that can do it and a demon who knows the way. I have some rudimentary knowledge of the place... I'm not trying to, err... condescend, but it seems to me that if we want our Rooney back, I'm the one to do it."

Rosalie hung her head. She hated it when he had a point. There were a lot of variables, however. It still seemed risky, even with the Vindicator and George. She took a long, hard look at the tunnel. What it stood for sent shivers down her spine, but there was nothing particularly menacing about it now that it wasn't on fire or anything.

"What if it was just a one-time thing, what we did?" She turned back to Eddie. "We're not supposed to travel between those worlds."

"People aren't, no. A Century Motors Vindicator, however..." Eddie wasn't actually sure how to make the soup, but he had all the ingredients. "Hey, if worse comes to worst, I'll just pop out the other end, right?"

"That's a derelict tunnel. I don't know what's going on in that darkness, but I'm pretty sure you're not just gonna pop out the other end."

"But we won't know if I don't try." Eddie put his arms around her. "And I have to try. It's Rooney down there."

Rosalie held him tight and sighed. For a while, she just enjoyed how he rubbed her back before eventually pulling back to give him a kiss. She wished there was a way to stop him from doing this but knew full well that he needed to find out for himself. If she kept him from this, he would come to resent her, and she'd even understand it. They were two people in an exceptional position; it was pretty much his responsibility to do this.

"Dammit, Sterling," she sighed. "I knew life with you wouldn't be regular, but damn..."

"I'm making it hard for you, aren't I?"

Rosalie let go of him and shot him a weak grin. "Oh, you know, my boyfriend is just going to pick up a friend in Hell. What's weird about that?"

Eddie looked at Jonah, who was doing his best not to be there during their loving moment. "Do you wanna try and talk me out of this too, before I go anyway?"

Jonah shrugged. Eddie and Rosalie were close enough to make light of this amongst each other, but he wasn't sure if it was something he could join in on, so he chose to err on the side of caution. He would have preferred to leave it at that shrug, but something in Rosalie's eyes made him say things he hadn't considered saying.

"Do you need me to come along?"

Rosalie jumped on it before Eddie could politely decline. "It would make me feel better if you had backup, babe."

Eddie smirked at her and turned his attention to Jonah. "I guess I do, yes."

He inched back to the Vindicator. "I'll be careful, okay?"

"Don't lie to me, babe."

He gave her a thumbs up and opened the passenger door for Jonah, who took his first encounter with a smoke demon relatively well.

"Hello," George said, still holding the empty paper bag in his hands. That he was done eating didn't mean he was done smelling.

Eddie leaned in. "Get in the back, buddy."

George complied without hesitation but that didn't mean

Jonah just got in. He saw the enormous fangs protruding up from that body-wide underbite.

"Is it safe? Like, that thing's not... I dunno. What does it do?"

"Hey, fuck you, man. George is better than either of us, and *he* is good people. He helped me get out of the Underworld, and now he's helping me get back in."

Jonah really regretted offering to come along. Whether or not Eddie was delusional didn't matter, even with that thing in the backseat. The more immediate problem was that he now took place in the passenger seat of a high-powered vehicle mostly known for its straight-line performance, piloted by a person who wanted to get to a make-believe place in a hurry.

When Eddie got in, he glanced over and grinned.

"She did the eye-thing, didn't she?"

"Yup."

"Regretting it?"

"Yup."

"Wanna get out?"

Jonah's lips started to form the Y in "yup," but then he locked eyes with Eddie. "Nope."

Eddie's cocky grin turned into an appreciative smile. "You sure?"

"The CDS brought me into this long before your girlfriend made eyes at me. I think I owe it to you, her, and Rooney."

Jonah turned in his seat and extended his hand to George. "Jonah Craig, nice to meet you."

George had seen humans do this and was reasonably sure how this worked. He grabbed Jonah's hand, shook it, and said his name, as was the custom. He went a little outside protocol by saying it like he always did: with the voice of all the disembodied souls he devoured echoing through the growling, ethereal bass that made the air around him visibly vibrate.

Gaeorghis.

Pale as a shroud, Jonah turned back and froze in his seat.

"Wanna get out now?" Eddie checked.

"I was not prepared for that." Jonah tried to swallow past his dry throat. "But I doubt it's gonna get much worse than--"

After the ungodly sound he'd just heard, it was quite easy for simple things to make it worse, so he nearly soiled himself when Rosalie tapped on the window.

Eddie rolled it down. "Sup, sexy?"

"Are you guys going today? Because I was planning on watching you go and stand here waving while the wind caught my hair and a single tear rolled down my cheek. But I've got stuff to do, so..."

"Aw, just like in the movies," he smiled, very much in love. "Just need to pick out the right music--"

"AC/DC, obviously."

"Damn, I love you."

"I know."

Rosalie smiled and tapped the roof to let Eddie know he could roll the window back up. She was going to stay and watch either way because he was about to do something dangerous, but he shouldn't be doing it with the window down.

"Alright then," Eddie hyped himself, "let's do this. George! Rock 'n' roll, baby!"

"Lillie!" George cheered.

His eyes lit up blindingly bright, and Eddie revved the engine until he saw the tunnel within the tunnel open up. The gaping black hole became a fiery inferno until the chaos organized into a twisting, burning vortex.

The Vindicator burst forward like it needed to set a quarter-mile record. Over the roar of the engine and the only appropriate song for driving to what many considered Hell, Jonah heard his knuckles crack from gripping the oh-shit handle.

"Ed! Ed! Ed!"

"Yeah?"

"It's on fire!"

"Awesome, right?"

"No! Don't drive into--"

"Too late."

Whatever smidge of color remained on Jonah's face after hearing George's demon voice now also faded as he watched smoldering asphalt in a sea of fire stretch out before them. Flames lashed out, the fiery tongues whipping around unnaturally as if each had a mind of its own. The Vindicator pushed forward angrily because it was born from fire. These bitch-ass flames didn't scare the machine. The engine snarled like it was cursing, saying nasty things about their mothers. The flames responded by twisting into a hellish tornado of death that no sane person would dare come near. Eddie technically wasn't insane, but he couldn't be considered sane enough not to do this. Sane people wouldn't have a maniacal grin on their face as fire enveloped their car.

Jonah just tried to find a feeling of normality by pretending he was touring along a coastal highway with the wind in his hair. It didn't work.

As quickly as it started and without warning, the terror stopped. The shaking and jerking were over, the flames withdrew, and all that was left was George lighting the way down an offramp until the car's headlights touched a hangar-sized garage door that opened automatically.

Almost confusingly calm, Eddie drove inside and stopped without finding a proper parking spot in an immense garage full of impressive cars. Jonah didn't mind. After that ride, illegal parking was far preferable to the complete lunacy he had just gone through. His respite was short-lived, though. The door of the office across from them opened, and a far-too-large balloony creature squeezed out of a far-too-small opening.

"What the fuck is that?" Jonah asked, worried as it approached them, seemingly eyeing them up for a meal.

Again, Eddie wasn't worried. "That's the Underworld's resident mechanic, Janick."

"Janick the mechanic?"

"I don't write the jokes, man."

Janick the Mechanic wiped his orange hands on a dirty rag, and even though each of his eyes seemed to be on separate errands, he examined the car and finished with a nod.

Eddie exited the car like he'd just driven to the shops. Behind him, George poured out and reformed into his regular self.

"Janick! What's up, Big Orange?" Eddie said jovially.

Janick twitched his left ear like he always did when processing something he wasn't used to, which happened a lot, considering he was solely created to care for the cars here.

"You come for tune-up?" he asked in his rather generic Eastern European accent.

"No. Why? Does he need one?"

"Bah!" Janick shook his head. He built this machine to last. "Who is pale friend?"

Eddie turned to Jonah and tapped the hood. "Come say hi. Janick's mostly harmless."

Jonah opened the door. "Mostly?"

"Yeah, just don't fuck with the cars."

That seemed doable, so Jonah got out and introduced himself to Janick, who didn't seem to have much of an interest in him anymore.

The last time Janick introduced himself to anybody was Eddie, and he did this by licking his hand, which apparently was not how you did it. Janick never bothered to find out how it was done because it didn't concern cars, so he chose not to do it anymore at all.

"Is he angry?" Jonah asked Eddie. "Because I kinda don't need a bear in overalls to be angry with me."

Eddie examined Janick. "I'd say he's more gorilla-ish..."

"Fine. A gorilla can also rip my arms from their sockets, so the main concern is with his emotional state as opposed to his genus."

"Ooh, fancy words for a carpenter. Did someone make you carve that into a wooden tile?"

"Jeeze, dude, what?"

"If he was angry, he would have pulled your arms out of your sockets already *and* beat me to death with them, but seeing as we're still bickering like we're married and he's bloody walking away, I'd say his emotional state is neutral. Hey, Janick!"

Janick turned around.

"Is Lilith in?"

Janick shrugged. That was also not his concern.

"Yes, she is!" a perfectly-timed voice sounded.

Eddie looked in its direction and saw Lilith approach with three security guards. George immediately hovered to her and gave her a big hug. "Lillie!"

She gave him a perfunctory hug back. "Why did you bring him here, George?"

George detected the disappointment in her voice, and it cut like a knife. He picked at his lip. "Uh... he gave me chickens."

Eddie came over to get a hug of his own in, but Lilith stopped him with a simple gesture. He assessed the situation quickly. If she brought these guards just for him, she should have brought more, though avoiding violence altogether would be preferable.

"What's going on here, Lil?"

She stepped closer to him with eyes of fire and poked him in the chest. "You pissed me off is what's going on."

"I've literally just got here. What the Hell did I do?"

"You're here!" Lilith burst, letting her temper get the better of her. "I told you not to come here. Not only did you ignore me completely, but you brought a goddamn friend while you're at it!"

Eddie looked back for a moment. "Err, yeah, Rosie kinda wanted me to bring backup. Just in case. And he's also my carpenter, actually. You saw the woodwork in the church, right? All his work. Fine job he did, too. Quality craftsmanship, if you ask me."

"Well, thank God I didn't ask you, else you'd drone on for hours about the fucking woodwork in your fucking church where you should have fucking stayed! I don't need every Tom, Dick, and Eddie going in and out of here as they please."

"It's Harry. 'Every Tom, Dick, and Harry' is the expression."

Lilith squinted and hissed, "No, it's definitely Eddie."

"In any case, he's my backup." Eddie gestured Jonah over and then held up a finger at Lilith's security detail. "So you muppets better not get any ideas."

Against his instincts, Jonah extended his hand. "Jonah Craig, ma'am. Carpenter."

Lilith merely glanced at it and crossed her arms. "Lilith. *Devil.*"

Her eyes glowed like melting glass, and Jonah retracted his hand. It was pretty clear to him they had arrived at a bad time, but Eddie seemed completely oblivious to the fact.

"Ehm, your lashes are melting," he said.

"They'll grow back. Why the fuck are you here, Sterling?"

"You know damn well why I'm here."

"Considering I told you Rooney is not here, I can only assume you think this place is like a bar, and you want to show me off to your friend. Other than that, I have no idea."

"Admittedly, you are quite a sight to behold, but not everything's about you," Eddie said. "Why don't you want to give back Rooney?"

"How many times are you going to make me repeat myself?" Lilith snapped furiously. "Because I don't fucking have him!"

"Well, I don't have him either, so one of us must be lying, and I've got a witness right here who says it ain't me."

Jonah took a step back. "Leave me out of this, would you?"

Eddie didn't pay attention to him and made the dubious choice of trying to anger Lilith into giving Rooney back.

"What kind of place are you running here if you're just losing souls like they're FedEx packages?"

Which backfired.

Lilith couldn't help herself anymore. She was really trying to be a professional Devil, and since her first day, she had vowed to do better than her father. Numerous improvements had already been made, souls were getting fairer treatment, and still she was getting looks because she was just daddy's girl taking over. Now this guy, who should definitely know better, was giving her lip; Lilith lost control, grabbed Eddie by his jacket, and pushed him up against a '55 Porsche Spyder.

"Whoa, is this--"

"Focus on me, you little bastard! I oversee everything that goes on in the Underworld, Eddie. And when you arrogantly call me to check up on trivialities, I do it, even though there are people who are supposed to do that for me because I'm *too fucking busy*! You think I enjoy never seeing my friends? Hm? Do you think I don't feel shitty for not visiting Phyx after her surgery?"

"Uh..." Eddie never really thought about it very much. "I think my lashes are also melting now."

Lilith let go of him. "Great, there he goes with the jokes again. You know what? Fuck you. Rooney's not here." She shot Jonah a quick, mean look. "Welcome to Hell, Mr. Craig." And then she turned away. "George! Come!"

George floated after Lilith as she headed for the door. Eddie would have loved to take a closer look at the Porsche she had him pushed up against, but instead, he quickly went after her.

To Lilith, death wasn't more than a transition—a triviality. Souls went on when they got here, and they came here because Fate required it. She knew Eddie knew this, too, and it upset her to no end that he'd callously come here to once again make everything the way he thought it should be. Right now, Lilith didn't even want to hear his voice, yet she did.

"Wait! I need George to get back!"

With her hand on the doorknob, Lilith took one more angry look at him. "I told you, you can only come here if you're invited or dead... And you were most certainly not invited, Eddie. Good luck and goodbye."

She slammed the door shut.

Obviously, Eddie wasn't about to take this lying down. He went to open the door again, but it was firmly locked. Worried, he shuffled back. This definitely wasn't good. He'd gotten himself and Jonah stuck in the Underworld's garage, but even worse, Rosalie was going to worry about him at some point.

"What now?" Jonah asked.

"Whelp... We might be dead, so..." He wandered back to his Vindicator and leaned against the hood for a proper make-a-plan cigarette.

Janick came up to him. "No smoking."

Eddie looked from the cigarette to him and then around the garage. "Man, there's a V8 Interceptor just behind you. That thing puts out more noxious fumes just by standing still than I ever could. Don't pull that no-smoking bullshit on me."

Janick came up close to Eddie and looked down on him. He pointed at a pump near his office. "No smoking around high-octane fuel."

Eddie dropped his cigarette and stomped it out. "My bad."

"Yes." Janick marched away and returned with a broom. "Clean up mess."

Apparently, Eddie was now an employee of Janick's Underworld Car Repair, which, admittedly, would look awesome on his CV. Still, he didn't plan on keeping the job any longer than he needed to figure out how to get out of here.

ELEVEN

If there were two things Lilith hated, it would have to be the elevator Muzak and the gnawing feeling that something wasn't right. At least she could try to do something about the latter, which meant she had to endure the former for a little longer. The door opened to the hallway by her office, and instead of getting out, she pressed another button. The doors closed again, and she was on her way down to Hospitality. Unfortunately for her dislike of the Muzak, Hospitality was at the lowest level, but it did give her enough time to think about Eddie's sudden arrival.

He was brash, that much was true, but she was confident not even he would just hop in his car to drop by for a visit... Well, on second thought, he might drop by for a simple visit, but that clearly wasn't what he was doing here today. If this had been a friendly visit, there would have been hugging, and drinks, and probably some innuendos. Things like that. Definitely not name-calling and saying things both of them would regret later.

He really thought he was coming to pick up Rooney, and Lilith didn't like that she was surprised by this. She didn't have the time or interest to keep tabs on everyone who arrived here, but for a select few souls, she made sure to stay updated. Part of the reason she went to Hospitality was to find out what happened, and the other part would come into play if she didn't like what she found out. If it was the case that she just hadn't been informed, somebody was going to catch on fire all of a sudden.

Lilith stepped out of the elevator in the grand Art Deco lobby and waited behind a partition wall until she heard the tour group that was coming through leave. She didn't mind posing for one or two pictures with a few starstruck tourists from Heaven, but she wasn't in the mood today.

Instead of taking the big doors into Processing, she went around back through the offices. Several employees dared to take a quick peek to see if it really was the new boss but Lilith just kept going until she came out the other end into Maintenance.

A giant octopus amid an array of imaginative machinery greeted her.

"Ma'am. Need me to fix your eyelashes?"

"No, thank you, Paul. Just passing through."

She went out the front door and walked onto the Hospitality landing to look around. It wasn't common for upper management to come down here, and from the arrival's point of view, it would be quite disconcerting to step out of their burial vessel to come face to face with the Devil. Lilith was aware of this and made it a point to keep her presence here to the bare minimum.

"Can I help you?" a young brunette in a baby blue uniform asked.

"Yes, err..." Lilith looked at her silver name tag. "Linda. I'm looking for Peter."

"Oh, he doesn't work here anymore," Linda responded, smiling nervously. She wasn't afraid of Lilith, per se, but she had a habit of making social faux pas around important people. She tried to keep her disbelief hidden. Peter's departure seemed like something the boss would know.

"Doesn't work here anymore?" Lilith asked as naturally as she could muster. "Was his time up?"

"Err... from what I've heard, he served his time even before I got here. He just enjoyed this."

Lilith remembered Peter from long ago. He was a nice man, so it didn't surprise her that he'd stick around after his ticket to Heaven became available. It felt right to him, making the transition for new arrivals that little bit easier, which made it all the more odd that he just up and left.

"If he enjoyed this so much, why did he go?"

Linda's mouth formed to make words, but she stopped to think about them, wanting to be sure she didn't sound disrespectful by accidentally asking how Lilith didn't know about this.

"A position for station master opened up, so he went there. He always had a thing for trains, so now he's making people happy *and* looking at the Number 9."

Lilith shrugged. It seemed a tad gratuitous to have a station master at a station that handled only one train, but then again, it was just as strange to give that single train a number. Either way, it was probably a position they could do without, but it wasn't a thought she entertained for very long. Liquidating Peter's new job just after he'd gotten it was a shitty thing to do, and shitty was more her father's game.

"Perhaps you could help me then."

"Absolutely, ma'am. What can I do for you?"

"I need to look at this week's manifest."

"Okay, follow me, please."

Linda led Lilith back inside to the offices, where she opened one of a seemingly infinite amount of filing cabinets and began riffling through the files.

"This may take a moment. I don't go in here often," she apologized.

"Take your time."

"It's kind of amazing," Linda said without looking up. "I've been here a little over six months, and I've seen not one but two bosses on the landing."

"I don't plan to make it a habit."

"Maybe you should." She handed Lilith a file. "So you know what goes on down here in the trenches."

Lilith took the file but kept direct eye contact with Linda, who started to realize what she implied.

"Err... Not that you don't know... Uhm..."

"Hm-hm." Lilith turned her attention to the file. All the names were organized per date, which made sense for dealing with arrivals but made things a lot harder if you just wanted to look someone up.

"Why is this still on paper?"

"We put in a request for computers a while ago," Linda said. "I guess it got lost in the transition of management?"

Lilith could have taken offense to that, but her answer was apologetic instead.

"I'm doing what I can to get this place in shape. My father left a real mess to deal with. It's probably a good idea if you put the request in again. I'm sorry."

Linda was surprised. This was not an answer she would have gotten from the previous Devil, and she couldn't help but feel a bit sorry for Lilith.

"That's alright," she chirped. "Everybody needs time to get acclimated to their new jobs, right? I remember my first day here. So nervous! All those coffins floating in. It's creepy, right? But I got over it, and I'm just down here saying hi to people. You've got, like, a whole Underworld to run. It's been, like, six months? I don't know much about what you do, but I think you're doing pretty well for only six months."

Lilith gave Linda a polite smile and went back to the file. With an average of 106 people dying per minute, it was a thick file, and a digital search option would have been a welcome relief. All the while, Linda waited politely. She needed to get back to the landing, but she hadn't been dismissed. Thankfully, Lilith was a fast reader.

"What does this mean?" she asked, showing Linda the file.

Robert James Rooney, status amended: Special Delivery

"I have no idea. First time I've seen it." Linda bit her lip, trying to think what it could have meant, but nothing she knew of made sense here. "My best guess is that his reservations were canceled, but this seems more like something above my pay grade."

Lilith looked at the words. *Status amended.* It looked alien, tucked in between all the regular, familiar arrival times. Statuses couldn't just be amended on a whim. It had to go through Legal, and only upper management could approve it.

Lilith took a picture and pushed the file into Linda's hands.

"Thank you, that'll be all."

Instead of going the long way around, she went straight through Processing. It really didn't matter that much, time-wise, but she didn't feel like pussyfooting around anymore. She had business with the Director of the Fates because this thing had to be controlled before it got out of hand.

Another Muzak-accompanied ride later, she stepped out of the elevator and marched to the steps of the House of Fates. Lilith pushed the button on the intercom, and it didn't appear to do anything until it crackled and Domino's voice sounded.

"Who's there?"

"Dom, it's Lilith. I need to talk to you."

"Hold on."

The intercom went silent again, and a minute later, Domino came to the door, which he opened only as far as the door chain allowed. Lilith looked at it for a moment.

"Really?"

"Yes," Domino simply stated. "You might imagine I'm a little wary after your father's shenanigans."

"You know we don't actually do the whole sins of the father thing, right?"

"And you know how long it took to undo the damage the father did."

Lilith groaned. If she was completely honest, she probably would have done the same in his position.

"Look, Dom, I need to ask you about Rob Rooney's fate."

"I can't give out any fate information pertaining to any persons living or dead as per Underworld Law article--"

"His status was changed."

Domino blinked at her a few times and shut the door. A moment later, the chain came off, and it opened all the way. "A status change?"

He let Lilith in and led her to the fate lines. Millions upon billions of domino tiles rattled on as they all fell where Domino wanted them to. Some fell faster than most eyes could perceive, others so slowly that it seemed they were standing still, but they all fell. In a manner that would make any domino enthusiast cringe, Domino gave the immense table a push. Line after line flew by until Domino stopped the table as suddenly as he had pushed it. He leaned over and examined a particular line.

"Hm," he muttered, rubbing his tattooed, bald head.

"What?"

"Nothing indicates his status needs changing. It was his time; he got shot; he should be on his way."

"Are you sure?"

Domino grimaced. "Of course I'm sure! The balance of the Universe depends on my work. It's flawless. 'Am I sure.' Yes, I'm bloody sure."

"Alright, alright. It's just that over at Hospitality--"

"You're going to take some paper-pusher's word over mine?"

"No, Dom. I have complete faith in your capabilities, but my paper-pushers also know what happens if they push paper wrong. This is delicate work, as you said, so I need to find out why the information doesn't match up. And, ehm... I may have locked Eddie in the garage because of it."

"Eddie's here?"

"Hm-hm." Lilith nodded. "Came to get Rooney's soul back."

"That's..."

"Typical of him, yeah."

Domino nodded and shrugged. "Well, all I can tell you is that Rooney's supposed to be here."

Lilith sighed. If Domino already didn't have an answer, it would be very hard to find one somewhere else. Maybe she could see if Dr. Ignacio had some clever insight into this, but even he wasn't privy to the workings of Fate and he preferred not to get mixed up in management affairs, as managers had a habit of getting in the way of development.

Lilith wandered back to the door. Domino could see she was a bit lost, and he understood. The gap between Fate and management was uncomfortable at the best of times.

"Lil," he said. "Sorry I couldn't help."

"It's okay... I'll figure... something out."

Back in the elevator up to her office, the Muzak was really getting to Lilith. The tones that were meant to be soothing did the exact opposite and started to test her patience. It was as if whoever was butchering "Crossroads" actively tried to annoy her. Almost like this mess was recorded specifically with her in mind. Hell, since she was apparently so out of the loop in her own Underworld, for all she knew there was a live band under a microphone somewhere, snickering at her displeasure. The corners of her mouth curled down as her shoulders pulled up and became tense. The Muzak didn't care. It just went on and on... and on... Her fists balled, her fingernails dug into her palms, and she would have drawn blood if she wasn't who she was.

Meanwhile, just outside Lilith's office, Ginger was filing her nails. Lilith had her reconstructed after she was accidentally killed by a demon with knife fingers. Normally, that would have been it, but Lilith thought it would be smart to have a receptionist who already had the necessary experience. Say what you will about Ginger, but she definitely had it. Nobody filed nails like she did. There was a brief moment where Lilith considered changing the color of her hair because hair that black was just weird on a girl with a name like that but, in the end, she decided it wasn't her choice to make and left it up to Ginger herself.

Ginger liked her jet black hair and that was why she was now sitting here, only stopping doing her nails to brush back a lock. She looked at the elevator as it signaled its arrival with a polite ding. The doors opened, and a light haze of white smoke dissipated as Lilith stepped out. Sparks emitted from a hole in the panel just above the buttons, and when she passed Ginger, she put a mangled speaker on the desk.

"Call Maintenance, please. There's something wrong with the... audio system."

Ginger confirmed, but Lilith barely registered it. She was looking forward to a shoulder rub from George and probably a big fluffy hug at some point.

That would have to wait, though. The second her hand touched the knob of her office door, her phone rang. She wouldn't have answered if she didn't see Domino's name on the display.

"Tell me something good, Dom."

Domino didn't. He had to fumble his words first. "Hey, it's... Dom-- You already know that. Let me get right to the point, then. Have you considered Helen?"

Lilith frowned. "What? You mean *Aunt* Helen?"

"Do you know any other Helens?"

"Actually, I do," Lilith said matter-of-factly. "Helen from HR."

"Oh, yeah... I don't like her very much."

"Nobody does."

"And she can't raise the dead either."

For a moment, Lilith was stuck on how that was a factor in liking somebody or not, although it would have its benefits. Then her mind wandered on whether that meant Helen from HR would be a friend with benefits, and when Domino inquired whether she was still there, she focused on the matter at hand again.

"Are you implying Rooney's been resurrected?"

"Yeah, but only implying. I have no hard evidence either way, but he should be dead, right?"

"Right."

"Since he's not here, that implies he's alive."

"I would like it to not imply that."

"So would I. And Helen can probably lend a degree of certainty here."

Lilith frowned, but realized Domino couldn't see it through the phone, so she frowned at Ginger, who didn't see it either. She had ten nails to file, after all.

"I don't wanna go running to Aunt Helen every time something's wrong here..."

"Lilith, I believe you make a great Devil. So does Helen. It's okay to ask for help every once in a while, and this is definitely an asking-for-help situation."

Lilith groaned. She didn't want to ask for help. It felt like letting down the people who had all that faith in her. On the other hand, not asking for help basically ensured she would let down those people as well, so perhaps it was time to choose the lesser of two perceived evils.

"Thanks, Dom." She ended the call and got Ginger's attention. "Get Aunt Helen on the line for me. I'm getting a massage in the meantime."

Almost offended that she had to do, like, *work*, Ginger picked up her phone and looked back before dialing.

"Would you like me to wait until you're done 'massaging'?"

"I don't care for that suggestive tone of voice, Ms. Ginger."

Ginger didn't care about anything at all. She'd seen a lot of crazy shit under previous management, and some of it was called a 'massage' too, even though it involved three girls sharing one bikini and a suspiciously shaped demon.

"But yes," Lilith added. "Give me fifteen minutes."

For an actual massage.

Twelve

Pushing a broom around was quickly getting old for Eddie, especially since Janick kept a pretty clean garage to start with. Aside from the cigarette he crushed on the floor earlier, there was nary an oil stain to be found. Impressive, considering some of these cars were from before the environment was invented.

There was very little point in aimlessly shoving a broom across the floor. Besides, if Eddie was going to work in a garage, he was going to be fixing cars. Or, at his skill level, looking at cars and assuming they were fine. He dropped the broom where he stood and went over to the car Lilith had pushed him up against earlier. As far as Eddie could tell, the Porsche was in mint condition, which was strange, considering this was *the* '55 Spyder.

Admittedly, he was better acquainted with American muscle than German sports cars but the number 130 on the hood and doors was unmistakable. This was the Little Bastard. A chill ran down his spine, and he made sure not to get too close to the cursed car. Although, rationally, it made sense to find it here, and it would be very unlikely to still have its 'curse' active.

"Hey, Jonah!"

"Yeah?"

"Do you have any idea if curses expire?"

"Like milk?" Jonah came to him and eyed the Porsche. "Curses are all in your mind, you know. The idea that you are cursed is what throws you off balance."

"I think James Dean is gonna have an opinion on that."

"Oh, James didn't think he was--"

"Hey!" Janick came from his office. "You don't stand around! You clean up mess."

Eddie looked around. There was no mess to clean up, and he didn't feel like being ordered around by Janick either.

"You think I actually work for you or something?"

"You're in here, you can't go anywhere. You work for me now."

Eddie rubbed his chin. This was something he could work with. While Janick squeezed himself back into the office, Eddie jogged to him. "Hey. So. Like, we're employees now?"

"Yes. But not very good ones," Janick answered matter-of-factly and came back out.

"Alright. Can we have our lunch break now?"

Janick looked around. The place was clean enough to warrant a lunch break. He snorted some sort of confirmation and went to squeeze himself back in *again*. Eddie walked back to Jonah and the Spyder and tapped him on the arm. "Come on."

"I thought we couldn't--"

"Yeah, but I think we can."

Eddie tried the door on the far side again, but it remained tightly locked for him.

"Told you so," Jonah said.

"Pff! You think I would have made it to Hell the first time if a locked door was something that stopped me?" Eddie turned around. "Boss!"

Janick came out again. It would have been perfectly understandable if he had let out a dejected sigh while doing it, but he didn't. He plodded to the other side of the garage and put his hands on his hips.

"What?"

"Door's locked. I think HR hasn't processed our credentials yet."

This time, Janick actually sighed. Those paper-pushers never had their stuff in order.

"Wait..." Something seemed wrong to Janick. There was something fishy about this, but he couldn't wrap his mind around what it was.

"Come on, boss. We can't work hungry. Are you gonna let some desk jockeys be the reason your garage gets messy?"

"Hmph." Janick opened the door for them. "Be back in half hour."

They stepped into an unremarkable hallway, which gave Jonah more than enough opportunity to look amazed at Eddie.

"There are certain natural laws that apply in every dimension. Those who do actual work will be at odds with those who ride a desk." Eddie wasn't very impressed with himself. He just exploited a simple rule. "Oh, and if it ever comes up, here's another one: kick 'em in the nuts."

"What?"

"If we get in a fight. Kicking someone in the groin works equally well here."

"I'll see what I can do..."

Eddie pressed the button at the nearest elevator as if he'd worked there for years. Of course, operating an elevator didn't take a very high level of competence—unless you were a lift attendant, in which case a degree of talent was expected—but Eddie made it look particularly casual for calling an elevator in another world.

Jonah wasn't very worried yet, either. Apart from being ready to get himself and Eddie out of the way should a Lovecraftian monstrosity lunge at them, he wasn't very impressed. Rightly so, as the doors opened to reveal a very mundane elevator.

Only when Eddie stared at the wholly ridiculous amount of buttons on the wall did Jonah feel a minor pang of concern.

"Where are we going?"

Eddie shrugged. "I have no idea."

"How about up?"

"Hm. No. Even if regular logic applied here, I'm not leaving without Orpheus."

Eddie's plan had always been to leave the way they came, even if only for the complete awesomeness of bursting forth from the tunnel in a torrent of fire. If it was up to him, he'd be doing that every other day and twice on weekends.

He reached for a random button with the idea that any point was a good point to start. Jonah vehemently disagreed and grabbed his wrist, though that meant he had to let go of the door, and it closed behind him.

"You're just pressing random buttons now?"

"Err, yah. I will accept better suggestions, though."

Jonah opened his mouth, but the elevator started moving. "At least give me a second to come up with something before you press the button anyway!"

"Nope. This is just how elevators work. It's gonna go if someone somewhere presses the call button."

The ride was long. Too long. Jonah estimated that they would have passed the top of the Empire State Building by now, assuming they were traveling at average elevator speeds, which, he had to admit, he didn't actually know. As far as either of them was concerned, there was normal and abnormal. And since Jonah was thinking about abnormalities, he noticed they were moving but couldn't tell in which direction. He didn't feel any lighter, nor did he feel gravity tug on him; all he felt was the subtle vibration of movement.

After what seemed like forever, the elevator signaled they had arrived, and the door slid open. A young Black man stepped into the elevator with a guitar case and tipped his homburg hat at them.

"Gentlemen," he greeted politely.

He was probably in his late twenties and his suit seemed to be from the late thirties. While unusual, Jonah thought nothing of it until he noticed Eddie had eyes wide as saucers, and if he did the universal "it's him!" look any harder, they might have popped out of his head.

Jonah examined 'him' again, and then he saw it. This wasn't just a guy with a guitar, and Jonah returned the equally universal "I know!" look.

Now it was up to Eddie to quietly check with Jonah if they should talk to the man, but he came to the conclusion that he didn't know what look went with that, so he improvised. Jonah then attempted to quietly convey he had no idea what Eddie's face was trying to say and at that point the young man looked at both of them.

"Y'all look like you need to break wind."

"Jesus!" Eddie exclaimed in absolute horror.

"I ain't him, sorry."

"No, you're Robert Johnson."

"That I am, sir."

Robert shook Eddie's hand, and a million thoughts shot through him. Out of all those thoughts, one was front and center and refused to be pushed back.

Oh God, am I blushing?

Eddie sincerely hoped he wasn't and quickly checked himself in the first reflection he could find when Robert turned to shake Jonah's hand.

"Coming to the show tonight?"

"You... You're playing?" Eddie stammered. "Like, here. In... Here?"

"I ain't playing in the elevator, if that's what you're asking."

Eddie shook his head. That was dumb. Goddammit, he was being dumb in front of the King of the Delta Blues.

"No. Yeah, I got that. No. I mean, Uh-Underworld. Why? How? Ugh, Jonah, help."

Robert turned to Jonah and looked confused. "Is he okay?"

"Yeah. He's just impressed."

"With me?"

"I don't know if you've managed to keep up with music since you came here, but you left quite a legacy. Hell, I'm a little impressed to meet you, too."

Robert wasn't sure what to say. "Aw, you know... I pick up things here and there and people seem to enjoy it when I play but I'm mostly just busy tryna get better. Kinda prove to myself I can do it without the Devil's help, you know?"

Eddie gasped. "You did sell your soul!"

Robert nodded. "I'm contractually obliged to do a show here every month. Kinda figured I'd be worse off when I made the deal, but it worked out alright."

"I'll say," Eddie scoffed. "Man, I could have been a rock star; instead, I sold my soul for a car."

Robert chuckled, and the door opened. He stepped out and greeted them, but Eddie followed and whipped out his phone.

"Would you mind if I take a picture?"

"Nah, it's fine."

Eddie waved Jonah over and took a selfie. He already knew what he was going to do with it, too: blow it up, print it on canvas, and hang it in the living room. Rosalie probably wouldn't want it over the bed.

"Thanks, man!"

Robert tapped his hat and walked off. Eddie stared at his phone as if he were watching stock prices rise.

"You're thinking about catching that show, aren't you?"

Eddie puckered his lips and looked at Jonah. Yes, he was absolutely trying to figure out a way to squeeze in a Robert Johnson concert while looking for Rooney, and the only reason it didn't happen was because he couldn't think of a way to do it.

"No. We're here for Rooney. I'll come back sometime to catch a show."

He looked around to get his bearings. They weren't going to find Rooney here, unless he was allowed to go out for lunch, because they were in the cafeteria.

"Come on. I know someone who might be able to help."

Jonah followed Eddie through the cafeteria. "Did you ever get your soul back, or does Lilith own it now?"

"Huh?"

"For the car. Because you actually have the car."

"Yeah, *and* my soul. But still, I always wanted to be a rock star, too."

"Maybe practice?"

"Pf, come on! That's not very rock 'n' roll, is it?"

He pushed a door open and wandered into the kitchen. Jonah was hesitant but followed anyway, which he regretted when a corpulent and slightly mustachioed woman laid eyes on Eddie and immediately barked, "You again?!"

"Ellis, hey."

"Oh, Hell no. Forget it. I'm not making you any more Vulture Legs."

Jonah looked confused.

"Long story, tell you about it on the way back," Eddie said and focused on Ellis. "I'm not here for that. I know how you feel about other people's recipes. I need to get to the Purgatory District. Do you know how I do that?"

Ellis tapped her lips with the ladle and thought for a moment, then she proceeded to stir something that was hopefully just tomato soup in the pot in front of her.

"I never go there. I wouldn't know."

"Okay. Alright. Good start," Eddie said. "Let's work our way up from there. Are you perhaps aware of any people who do know how to get there?"

Ellis hummed something and leaned to look out the serving hatch. She banged the ladle on the counter to get the cashier's attention.

"Milo, get Captain Fokke over here, please."

Eddie chuckled. Jonah started to chuckle because Eddie did, but Ellis wasn't amused. "Oh, grow up. It's Dutch. He runs the postal service for stuff that doesn't fit in the tubes."

Eddie didn't grow up. If anything, he became more juvenile. "So you might say he's been fokking everywhere?"

Before Eddie's material could sink any lower, an imposing, well-coiffed man of regal stature approached the window. He leaned on the counter, careful not to ruin his uniformed sleeves in the soup spatters Ellis had left there, and greeted them in a thick Dutch accent.

"I'm lunching. If you need anything sent, it will have to wait."

"Nothing like that, Bernie. These guys need to know how to get to R&D."

The man examined Eddie and Jonah before deciding he didn't want his eggs going cold. "Go to the lobby. Seventh elevator, sixth floor."

And that was all Bernard Fokke had to say about it; he needed to get back to his table. Ellis had enough of this interruption as well.

"There you have it. Now get out of my kitchen."

It was exactly Eddie's plan because they had a Rooney to retrieve, and he didn't want to leave Rosalie alone for too long either. She was definitely good in a fight if anything happened, but he hated leaving her to fight alone.

Soon enough, they were in the lobby, and Jonah was fairly impressed by it. While the elevator already came with some art deco elements, the lobby went all out.

"Nice. Professional job."

Eddie looked around, realizing that he didn't really have the time to take in the place the last time he was there. There was something cocky about the style, and he was quite fond of it. It seemed to be saying, "I'm here. Deal with it," which was a sentiment Eddie could relate to. Especially right now.

"You're taking this whole Underworld thing rather well," he said. "I figured you'd be freaking out."

Jonah just shrugged and went to the elevators. "I've been around, man. To be honest..." he pressed the button for the seventh elevator, "with the ever-increasing droves of assholes shooting other assholes over asshole reasons, this place is a breath of fresh air."

While they waited, Eddie realized that Jonah had a pretty sharp point there. Sure, there was some heinous shit going on in Purgatory, but all those people were paying their dues for the sins they committed while alive. As far as wanton violence went, Eddie had yet to see the kind of viciousness that seemed to be standard issue for humans. And for the sake of the argument he had with himself, he conveniently overlooked that time he tried to have a fistfight with the Devil.

The elevator dinged, and the doors opened. To cheer himself up, Eddie pressed the button for the sixth floor three times.

THIRTEEN

There's a saying that proposes gambling is the Devil's way to poverty. This might have been why more Las Vegas elevators than you'd care to know were able to go considerably lower than basement level, as long as you knew which buttons to press. Or if you were dead enough. Troubling as it may be that there were so many ways for traveling to and from Hell, Lilith found it quite convenient. It would be very tiresome if she had soul-business in, say, New York, and she had to drive all the way there from Herringwood.

The next time you walk down a seemingly deserted alley, look at that one rusty steel door that's just a little out of place. You never know.

This elevator didn't open into a deserted alley, however. Lilith stepped into an elegantly lit hallway leading to a penthouse on the Las Vegas strip.

The first thing Helen did when she arrived in Vegas was talking herself into the fancy suite because, when you're God, you get used to a certain level of comfort. Lilith understood. She would have done the same if she was planning to stay somewhere for longer periods.

However, she hoped not to be here so long that she needed residence. That said, she would have liked to hang out with cool Aunt Helen for a while, but there were just too many work-things to deal with. Lilith's days of hanging out were mostly over.

While Helen did expect her, Lilith knocked anyway because she knew one of the main reasons Helen enjoyed being in this world, and that she could be... impulsive.

"It's open!"

Yeah, that still left room for interpretation, but Lilith went in anyway.

Helen was standing in front of a large panoramic window, silhouetted against the day's end and the city's bright lights. She was wearing the Hell out of a short black dress, but what actually caught Lilith's eye was that she stood barefoot.

"Are you going to stare for long, dear?" Helen asked without looking back. She took a casual sip of wine from the glass in her hand. "Because at some point it's going to get awkward."

"What? Err, no. I was looking at your feet."

Helen turned around and smiled. "It just got awkward, hon. You're not going all Tarantino on me, are you?"

"No, but if I write some killer dialogue I will let you know," Lilith sighed. "I just can't remember the last time I saw you without your heels on. If ever."

Helen grabbed an extra glass and put it next to the bottle that was standing on a designer table. She sat down on a couch so expensive it couldn't possibly be comfortable but she effortlessly made it look like it was.

"Even the creator of the universe needs to rest her feet once in a while. Wine?"

Lilith nodded and sat down on a chair that matched the couch, both in high-end design and lack of comfort.

"I did go barefoot once or twice when I wore the habit," Helen added. "But, eh... a good pair of stilettos does something for my attitude, you know?"

Lilith nodded again. She never managed to make walking on stilettos look sexy or confident. She was very good at making it look like she was a newborn deer in an ice rink, though. That was probably someone's fetish, right? Fetish or not, she usually stuck to a comfortable pair of black boots.

Helen waited for Lilith to speak, but all she got was a deep, anguished sigh. She leaned over and patted Lilith's knee.

"Tell crazy Aunt Helen what's up."

Lilith sighed again and said, "I've got Eddie locked up in my garage."

Helen sat up straight and processed it. Then she started to laugh, which wasn't exactly the reaction Lilith expected.

"Aw, my little niece the serial killer," Helen giggled. "Why don't you explain a bit further for me. I might not be up to date on your hip young lingo."

"No, it's literally that."

"I'll literally still need an explanation then."

Lilith shook her head and slumped. "It feels like I'm losing control of everything. I don't think I can do this, Aunt Helen. I should quit... I want to quit."

Helen got up and grabbed the phone. She gave Lilith a quick "I've got your back" nod before somebody answered her call.

"Hello, room service? Yes, this is Helen... Oh, hello, Meredith! How's your mother? ...Good, good. Tell her I said hello. Listen, we're going to need more wine. Yes, it's an emergency... Alright, thank you."

She came back to the couch and sat down. "Medicine is coming up, sweetie. Tell me everything."

Lilith wasn't so sure drowning her problems in alcohol was the best course of action, but it couldn't hurt to try. She took a good swig from the wine they already had and leaned back, which the chair didn't really want her to do. It made this clear by becoming a little more uncomfortable because chairs this expensive have an attitude. Lilith sat back up.

"Eddie called me to ask if I had Rooney's soul--"

"Excuse me?"

"Oh, yeah. Rooney was shot. He died... So, of course Eddie called me. Can't blame him, right? But I had to tell him I can't just send souls back."

"Not if it's their time, no," Helen confirmed. "Was it?"

"I didn't know yet, at that point, but I should be able to trust Domino's work, right?"

Helen nodded and got up to answer the door. A Latin man somewhere in his thirties brought in two bottles of wine. Lilith could see he worked out, even with the unflattering bellhop uniform.

"Ooh, Tomás! Meredith sent you up, did she?" Helen added a wink, just in case she wasn't obvious enough.

Tomás just smiled and glanced at Lilith, before answering with the same unsubtle wink. His smile disappeared when Helen gave him a fifty-dollar bill.

"I'm sorry, Tomás. It's not *that* kind of emergency. She is my niece, and we have things to discuss."

Tomás pocketed the money. "Then I have some free time on my hands all of a sudden."

Helen sent him off with another sweet smile. "I'm sure Meredith will find something for you to do until I require your *services* again."

Tomás left, and Helen came back to the couch. Lilith gave her the look that said it was now her turn to explain.

"You should consider getting a room here," Helen casually said.

"Room service is... divine."

Lilith decided not to dwell on that. "Yes, well... Eddie and I got into a fight and he threatened to come get Rooney himself. Which he did. We saw him coming from miles away, so I met him in the garage. He actually brought a friend! Can you believe that?"

"Yes, I can."

Lilith took a big swig of wine. "Hm-hm." And refilled her glass.

"Anyway, I told him we didn't have him, but he insists Rooney's dead. We got into a fight, again. I lost my cool, and now he's locked in the garage."

Helen nodded. She knew Eddie well enough. A charming idiot, especially for a human, but she could see how he could get under your skin if he thought that would get things done. Something like the barrier between life and death definitely wasn't going to stop him.

"You know he's busy finding a way out as we speak, right?" she said, grinning.

Lilith groaned. "Ugh! I know."

"But I'm not willing to believe you let Eddie bully you into thinking about quitting."

"It's just one thing on a pile of things. I don't get the respect my father did. They're just looking at me like the girl who got daddy's job."

"Aw," Helen cooed. She moved closer to Lilith and tried to put an arm around her, but they were too far apart, so she grabbed a hand and pulled Lilith to the couch. Then she put an arm around her.

"There's a difference between being feared and being respected. But if you want, I can drop by and go Old Testament in there."

Lilith chuckled. "Yeah, I'm sure that'll make a good impression. Look, I'll get the respect I deserve by proving I deserve it, but it's like the whole place is trying to work against me. According to the system, Rooney didn't even have reservations."

"So he's not dead?"

"No, he's dead. Say what you will about Eddie, but even he isn't dropping by uninvited and starting a fight for shits and giggles."

Helen frowned. There was definitely a misunderstanding here. "So what did the manifest say?"

"'Status amended: Special Delivery.' Do you know what that means?"

"Yes. And that can't be right." Helen grabbed her phone. "Let me check with the office real quick."

Lilith looked at the phone in her hand. "Not using the old rotary anymore?"

"No, it's almost impossible to find a place to plug in anymore, so I just had IT clear a line for me."

She dialed and put the phone to her ear. "Just calling Mike. If this is what I think it is, he should know more-- Michael, hello! It's Helen."

"Helen," Michael answered coolly. "It's been a while. When do you think you'll be coming back?"

"I don't know if I appreciate that tone, Michael."

"And I don't know if I appreciate running the place on my own. Are you ever coming back?"

Helen put the phone to her chest and whispered to Lilith. "Mike is a bit salty sometimes."

Lilith nodded. She knew Michael used to be a soldier. He dealt well with orders—perfectly even, in his case—but had trouble adjusting to the corporate setting.

"I will come back when I come back," Helen told him.

"That statement makes very little sense."

"Well, I work in mysterious ways. Deal with it." She gave him a moment to deal with it by sipping her wine. "Mike, hon, you wouldn't be assistant manager if I didn't think you could hack it. Now, could you find it within your busy, busy schedule to answer a question?"

"Now I don't know if I appreciate your tone, Helen."

"I'm your boss, Michael. It's my mighty, mighty bosstone."

"What did you want to ask, ma'am?"

"Could you confirm if we have a Robert James Rooney of Herringwood?"

Lilith frowned. Though it would have been nice to have this mystery solved, she really wanted the answer to be no. What was the Afterlife coming to if Heaven just let in unpurged souls? And even if they were suddenly okay with that, why wasn't she told about it?

Helen caught her looking. "Michael's gonna check, but he needs to log in to the computer first."

"Oh good, you have computers."

"You don't?"

"It's just one of the many piles of shit my father left for me to clean up."

Helen held up a hand. "Yes, Michael?" And then she looked at Lilith. "Hm-hm, and how did that happen?"

Lilith wasn't sure if she was supposed to answer the question but didn't have to wonder long as Helen thanked Michael and ended the call.

"He's upstairs."

Indignantly, Lilith repeated her aunt's words. "And how did that happen?"

Calmly, Helen put her phone on the table and refilled her glass. She took her time leaning back and getting comfortable before putting a subtle but haughty smile on her lips.

"Because *somebody* blacklisted Eddie."

"Okay. If *somebody* rightfully blacklisted the Herringwood nuisance, how does *somebody else* have his friend?"

Helen laughed. She liked how her niece had already grown in the short time she'd taken up her position, but there was some more growing to do.

"Let me guess," she said. "You went to Administration and at some point told them to blacklist that 'Herringwood nuisance,' didn't you?"

"Almost verbatim… But I mentioned Eddie!"

"Yes, and if you'd mentioned cake, they would have blacklisted that, too."

Lilith grabbed her head and fell back on the shitty chair that suddenly felt a little more shitty. "Oh, goddammit, I blacklisted the entire town of Herringwood?"

"Yes, you did."

"Oh-shit-oh-shit-oh-shit!" She jumped up. "We're going to miss an entire town's worth of sinergy! I need to… This is bad. What do I do?"

Helen got up and put her hands on Lilith's shoulders. The touch calmed her somewhat, but tears still welled in her eyes.

"Relax, sweetie. Nothing is ever as bad as it looks."

Lilith wasn't so sure. This looked very bad. Even overlooking the consequences, this was really just a gross amateur mistake.

"I'm gonna lose my job over this…"

Helen looked at her. "You're pretty worried about a job you didn't want. That's a good thing."

Lilith didn't understand and still felt crying over a monumental fuck-up was warranted. Helen less so.

"Shows a sense of responsibility. But really, who's gonna fire you?"

That hadn't occurred to Lilith yet. The highest tier of management was currently drinking wine in a Las Vegas penthouse suite. The worst that could happen was her pissing off Helen enough to make her send Eddie to run her over.

"So, cheer up," Helen said. "Finish your wine and stroll your gothic butt back to the Underworld to fix your little faux pas with Admin."

"How do I fix this?"

Helen made her sit down again. "Hon, do you have any idea how many memos are instantly followed by a correction memo on a daily basis? Your thing isn't even a thing. Just tell Administration to change Herringwood to Eddie Sterling, and you're good."

"And what about Rooney?"

Helen took a sip of wine and wandered back to the panoramic window. "Look."

Lilith went over and looked. The Strip was colorfully lit with lights and billboards vying for tourists' attention. None of these tourists had any idea who was looking down at them.

"You could grab any random five people from the street and get more sinergy from them than ten Rooneys," Helen said. "Let's not make the poor guy's death more stressful by sending him to Purgatory."

Lilith thought about it. Purgatory could be stressful, and she had no idea what Rooney's torment would be. It probably wouldn't be anything gruesome since Rooney was a good guy, but why risk it? And as a bonus, she'd get Eddie off her back. If she didn't have Rooney, he didn't need to be in her Underworld.

"Oh, I need to call Ignacio so he can send Eddie home."

"Maybe have him take away Eddie's car too. That's the whole reason blacklisting isn't really working out."

Lilith looked dumbly at Helen. "Are you hearing yourself?"

"What?"

"You want me to take away the car he sold his soul for? Look, if I want trouble, there are easier ways than trying to take his car."

"You're the boss, hon," Helen lilted and returned to looking out over Sin City.

"I should get going. I'll call Ignacio on the way."

Lilith went to the door and looked back at Helen in front of the large panoramic window, silhouetted against the day's end and the city's bright lights.

"You're welcome, hon," Helen said without looking back.

"Yeah... Ehm, do you just stand there and pose all the time?"

"Honey, if it impresses you that much already, imagine what it's gonna do to Tomás when I have him sent up again."

Lilith took that as her cue to leave. As attractive as Tomás was, she didn't want to be here when crazy Aunt Helen got her hands on him.

FOURTEEN

J onah leaned out of the elevator and saw only a short, featureless dead-end hallway. He put his hand on the door to keep it open and turned back to Eddie.

"Are you sure we're on the right floor?"

Eddie took a look for himself. The only things of note were a steel door a few feet away and a factory light against the ceiling. Somehow, several flies had managed to work their way in there and die.

"Makes you wonder how they got in there, huh?" Jonah remarked.

"Yeah, I think they're sold like that. I used to fix those kinds of lights in a factory that isn't there anymore. There's no way a fly could get in unless they came with the light. That said, we're on the right floor."

Eddie stepped out and went to examine the riveted steel door. It didn't have a handle, and it didn't look like he could kick it down.

Aside from the impressive feat of a dumbass insect that couldn't find its way out of an open backdoor magicking itself into a light fixture, Jonah didn't think there was anything interesting here, so he reached for the lobby button.

"Don't," Eddie said. "We need to get through this door."

Jonah watched how Eddie tried to pry the door open with his bare hands.

"You're just gonna hurt yourself, man."

Good advice never stopped Eddie from doing anything, and he kept trying to make the door budge. What usually stopped him from doing something was getting hurt by doing it, so when his fingers slipped and nearly tore his nails off, he groaned in pain and blew on his fingers.

"Ow. That's not gonna work..."

"Yes, much like I said."

Eddie looked at the door. It was the only thing between him and Rooney, which meant that it needed to be dealt with. Violently, if need be.

"Look, there are a bunch of cells behind this door, and in one of those cells is my best friend--"

"Come on, man. The Devil herself just told you that she doesn't have Rooney."

"And that's why they call the Devil the Prince of Lies. Now help me get this door open."

Jonah crossed his arms. Wood was more his thing, but there was clearly no way to open this door, and he didn't feel like exerting himself to prove it.

"Prince of Darkness."

Eddie looked back at him. "What?"

"The Devil is the Prince of Darkness. Princess, in this case. Does she even identify as--"

"That's Ozzy Osbourne. And he's definitely a prince. If you're not gonna help, get your surprisingly woke ass out of the way and let me do my thing."

His thing turned out to be running into the door shoulder first—completely overlooking that the hinges were on this side—and grumbling about Lilith.

"She made that body..." *Bang!* "I think it's pretty obvious..." *Bang!* "That she identifies as a woman..." *Bang!* "Ow."

He stopped to rub his arm and shoulder. He should have stopped somewhere around the second 'bang,' but he was far too macho for that. He hissed through his teeth as the pain started radiating further out from his arm. To counter it, Eddie did what science proved to be an acceptable substitute for actual painkillers: cursing like a longshoreman stepping on a Lego. While it did help with subduing the pain from running into a riveted steel door, it did absolutely nothing for opening said door.

Jonah leaned against the wall.

"Is Sterling an Irish name?"

"It's my name... But that's all I can tell you. Why?"

"Because you're being incredibly stubborn." He scratched his beard. "I'll be right here when you're ready to give up."

"I'm gonna get that door open--"

The door swung open, and Eddie turned back around. A guard in a royal blue uniform and white Bobby helmet stood half in the doorway, propping the door open with his shoulder.

"Would you knock it off?" the guard snapped.

Eddie came a little closer and examined him. "Are you a prison guard?"

"Yeah."

"Since when do they have prison guards here?"

"Guard. Singular."

"Okay, since when do they have a singular prison guard?"

"Since some asshole waltzed in and left with a condemned demon. Now I'm stuck in here to keep an eye out for unauthorized people. And I'm thinking I'm seeing some now."

Eddie grinned at the idea that his previous visit had caused the tightening of security. It felt pretty boss to influence the Underworld like that, and this feeling of grandeur would probably influence it some more, because one guard wasn't going to do what his superiors thought it would. Eddie took a quick look back at Jonah.

"Oh, don't..." Jonah said.

"Don't what?" the guard asked.

"Sorry, man," Eddie answered and punched the guard in the face. He stumbled back, holding his nose, and Eddie caught the door to go after him. The last thing Jonah saw before the door fell shut was Eddie reaching for the guard's nightstick.

Jonah listened, but this was a very good door, so he heard nothing, and after a while of hearing nothing, he began to get worried. He'd been alone in unfamiliar places before, and even if those places weren't the Underworld, it didn't bother him much. The main problem was that Eddie had the car keys.

"Ed?" Jonah banged on the door. "Eddie?"

Jonah looked at the elevator. If he could find his way back to the garage at all, he had no idea how to get back to the land of the living.

The lock on the other side clicked, and the door opened. Behind Eddie, the guard lay unconscious on the ground.

"Boy, he did not go down easy," Eddie said and wiped his forehead. "Let's go find Rooney."

Jonah recoiled when he stepped through the door. He would definitely not describe this as "a bunch of cells." These were infinite cells, and those were just the ones he could see. It would take a lifetime to even make a dent.

"Too bad you knocked out the guard. Maybe he could have told us more."

Eddie looked down on his most recent conquest. "No sense crying over knocked-out guards. But I have his keys. I'll just have to think of a different plan.”

“Like?”

Like the very typical plan Eddie immediately put into motion.

“Rooney!” he belted. “Dude!”

Part of this plan involved walking around, so he also started doing that. Jonah wandered after Eddie for a couple of blocks as he yelled at semi-regular intervals, but he didn’t have the same kind of confidence in this plan. Every time he looked down any of the side aisles, all he saw were more cells divided into blocks that stretched so far he couldn’t see the end of them.

“Maybe we should go to that guard’s office? See if he has any prisoner logs or something.”

“Hm-hm,” Eddie answered, looking around. “Thought of that, too, but I don’t see an office, do you? *Rooney!* It’s gonna be just as hard to find, and at least Rooney will answer if I call. *Rooney, dude!*”

Though Eddie produced quite some volume, it could never have been enough to reach all the way across Purgatory. All of a sudden, Eddie decided they had to go right.

The stench of despair was palpable through the square openings in each door and Jonah decided to have a look.

“Yeah, you might not wanna do that. Some fiendish shit goes on in there,” Eddie warned him, but it was too late.

“Jesus, fuck!” Jonah exclaimed and pushed away from the door. “Why is that pineapple... *How?!*”

Eddie stopped his yelling and walking to turn around and have a look for himself. Inside the cell was a naked man in terrible pain, but other than that, Eddie could see no pineapples anywhere. Considering Jonah’s reaction, he didn’t mind either. Still, torments were a personal thing.

“You can see it?”

“And I really fucking wish I couldn’t.” Jonah leaned on his knees and tried not to hurl.

"You're not supposed to be able to see it."

"It's pretty fucking clear why, it is!" When he was sure he wouldn't throw up, Jonah righted himself. "That's sick, man."

"Hm-hm, sure, horrible. How can you see it?"

"I don't know! How are we even here? That's not supposed to happen either, is it?"

"Yeah, I guess." Eddie looked into the cell again but still didn't see anything. This wasn't something he had time for, so he refocused on his search for Rooney.

"Rooney! Where are you, dude?"

Jonah followed again, this time making absolutely sure not to accidentally peek into a cell. They both stopped in their tracks when a voice spoke in a thick Scottish accent.

"I know where Rooney is."

They looked for the cell around the voice but had a hard time finding it until the man stuck a meaty arm out and waved.

"Over here, lad."

Eddie made sure to stay out of range of the arm and had a look. An unkempt face, sweaty and tired, looked at him. His black hair was stuck to his forehead in greasy locks.

"Shouldn't you be in torment?"

"Healing break," the man said. "So if you use that lovely set of keys you got on ya, I can be out before the whole thing starts again."

Not even Eddie thought it was a good idea to start releasing prisoners at random, but if this guy knew where Rooney was, he would at least consider it.

"What are you in for?"

"Oh, this and that, you know?"

"I don't. Enlighten me."

The man seemed hesitant to talk about it, which was a nice clear red flag to start with, and like any red flag, it drew Eddie's curiosity like a bull.

"If you want me to let you out, I should at least know *who* I'm letting out."

"Seems fair," the man said. "Dirk Paisley. Prestonpans, Scotland."

"Alright, Mr. Paisley. That's not what I asked."

"Fine. I set twenty witches on fire."

Eddie frowned. "Twenty?!"

"Not all at once!" Dirk genuinely thought that made a difference. "Either way, doesn't matter. Turns out that it's not the Lord's work after all."

"No, Helen tends to frown upon that."

Dirk squinted. "Who's Helen?"

"Heh. The 'Lord.' You've not met, I take it?"

"No. You have?"

Eddie nodded rather proudly, though he never thought of meeting Helen as something special. Sure, she was God, but she wasn't a diva about it or anything. In fact, she was rather pleasant to be around. Seeing how this impressed Dirk, Eddie added, "Rumor has it I slept with her too."

"That's great!" Dirk exclaimed. "You can let me out and put in a good word for me. I thought executing witches was God's work."

"It's not, and I'm not letting some pyro run free."

"Then you're never gonna find out where your Rooney is."

Eddie looked around. It would make things a lot easier if he knew exactly where Rooney was, but, all things considered, it looked like he was just going to have to do his own searching. Still not the worst puzzle he had to solve, and maybe he could still talk his way into finding out where Rooney was.

"Why don't you tell me where Rooney is as a show of good faith? If you speak the truth, we'll come back and let you out." Eddie leaned against the door. "How about that deal?"

With surprising agility, Dirk's flabby arm lashed out and grabbed Eddie's hair, pulling him against the door with a thud.

"How about I just take those keys off you right now?"

Eddie flung the keys away, and they landed on the floor at Jonah's feet. Dirk looked out the hatch as much as possible while holding Eddie in place.

"Let me out, or I break ya wee friend's neck."

Jonah picked up the keys.

"Don't you open that door!" Eddie groaned.

Dirk really wasn't kidding, and that was all the reason Eddie needed to not let the guy out. He hoped that breaking his neck while already in the Afterlife wouldn't make him extra dead. Up until this point, he never really wondered what would happen if he got into a situation here that would have meant his death in the normal world, but at least he'd have a new experience. Every cloud has a silver lining.

And that cloud apparently also had a bolt of lightning. A flash of it sent Dirk yelping back into his cell, and Eddie tripped, trying to get away from whatever was happening now.

"Mr. Sterling, nice to see you again."

Dr. Ignacio tapped the cell door with a cattle prod. "This is your last warning, Mr. Paisley. Misbehave again, and I *will* set Dr. Fian loose upon you."

That seemed to put Dirk right in his place. Eddie got up and greeted the small scientist, whose cattle prod made him look like a small wizard. It didn't really look like a good tool for science, though.

"Thanks for the save, doc. You carry that thing around with you now?"

"Only when I know I am looking for you, Mr. Sterling. Come, I shall escort you back to your car before you get into any more trouble."

Ignacio started walking, casually greeted Jonah as he passed him, and turned into the main aisle as Eddie caught up with him.

"I can't go back yet, doc. I'm looking for Rooney."

Ignacio stopped walking and turned around. "You won't find him here."

"Where would I find him, then?"

"An administrative error sent him straight to Heaven. Now, if you would just follow me..."

"If you're not going to Heaven, I'm not following you."

Ignacio pointed the cattle prod at him. "Unless either of you want to see me use this, you will follow me."

Eddie looked from Ignacio to Jonah. "Yeah, so... Jonah Craig, meet Dr. Ignacio—the smartest man in any world. Yet he still doesn't know better than to threaten me."

Ignacio knew better. He knew everything better, and so he knew he could drive his point home by delivering a quick jab with the prod, which he did. Eddie jumped and held his hands up.

"Point taken."

Jonah chuckled. "I should get me one of those in case he gets more ideas like this."

Ignacio studied him with an intent squint, and Jonah took a step back.

"Hey, I'm following, man. Don't prod me."

"I won't, but... Have we met?"

"I think I'd remember a scientist with a cattle prod."

Ignacio grinned. "Well, nice to meet you, Mr. Craig."

Meanwhile, Eddie quickly did the math to see how outnumbered he was. According to him, he could take a bowling-pin-shaped scientist, even with the cattle prod in play. Should Jonah choose to side with Ignacio, the balance would shift, but the prod would probably help shift it in Eddie's favor.

The whole thing was moot, he decided, because he didn't want to hurt either of them. However, that meant the only weapon he had at his disposal in his quest for Rooney was talking, so he did that, and Ignacio quickly put an end to it.

"Our mutual friend and my direct boss has found it within

herself to allow you passage home and, unfortunately, tasked me with making sure you do, even though I have several experiments running that would benefit from my attention far more than you." He pulled a flash drive from his breast pocket. "To expedite your departure, I have here an update for the GPS of your car, which will allow you to travel to your world."

"Ooh, handy."

"Wipe that look off your face, Mr. Sterling. It's single use, and we're closing the door for you."

Eddie took the flash drive and pocketed it. "What do you mean?"

"This will be the last trip you make between our dimensions. The next time we meet, it will be through conventional means, and you will be staying."

"Pff. Right."

Ignacio held up the cattle prod. "I mean it."

Eddie relented for now. The cattle prod made a solid case, but as soon as someone close to him kicked the bucket, he would be right back in the Vindicator, and pointing it towards the tunnel with George in the backseat. If Rosalie would let him, anyway. She didn't exactly have him whipped, but, like the cattle prod, she simply knew how to make a convincing argument.

The elevator ride felt like it was much shorter than the previous time and the polite ding signaled the end of it. Ignacio walked them to the door and took out his keycard.

"This is where we part ways, Mr. Sterling," he said. "Have Janick install the update, and then be on your way."

He opened the door for them, but Eddie lingered. Ignacio sighed and shook his head before adding, "No. I'm not going to send any more souls back."

Eddie hadn't even considered that, though now that it came up, he would have liked to see Robert Johnson back and making music. Correctly assuming that was too big an ask, he got back on his previous train of thought.

"You don't have to send anybody back, I guess... But if Rooney shows up after all, could I, like..." Eddie tried to swallow his emotions. "Say goodbye properly?"

Ignacio puckered his lips. He was supposed to say no but just couldn't. "Alright. My people will call your people. Now go." He held the door open a little wider. "I hope you've enjoyed this brief tour of our facilities, Mr. Craig. I look forward to giving you the full tour when your time comes. Now if you'll excuse me, I have experiments to run."

Eddie caught the door when Ignacio hobbled away. With the flash drive in hand, he walked into the garage with Jonah in tow and found Janick waiting for them outside his office.

"That was more than half hour," he stated.

Though Eddie always did have some difficulty grasping time passed, he suspected as much and nodded.

"I know." He just kept on walking to his car.

Janick took a few steps toward him. "Back to work now."

"I quit."

"You don't quit until boss says--"

The phone in his office rang, so he raised a finger to indicate this wasn't over yet and walked back. To avoid having to squeeze back in, he just reached inside and answered.

"Hello?"

Eddie leaned against the hood and grinned at Jonah while he waited for Janick to finish the phone call. He would have lit a cigarette for added nonchalance, but the risk of a fiery explosion outweighed the need to look cool. Janick wouldn't comprehend that kind of cool anyway, and Jonah wasn't that easily impressed, judging by his overall reaction to a walking tour of the Underworld.

Janick hung up and came to the car. "Give flash drive."

Eddie handed it over and Janick went around to the passenger side to install it. It was rather amazing how the large mechanic fit into the car at all, let alone allow himself space to work, but after a minute, Janick came back out.

"Go straight home," he ordered. "It is single use. Good luck. Take care of car."

He walked away. Whether he didn't expect a thank-you, or just didn't grasp the concept of common courtesy—Eddie assumed the latter—all he knew was his work on the car was done, and he wasn't needed here anymore.

"Alright, let's get undead," Jonah said and got into the car.

Quietly, Eddie did so as well. He managed to put the key in the ignition, but then he just stared out with his hands on the wheel.

"Ed?"

Eddie didn't answer.

"I don't like that look, Ed. Whaddya say we start the car, put on "Hellraiser," and go home? Huh? Back to Rosalie? And life and shit."

Life and shit was not what Eddie was thinking about. At least not for himself. He got back out of the car and jogged to the office.

"Janick!"

Jonah watched how Eddie leaned in and discussed something with the demon mechanic. He couldn't hear what they were talking about, but it wasn't hard to imagine. There wouldn't be any "Hellraiser" yet. He should probably start looking for "Stairway To Heaven" in the playlist.

Eddie came back to the car and proved him wrong on that as well.

"Come on. We're going to hitch a ride on a train."

FIFTEEN

Yaeger bit his tongue, leaning on the jagged piece of rust that had to pass for a car door. In any other normal situation, he would have had plenty to say about this downgrade, but considering the circumstances, he did what he could to not sigh or make any snide comments.

The scrapyard owner had indeed been the kind of man who didn't ask questions. That was a good thing, from a fugitive's point of view, but Yaeger thought the man could have asked *some* pertinent questions, like "Really? That thing?" or "Did you get your tetanus shots?"

But "no questions asked" really covered it all. Like the question of the rat droppings in the backseat. Fortunately, Yaeger couldn't see a way to get to the backseat anymore, so that was less of a problem than he initially suspected. Unless the rat still lived in the car, in which case it was probably the previous owner, judging by the size of the droppings.

Yaeger knew a little about automotive mechanics—though not so much he could be considered an expert—and he couldn't figure out how this thing was still roadworthy. It was rusting almost fast enough to see it happen live, the passenger side mirror was on the remains of the dashboard, and every time Rigby started it, people came to see what kind of bear was loudly dying in the street.

If he tried really hard, Yaeger could see a silver lining. But it was dull and unpolished silver, and probably just that thin layer they put on pewter rings to make them look expensive. At least they didn't have to start the car a lot because they were now parked in an alley by a dumpster with a good view of the hospital that housed the morgue where Rooney's body was kept.

Yaeger realized there was another silver-coated pewter lining. Sitting next to this dumpster, the car blended in like an octopus on a reef. That did come with all sorts of interesting new smells floating into the car because the driver's side window didn't go all the way up anymore. Or down. So... win some, lose some.

When another breeze of formerly fresh air crawled into the car like a clutter of hungover spiders, Yaeger couldn't hold his tongue anymore.

"Brother, I get that we needed another car but couldn't we have gotten one from Salt Creek?"

Rigby disapprovingly glanced at Yaeger. "You have the gall to complain right now?"

"Just asking questions."

"Salt Creek's funds are stretched thin enough without handing out new cars to every brash young missionary that shoots people at the drop of a hat."

Yaeger slowly shook his head. "I'm never going to hear the end of this, am I?"

"Literally only the Good Lord can help you there. Now enjoy the car because it's the only option found in the Venn diagram of availability and my personal budget."

Yaeger tried. It had to be said. His eyes scanned the car inch by inch to find anything worth enjoying, which he didn't manage. Eventually, he noticed the AC button and a train of thought left the station in his head. It was going fast—too fast, and in danger of derailing.

This car was the polar opposite of the SUV they'd lived in for so long. Everything in the SUV was well maintained, not a spot of rust on it and there were no rat droppings to be found anywhere. Only the AC didn't work.

This Gremlin was a wreck, rusty, and full of droppings. According to Yaeger, this meant that when God closed a door, he repaired the AC button. He reached out to it.

"Are you sure you want to do that?"

"Just humor me. What's the worst that could happen?"

Rigby quickly aimed the vent on his side away from him. The AC button squeaked, and that was it.

Yaeger grunted. "Can't catch a break."

"I guess--"

The AC suddenly went full blast and coughed a cloud of fruit flies into the car. Rigby got out, but Yaeger didn't. He just sat there and stared as the tiny flies frantically hovered around him until the smartest one among them managed to radio his buddies about the open window.

"Is it cooling, at least?" Rigby asked.

"I'm pretending it is."

"Good for you, kid."

Rigby started to feel bad for him. The Lord had His ways of testing them but Yaeger seemed to be getting the short end of the stick on all fronts.

"Rigby?"

"Yes?"

"I swallowed one."

Rigby went to the back and got him a bottle of water. At least these were cooler than in the SUV because this car was full of holes that doubled as ventilation.

"Here."

"Thanks."

Rigby leaned on the roof and looked at the hospital without really seeing it.

When he first joined the Current Day Saints, things were so very different. The worst they ever did was getting a little too close to a subject and pretending they were someone else. Never did they get out the gun for anything other than self-defense. Even that was only three times that Rigby knew of, and all three times, it was hearsay from other teams in locations that required the occasional self-defensing.

Now, for the first time, they'd shot a man in cold blood, and to make the whole ghoulish circle complete, they were watching the local morgue to see if he was walking out anytime soon.

A soft ping pulled Rigby from his musings, and he looked at his phone. "Darn."

He had no idea how to open the email he apparently got. These blasted things were far more complicated than the rotary phones he grew up with. Still, he was a grown man who didn't want to have one of those newfangled devices explained to him by the closest available kid, so he resorted to trying himself.

Pushing the screen really hard in the general area of the email notification did nothing. He had to find another way and, by sheer luck, managed to swipe his way to an envelope icon.

Just not the right one.

"Oh... dear."

Rigby didn't want to have his penis enlarged, nor did he want to talk to the large number of women who were willing and able to have intercourse in his neighborhood. How did they even know where he was? He pressed the back button, which was one of the few buttons he understood. Now, back where he started, he tried again and eventually managed to dim his screen just enough to make it unreadable. It was about time to give up.

He got back in the car and held out his phone for Yaeger. "I think I have an email."

Yaeger just chuckled weakly and took the phone. With a swipe and a tap, he handed it back, and Rigby was finally able to check his messages.

"Holy fuck!"

Yaeger physically recoiled and pressed himself against the door as if venomous snakes slithered from Rigby's lips.

"Excuse me, infallible Elder Rigby?"

Rigby cleared his throat. "What's with the face?"

"You cursed."

"No, I didn't."

"And now you lied."

"No, and I'll tell you why. Err... To lie with a loving woman is close to divinity. Therefore, the, ehm, fuck, is holy."

Yaeger's mouth fell open. Rigby's righteousness seemed to have taken its final form. Perhaps the whole situation was getting to him more than he wanted to admit.

"Fine. Then just tell me why you weren't cursing."

Rigby held his phone up. "Mr. Hall is coming."

Yaeger lunged at the phone, hoping Rigby simply misunderstood it.

"Why?!"

"Because he apparently believes that when he orders someone shot, there should be instant results!" Rigby waved the phone around too angrily for Yaeger to read anything. "We've got nothing!"

"I'm fully aware of that, yes," Yaeger hissed. "Did you not brief him about the four days we're waiting?"

"Mr. Hall is a hard man to reach! I left the message with Vanessa."

Yaeger threw his hands up and hit the roof. Flecks of rust fell down, but he hardly took notice.

"Bah! Vanessa!"

"Oh, right. I know you have your eye on Vanessa. I'm sure it'll increase your chances if you throw her under the bus first chance you get."

"Psh! I have my eye on her breasts at best."

Out of nowhere, Rigby slapped him. "You will not speak ill of Vanessa. You are better than this, young man."

Yaeger rubbed his cheek. Rigby was right on all points.

"I'm sorry. I'm at the frayed ends of my rope, Brother Rigby."

"I know…" Rigby sighed. "And your rope will fray more still, but I'll see to it that you make it through."

Yaeger appreciated the sentiment, but something in the way Rigby spoke bothered him.

"Is there something specific I need to make it through?"

"Mm." Rigby thoughtlessly shrugged. "I honestly don't know. On very rare occasions, Mr. Hall has shown quite a temper. If this turns out to be one of those occasions, I'll take whatever blame is cast."

Yaeger brushed away the final fruit fly. "I appreciate that, I do. But the guilt would eat me--"

"I think this will be my last time."

Yaeger stared dumbly. The words didn't make sense to him.

"I think I'll ride this one out and then tender my resignation," Rigby explained himself. "I miss my wife and my boy. I'm afraid the next time they see me, I won't be the man they knew."

Yaeger frowned. "Why now, all of a sudden?"

Rigby rubbed his chin and nodded at the hospital. "I've been doing this for… let's say thirty years. I've never staked out a morgue."

"It's a hospital."

"We can lie to ourselves as much as we want, but it's the morgue we're here for, and it would appear to be my limit."

Yaeger stared at the hospital, trying to think of the right thing to say, but everything that came to mind was stupid or sounded like a threat. He was even losing faith in the argument he finally settled on.

"He could still be our guy, that Sterling."

Rigby snorted dismissively. "He isn't."

"What makes you so sure now?"

"When you've been spying on people as long as I have, you know what a regular guy looks like. I'll grant you, Sterling isn't your average kind of regular, but he's not the Son of God."

There was a lot riding on this for Yaeger. He needed Sterling to be the son of God. If he wasn't, it meant imprisonment for a large chunk of his life, not to mention damnation for a large chunk, if not all, of his death. He wasn't even sure he'd avoid damnation in the current situation, either. The only chance at any kind of redemption was if Sterling turned out to be the Lord, and he couldn't bear not to argue for it.

"That's just your mood talking. The dumpster, the house full of sick people, and the basement full of dead, all that has you depressed. No wonder you don't believe Sterling is the Christ."

Rigby flashed a wry smile. "The flies didn't help either."

"I ate most of them."

At least that got a big laugh out of Rigby.

"Look, Yaeger... Just learn what you can from this one and manage your disappointment. One day you'll meet the Lord, but that's not this day."

They sat quietly for a few moments until Yaeger thought the sincerity might be a good moment to ask about his future.

"Now that you've decided to quit, will you still report me to the police?"

"You killed a man. Your intentions were good, I'm sure, but the Lord is gonna have to pick you up at the State Pen."

"Dang it."

It seemed Yaeger couldn't catch a break. For the briefest of moments, his thoughts focused on the glove box where they kept the gun, and he scolded himself quietly but harshly. This was not what he wanted to become.

"Rigby?"

"Hm?"

"Could you keep the gun on you?"

Rigby turned to Yaeger. "Why?"

"I..."

Yaeger couldn't finish, or barely start, for that matter. He hoped a pained look would get the message across.

It did. Rigby took the revolver from the glove box and emptied the chambers. Herringwood was a lot of things, but not a town where your survival depended on a loaded gun.

He chuckled at the irony.

Sixteen

Eddie and Jonah walked up a wide stairway leading them onto the station platform. It was large, with tracks on either side and a handsome Roaring Twenties aesthetic. Very nice and all, but as of yet, Eddie couldn't see a way of sneaking into Heaven.

"I'm not sure what to do here yet," he told Jonah. "Any ideas will be genuinely considered."

Jonah didn't have any ideas either, but since they'd barely walked onto the platform, perhaps some further investigation would yield answers. It might have been as simple as stowing away in a luggage compartment, though they'd have to wait for the train to arrive before trying that.

"Maybe there's a secret stairway somewhere?"

Eddie smirked at him. "A stairway? To Heaven?"

"Yeah, I heard it when I said it."

"As much as I'd love for you to be right, I still don't wanna climb all the way to Heaven."

"Obviously. But you'd think there would be some sort of maintenance access..." Jonah looked around. Amongst the ticket booths, one window caught his attention. "Why don't we start by asking the station master?"

"Because he's gonna figure us out and send us back to square one?"

"Just ask for directions or something."

Eddie looked at the window. It was fancier than the ticket booths and currently unmanned. Maybe he could worm his way into the office and forge a ticket or something. For lack of any better ideas, or *good* ideas, he sauntered over. Before he was going to try anything, he told Jonah to hang back a bit.

"No point in us both getting caught if shit goes down. I mean, I can handle a couple of security muppets, but if they swarm me, you'll have to break me out of Purgatory."

Jonah nodded and hung back. He had no idea how to break Eddie out if he was sent to Purgatory or anywhere else, but on a broad scope the idea was sound.

Eddie skulked up to the window and looked around. There was an office in the back that was mostly hidden by the booth partition. Before any breaking-in was going to take place, he'd need to establish there was nobody back there, and he did so by ringing the bell.

He probably would have rung the bell anyway. Something about these service bells just compelled him to push them even if somebody was already at the counter. He briefly owned a service bell when he was young. A hotel clerk who was tired of his shit gave it to him, but it mysteriously disappeared not long after Eddie's father asked him not to ring it every other minute.

A man with a well-coiffed beard came from behind the partition. He was older than his gray hair already suggested but still quite spry, judging by the way he moved into the booth. He wore the same baby blue uniform they wore down at Hospitality, which led Eddie to believe they were of the same branch. His platinum nametag read, "Peter."

"Shit..." Eddie said under his breath.

Peter examined him. "Have we met before?"

"No."

"Yeah, you look familiar."

"I don't think so. I've got a very unfamiliar face."

"Give me a moment. It'll come to me."

"You don't know me!"

Unfortunately, Peter was very good with faces, though faces that weren't supposed to be in this dimension took a little longer.

"Edward Sterling. How's your groin?"

Eddie grimaced. "Still a little sore after six months. You've got quite the knee on you."

"I'm sorry, but you were making a lot of trouble, and I had to show Linda how we deal with troublemakers."

If it hadn't been for Peter, Eddie would have been loose in the Underworld without delay. While getting kneed in the nuts only slowed him down for a few hours or so, it did save a lot of security guards from broken noses.

"What are you doing here?" Eddie asked, hoping to smalltalk his way onto the train. "You were in Hospitality, right?"

"I still am, but when this position opened up, I jumped at the chance. I like trains, so now I can enjoy the marvelous Number 9 and still help people deal with the Afterlife."

Eddie amicably leaned on the small counter. "Since you like to help people, could you help me get on the train?"

"No."

"How do you know I don't have a ticket?"

"If you had a ticket, you'd know it, I'd know it, and you wouldn't need my help getting on the train. You are thusly here to once again stir up trouble, and I worry about the state of the Underworld that you have made it this far to do whatever it is you're planning to do--"

"Picking up a friend in Heaven."

"Of course you are. Well, let's put a stop to your shenanigans before you do any serious damage. One moment, please, while I call for security." Peter reached for a button under the counter, but when his eyes shifted away from Eddie, he turned pale as death and froze.

"You wouldn't do that to me, would you, Cephas?"

Without so much as a touch, Jonah pushed Eddie aside and leaned on the counter directly in front of Peter, and for a few endless moments, they looked at each other. Jonah with a cool, confident look in his eyes, Peter with utter terror and regret.

Eddie made a bet with himself who would say something first but it started taking too long. He had a Heaven to get to and no idea when the train would arrive.

"You two know each other?"

Eddie kind of assumed Peter had been here far longer than Jonah had been alive, but clearly, they'd met before.

"Yeah, we know each other very well," Jonah said without taking his eyes off Peter. "Though he'd deny it. About three times."

Eddie lit a thinking-cigarette. Instead of explaining how they knew each other, Jonah thought it was funny to waste time by only giving some bullshit hint. And on top of that, it only made sense if Peter was *Saint* Peter and Jonah was--

"Jesus!" Peter finally managed to exclaim. "My Lord, you've returned to me!"

"Oh, fuck you, you sanctimonious hypocrite."

Peter answered with an expression of utter shock. This was not the Jesus Christ he remembered. It looked like Him, sounded like Him, but didn't quite speak like Him.

"My Lord?"

"My ass," Jonah snapped. "You were blowing smoke up my ass the whole time, but you make yourself scarce when things get a little hairy."

"I remained faithful even after your arrest."

"At a fucking distance you did, yeah. And when they asked if you were with me, you denied it because you didn't want your faithful ass nailed to the cross next to me, did you?"

Peter was at a loss for words. He wanted to deny it, but that seemed like playing right into Jesus' argument, and in all truth, he couldn't either. He thought it better to change the course of the conversation entirely.

"I returned to lead your followers. The church--"

"You lived the good life off my stardust, is what you did. You just went around telling people you saw me resurrected, which you bloody well didn't, and you know it. Then you used that to rake in riches under the guise of a church."

Tears of genuine regret started to well in Peter's eyes. At the time, he never considered there being any repercussions for what he did. He gave people hope with a little white lie, and whatever coin he got from it was a nice bonus.

"I never lost faith in you," he spoke, averting his eyes and bowing his head.

Jonah looked down on him, and then at Eddie, who leaned in and whispered, "We're definitely talking about this later, but right now you're gonna guilt him into getting us on that train."

Jonah quickly weighed his loyalties. Peter was a faithful disciple for the better part of three years until it all went sour. Eddie, on the other hand, was a good friend who didn't screw him over three times, and Jonah felt closer to him in six months than he did many other people in the past two thousand years. Eddie's love for Rooney seemed more genuine than Peter's love for him, so the choice was made.

"Look at me, Rocky."

Peter looked up.

"Why did you do it? Why did you deny me?"

"I feared for my life, my Lord."

"So did I, and only one of us was right to. The other one might have been able to do something if he'd had the balls to speak up."

Peter looked away again and folded his hands. There was nothing left of the man who decisively kneed Eddie in the groin and was just about ready to sic security on him.

"No, old friend. Look at *me*." For a moment, Jonah's posture changed, and Eddie was impressed, though not as much as Peter. "Look upon my face and see the pain your denial caused."

Peter broke and tearfully pleaded, "I'm sorry, my Lord. I beg your forgiveness."

Jonah put his hands firmly on the counter and leaned forward. "I'm not your lord anymore, and I'm kinda over that whole forgiveness bullshit, too. But maybe one more, for old times' sake?"

Peter looked back and forth between Jonah and Eddie, fully aware that he was being emotionally blackmailed. Yet the yearning for forgiveness was greater than his sense of duty.

"What would you have me do, my Lord?"

"First you're gonna knock it off with that Lord-nonsense. I didn't care for it then, and I don't care for it now. Second, you're gonna get me and my buddy here on that fancy train of yours, and then we'll call it even. How's about that?"

Peter loved the idea, but he could only do half of it.

"You actually have a ticket waiting, but I can't get Mr. Sterling on the train."

"Sure you can," Jonah said.

"How?"

"Pete, I don't know. That's your part of the deal. You can't expect me to do all the work *again*."

Peter was already feeling guilty enough to help his old friend with just about anything, but now he was asked to do the impossible.

"My Lo-- Sir... Jesus, it's impossible. Nobody gets on the train without a ticket, and nobody gets a ticket without paying their dues. I don't know where the tickets come from or who decides when they are given out."

Jonah stood up straight, clearly showing he was about to walk away.

"Look within thyself and find that can-do attitude you used to have. Lest I look within myself and find some dirt on you that'll get you booted right off this platform you so covet."

And then he did walk away. Eddie quickly followed and took a seat with him on the nearest bench. Jonah stared in front of him quietly and Eddie played along for a while, but there were questions burning inside him that couldn't be kept down.

"When were you planning on telling me you're Jesus Christ?"

"Never."

"Dude, you should have said *something* before I made you listen to Judas Priest."

Jonah snorted. "That's what you're upset about?"

"I'm not upset," Eddie clarified. "Everybody's entitled to their secrets, but if I knew, I wouldn't have suggested the band named after the guy who ratted you out and got you killed."

"Who? Judas?"

Eddie nodded.

"I don't actually know a Judas."

"Wut?"

Finally, Jonah turned to look at Eddie. "Yeah, who knows how these stories get started, right? Closest I can think of was a guy called Jedidiah. He thought he was my right-hand man. Got kinda pissy about it when he realized he wasn't. Used to call him Jedi, too. He hated that, so he did his best to be a dick, but I know for a fact he didn't kiss me."

"Jedi?" Eddie chuckled.

"Heh, yeah. Took about two millennia for that to become

funny, but I'm glad it finally got a laugh."

"So, you just hung out for two thousand years?"

Eddie lit another cigarette and offered Jonah. Though he didn't smoke, he assumed it couldn't do any harm now that he was theoretically dead and took one.

After Jonah was done coughing, he answered.

"I was thoroughly confused for a long time. When God gave me the power I have, she overdid it, I think. It screwed with my head, hence the preaching and attention-seeking and whatnot. Not to mention getting crucified."

Eddie grimaced. "That must have sucked ass on a whole other level."

"You have no idea." Jonah rubbed his palm through the leather fingerless gloves he always wore for reasons that were now clear to Eddie. "If you've some spare time, try pulling yourself up using nothing but the nails through your hands. Believe you me, bud, you'll literally be thanking the guy who sticks a spear under your ribs." He held up the cigarette. "You do this for fun?"

"Uhuh. And a bit to annoy people. It relaxes me to see hypocrites throw a hissy fit over what I do with my body. Talking about bodies..."

"Nice segue."

"Better than my usual work. You did die?"

Jonah coughed again and nodded. "That part's actually reasonably accurate. They did stick me in a cave after I expired. I was lost in darkness for an indeterminable amount of time--"

"Three days."

"So I hear. However long it was, I met God again. This beautiful woman appeared before me... Man, those eyes... Well, it seems you would know."

"Dude, I know, right? And apparently I had an affair with her, too."

Jonah looked surprised. "Seriously? You cheated on Rosalie?"

"I would never!" Even just the simple inquiry made Eddie angry. "But we were hammered on Jolene's moonshine. All we know is that the next morning Helen left her panties and a message that I was great. Still have 'em in my pocket, now that I think of it."

"Lucky dog."

Eddie didn't think so. It was bad enough he didn't remember lying with God, but it was worse that he probably cheated on Rosalie.

"Helen didn't come to me for that," Jonah continued. "She just apologized for letting things get out of hand and said she'd personally see to it that I'd be treated well. Nice of God to tell me that, but you can imagine that I was pretty apprehensive after what the Romans did to me. Everything inside me told me to bolt, and I did. I ran through the darkness until it turned into light. Or, less darkness, anyway. I woke up in that cave, knocked the door out with strength I didn't know I had, and went into hiding."

Eddie had been listening so intently that his cigarette burned down to his fingers, and he flicked it away when the burn bit him.

"Jesus, man. Why are you here? We're going to where God lives. Why risk coming out of hiding now?"

Jonah leaned back and stared up. Maybe to Heaven, maybe to nowhere in particular. He sighed deeply. "I feel responsible. Those CDS types were looking for me. They shot Rooney to get me out of hiding."

Eddie stood up and stretched his back. "For the last stop before Heaven, these benches are definitely Hell on your back. It sucks, though, that the CDS is actually getting what they want then. And if you were coming into the open, why not resurrect Rooney and save us the trouble of finagling ourselves onto a train?"

Jonah extinguished his cigarette and put the butt in his pocket so as not to litter. "I never resurrected anyone. Those are stories from a time where they'd bury you if you were a particularly deep sleeper..."

A steam whistle ended their conversation.

"Well, ain't that a sight..." Eddie spoke with awe.

A massive streamliner locomotive pulled a long line of finely crafted carriages into the station. The Art Deco lines starting on the plow ran up and to the sides along the length of the train, giving it a feeling of speed, even rolling in calmly like it was now. The front of the boiler jutted out like a bullet escaping a barrel, and on the side, 'United Afterlife Railroad' was written in proud silver letters.

Steam jetted onto the platform, but by the time it reached Eddie's legs, it was a calm cloud.

"The Afterline model S1," Peter said, who had come out of his office at the sound of the whistle. "Pride of the Afterlife Railroads, even if we have only one train. She's a beauty, huh?"

Eddie nodded while he took in every line, curve, and form of the magnificent engine. Though Jonah was impressed with it as well, he had more urgent matters to deal with.

"Got some good news for me, Pete?"

Peter handed him his ticket and then held one up for Eddie. "I had to dig deep but I found a tiny little loophole that has a sliver of a chance of working."

"Sounds promising..." Eddie scoffed and took the ticket.

"You're Jesus' spirit guide now," Peter said, tapping the ticket. "Officially, we haven't allowed spirit guides anymore since the early 19th century."

"Why's that?"

"Because people were sneaking other people on trains under the guise of spirit guides. So... exactly this. But considering Jesus' reservations were from far before the amended rule, one last exception could possibly be made."

Eddie didn't feel so sure about it. Illegally riding a train wasn't normally a top concern for him, but he had no idea how they dealt with fare dodgers in the Afterlife. "And you're sure this will work?"

"I'm sure this will get you on the train, yes. What happens when you get off the train at the next stop is beyond my control and, quite frankly, I don't care. My Lord's ticket is legit, that's what matters."

Jonah quickly stopped Eddie from starting an argument by nudging him toward the train.

"Thank you, Peter."

He could have shown more gratitude, perhaps, but considering the circumstances, this seemed like more than enough. Now he just wanted to get on the train and figure out what a spirit guide was supposed to do.

SEVENTEEN

"Joachim Cohen, Jack Coltrane, John Carpenter, but that was in '78, so it drew a little too much attention. Changed it to John Connor. Didn't have a lot of luck with names around that period. Ehm... James Callahan, Jim Cullen..."

Eddie regretted asking. He should have known Jonah used quite a few different names over two thousand years.

"Frank Shepherd, Jesús Salvador, because I was feeling cocky--"

"Alright, I get it!"

"Josephus Colt-- Oh..."

"Wait, as in Joe Colt?"

Jonah nodded.

"You are famous gunslinger Immortal Joe Colt?"

Jonah nodded again. "Was. And the legend is far bigger than the man, I promise you. Survive getting shot one time, and all of a sudden, you're immortal."

"But you are."

"And yet we're still standing at Heaven's gates."

Eddie took a good look. Up to this point, he'd been focusing on all of Jonah's names and somehow missed these enormous wrought golden gates that looked exactly like he expected, down to the inset pearls and the cloudy ground they had stepped on after leaving the platform.

"That is some tacky shit."

"Well, we're not staying." Jonah checked out the line. "But we're gonna be here longer than we planned."

Eddie saw it, too. Every soul that was on the train needed to be checked in one by one, and this train held a lot of souls. Maybe they would have been more to the front of the line if they hadn't spent all this time talking about aliases. And maybe this would have gone faster if there was more than one check-in window for this entire crowd. Eddie pulled his phone from his pocket.

"Hey, whoa, what are you doing?" Jonah exclaimed nervously and tried to push the phone out of sight.

"Seeing if I can call Rosie. Time is weird in the Afterlife, and for all I know, this line is going to keep us for months."

"You are a spirit guide from the early first century--"

"Ooh, Captain Arrogance. You should know the count didn't start when you were born, man."

"It's the count the whole world is using, and at that point in the count, you didn't have a phone."

Some souls in front of them turned to see what the fuss was about, but Eddie dismissed them with a wave and tapped the pocket of Jonah's leather cut.

"Is that a phone, Mr. First Century?"

"Yeah, but..."

"But my ass. I'm seeing if I can get my girlfriend on the line, and maybe you should too."

Jonah put his hand on his pocket and remembered Eddie ranting about things screaming at you if you called the

Underworld. Technically, they weren't in the Underworld anymore, but he was going to wait and see what would happen before calling Jolene.

Eddie put the phone to his ear and gave Jonah the I-got-this nod. The kind of nod that was without fail followed by the person doing the nodding absolutely not getting what they thought they got.

The shrill, bone-chilling scream pierced Eddie's ear like a barbed icepick, and in an uncontrollable reflex, he tossed the phone away like he was trying to shake fire ants from his hands.

"Jesus Christ!"

"She didn't answer?" Jonah said smugly.

"As your spirit guide, I advise you not to use your phone and also, kiss my ass."

"I'm only gonna do one of those things, okay?"

Eddie shrugged. "I just advise; what you do with it ain't my bitch."

He stepped out of line to find his phone, which was a little impractical in the misty cloud. Shuffling around in the general area where he'd flung his phone, he hoped his feet would touch anything out of the ordinary. After getting much farther away from the line than expected, he found it and put it back in his pocket. Even if he couldn't call anyone, it was always handy to keep a phone around. Like now, to take a picture of this line in front of the pearly gates while a strange sort of sunlight hit them just right.

Without the crowd blocking his view, Eddie saw another check-in window. It was definitely occupied but there were no people queuing up for it. That might have had something to do with the sign saying *VIP Check-in*, but to Eddie, it said *Shortcut*.

"Jonah! There's another window."

"Yeah, the VIP one. I saw it."

"You didn't think that was worth mentioning?"

"It's for Very Important People."

Eddie slumped his shoulders and looked at Jonah like he was

stupid. "Remind me again, what's your name?"

Jonah wasn't sure what Eddie was asking at first until he looked at the VIP window again, and it hit him.

"I'm Jesus H. Tapdancing Christ. Come on."

Eddie followed him up to the window, trying to look as much like a spirit guide as he could. Which was a hundred percent, if spirit guides walked like people from Herringwood who wore leather jackets and Judas Priest t-shirts.

Regardless of Eddie's performance, the girl behind the window received them with a friendly smile. "Hello, how can I help you?"

"Ehm..." Jonah started unsurely. He thought it would have been obvious why they were here. There weren't exactly a lot of options. "We would like to go to Heaven?"

"You've come to the right place," the girl laughed. "May I see your ticket and VIP pass, please?"

"Oh... I don't think Peter gave us VIP passes."

The girl's genuine smile turned into a forced one. "I'm afraid you'll have to queue up for the other window then."

Polite as he was, Jonah was ready to accept this answer but his 'spirit guide' wasn't as enthused about the idea of getting back in line. Eddie didn't step in line very often to start with, especially not if he had important business. He leaned on the stubby counter and turned on the Sterling charm.

"Are you sure you can't just have a quick look at our tickets anyway? There's nobody here, and he's single."

Eddie nodded at Jonah, who understood the general plan but ruined it by trying very hard to look single and achieving the opposite.

"You will have to get back in line, sirs."

"Alright." Eddie straightened his back. "But if we do, you'll have to start thinking of how to explain to Helen that you dismissed Jesus Christ."

Surprised, the girl squinted at Jonah, hoping to recognize him.

She didn't because she had never met him in any capacity, but that made it all the more critical to at least check the name on his ticket. She wouldn't even have entertained the idea if it had been anyone else, but this was the last name on the list of must-have souls.

"May I see your ticket, please?"

"Sure." Jonah pushed the ticket through the slit between the counter and the window.

The girl picked it up and examined it. The golden sheen reflected a shimmer on her face as she flipped it around and around to check it for authenticity, and her eyes kept getting bigger. They showed amazement and flashes of pride. She never thought *the* Jesus Christ would show up at her window.

Ooh, Sally, you hit the jackpot!

When she got up this morning, it felt like a good day, and her coffee tasted better. Just before she left her small apartment, she psyched herself up in the mirror like she always did, and this time she believed herself. Now she finally understood why.

"I'll be happy to check you in, Mr. Christ. And your friend?"

Eddie handed his ticket over. To his chagrin, she was far less impressed with it.

"We don't accept spirit guides anymore. You'll have to get back in the other line."

Before Eddie could start an argument, Jonah took the lead. He knew Eddie well enough to know it would be far more beneficial if he did the talking now.

"Yes, Peter told us. But my reservations were made long before that rule was implemented and I was at no point informed about it. I need my spirit guide."

Sally examined him and then Eddie. He didn't look like any spirit guide she ever saw but then again, she hadn't been here long enough to ever see one at all. Still, spirit guides were more an ancient people's practice, she knew from the manual. It was rare for modern people to have one even before the rule was created.

"What kind of a spirit guide are you, exactly?"

"Uhh… A pretty good one," Eddie said. "I even saved you from screwing up just now. Imagine what I do for my homie here."

Jonah put an arm around Eddie. "You don't get to be the Great Redeemer on sheer luck, you know."

Sally bit her lip and looked at them both. Some quick considerations later, she made a decision.

"And you don't get to be employee of the month two times in a row if you don't do your job properly. I'm sorry, Mr. Christ, but I can't let your friend in."

"Fine. If I don't get my spirit guide, you don't get me." Jonah turned away. "Come on, Ed. Let's see when the next train is."

Sally watched them walk away. She wasn't worried. They couldn't just get on the train and go back… *Could they?* Tour groups did it, though. *But why?* Who wants to go back to the Underworld? Unless they wanted to go back and inform Peter about this… They clearly knew him.

And now she was worried.

Meanwhile, Eddie checked if they were out of earshot and whispered to Jonah, "We're not actually getting on that train, are we?"

Jonah chuckled. "I briefly sold used cars in the eighties. Did you see the look in her eyes when she realized it was me? Only place we're going is Heaven."

"But we're still kinda walking to the platform."

"And we'll kinda keep on doing so. I guarantee you she'll be running after us before we get on a train."

Sure enough, and to nobody's surprise, Sally's voice rang out the moment Eddie's boot made contact with the platform.

"Mr. Christ! Please, wait."

Eddie and Jonah turned around. Now that he had her in full view, Eddie noticed how Sally's hospitality uniform fitted her as perfectly as a uniform could. And because he was but a man, he needed to relay this information to someone. It needed to be stated, preferably to another man, and he just so happened to have one near.

"Damn, she's sexy," he quickly passed on to Jonah. Not quickly enough, though.

"And also not deaf, Mr. Sterling."

"Just spirit guiding and shit. If I don't tell mah Jeezy this stuff, I'm not doing my job."

"Sure." Sally chose to have the rest of this conversation with Jonah. "I've spoken to Peter, and ehm... Well, I'm sorry for the inconvenience. Here are your passes, and these are coupons for free drinks."

"Wait, what kind of a Heaven is this if you have to pay for your own drinks?"

Sally ignored Eddie. She was aware that she was an attractive woman, but having it pointed out regularly quickly wore thin, as did her patience with the ones insisting on pointing it out.

"You can have a seat in the lounge while you wait for your tour guide."

Jonah took the fancy envelope she held out for him. "Tour guide?"

"Oh, yes, Mr. Christ. All our VIP guests get a fully guided tour of our facilities. And as a bonus, you'll get an in-depth evaluation to see which district is best for you. Though I'm sure a man of your stature will be able to get a whole new district if need be."

"And Eddie?"

"He should just be happy Peter will have me fired if I don't play along with this blatant lie."

She shot Eddie one fierce glare.

"I'm sorry, okay?" Eddie tried. "It was a compliment."

"Which I might have taken as such if you said it to me instead of about me."

Jonah saw Eddie open his mouth for reasons that couldn't

possibly be helpful at this point and spoke before he could. "Luckily, my spirit guide knows when to shut up."

Sally looked at Jonah, and her face turned nice again. "Another lie I will choose to believe. Now, if you follow me, I will show you to the lounge."

She started walking to the gates, and Eddie did his utter best not to watch her hips sway as they followed her.

Eddie wasn't a stranger to the concept of lounges, and he'd even seen some on TV, but none of what he had imagined measured up to what he was seeing here. The centerpiece of the spacious room was a long U-shaped bar, lined with comfortable-looking leather stools. He wasn't planning to sit on any of them because dotted all through the rest of the mahogany-paneled room were royal armchairs and the fluffiest-looking sofas in cozy arrangements. Before he took a seat in one of them, however, he did saunter up to the bar, because it was a sin to let a free drink coupon go to waste. A tall, well-built barkeeper immediately came up to him because there was currently nobody else to serve.

"Good day to you, sir. How may I help you?"

"Good day right back at ya," Eddie said and leaned on the bar to prepare for what he was going to ask. His mind couldn't quite construct a scenario where this question wasn't utterly ridiculous, so to counter that, he made sure he looked utterly cool while asking it.

"Do you have a Macallan Reach, and is that covered by the coupon my good friend is about to hand you?"

Jonah, who already had the chance to taste a Macallan Reach, whipped out the coupons, ready to pay for a vulgarly expensive whisky.

The barkeeper laughed, and for a moment, Eddie thought he was being laughed at, but then the bottle came off the top shelf.

"Excellent choice, sir. Not a lot of souls even know of it, let alone dare to ask for it." He poured a dram and showed the bottle to

Jonah. "For you as well, sir?"

"Just a Coke, for me, please."

The barkeeper showed no signs of contempt and treated pouring a fizzy drink the same as pouring a six-figure whisky. For once, Eddie decided to follow a good example. If Jonah wanted a Coke instead of the finest spirits he could dream of, then he got a Coke. Eddie had his unicorn.

He'd always been a fan of a good whisky and, at one point, considered whisky-tasting as a career until he realized you're supposed to spit it out. Nevertheless, he did manage to rack up a nice list of sampled whiskies recreationally, but for obvious financial reasons, The Macallan The Reach was always—and perhaps ironically—out of his reach.

He picked the glass up and studied the deep auburn liquid in the brilliant crystal.

"Sir, before you taste..." The barkeep put a box of cigars in front of him and opened it. "A Montecristo would complement your Macallan exceptionally well. If you are of the smoking persuasion, of course."

"If I wasn't, I'd be persuaded now. Thank you very much, good sir."

Promptly, Eddie stuck a cigar in his face and lit it with his trusty gasoline lighter. Both the barkeep and Jonah showed a little bit of contempt this time.

Eddie neither cared nor noticed. A large framed map caught his attention, and together with his new friends Monty and Mac, he went to have a closer look.

The map appeared old, and from a distance, the illusion held up. On closer inspection, it became clear that it was merely treated to look centuries old. The layout of all the current Heavenly districts included, for example, more recent additions like Pastafarian Heaven and a Jedi Academy.

Jonah joined him. "Hey, look. Fallen Kingdom."

Eddie nodded and took a thoughtful sip of whisky.

"Mm-hm," he said, long after swallowing and shortly after the lingering sweet and smoky taste politely excused itself from his tongue. "I'll give you two guesses where Rooney is."

"Why two?"

"Because maybe you wanted to get a joke in or something?"

"Eh." Jonah shrugged a little. The glorious calm here had a relaxing effect on him. He preferred to enjoy that while he could, and leave the smartassery for later. Undoubtedly there would be moments where it was called for, but this was not one of them.

The calm was briefly and only mildly disturbed by a golf cart pulling up a little too enthusiastically. Seconds later, a young man walked in and headed straight for them with an outstretched arm.

"You must be Jesus Christ," he said with a big, wide grin. "Nice to meet you. I am Raphael and I'll be your guide today."

"Nice to meet you too, Raphael," Jonah said. "I go by Jonah Craig these days, though."

"If it's all the same to you, I'd prefer to use your given name as to avoid confusion. And I'd be remiss if I didn't say I am quite honored to show you around our facilities, Mr. Christ."

"And my spirit guide."

Raphael took a dismissive look at Eddie. "Hm, yes. I was informed you were traveling with a... spirit guide. Hm. Well. He's here now. Might as well."

Eddie took another sip and chased it with a good drag of cigar. "Love your enthusiasm, Raph."

"Yes. If you don't mind, I'd like to get going."

"I mind."

Of course Eddie minded. He had one more sip of fine whisky, and he was going to savor it. Not to mention the indeed perfectly paired cigar that was going to take quite some more time to savor. Then again, he could savor that on a golf cart.

"I'm really sorry, but I have to be back here in three hours to pick up David Jones, and there's a lot of ground to cover."

"Who's that?" Eddie asked, trying to stall so he could do the whisky thing.

"Err, I'm not entirely sure, actually." Raphael seemed to hate admitting it. "The briefing was a little confusing, but he had something to do with documenting the rise and fall of a person named Ziggy Stardust. It's strange, though. I pride myself on keeping up with all our new arrivals, but I don't recall ever seeing that name on any list."

"Yeah, I don't think Ziggy will ever be dead enough to get here." Eddie raised his glass in a toast to Ziggy Stardust and closed his eyes in a quiet farewell to the whisky he would likely never taste again. He needed this memory to last. Licorice. Bramble jam. Crystalized ginger? This was a hard taste to store in his memories. He wasn't sure if he ever consciously consumed ginger, let alone crystalized.

"Fine," he finally said. "Let's go."

"Oh, you'll have to leave the cigar. Smoking is only allowed in designated areas."

"What the fuck kind of a Heaven is this? Stinks a whole lot like Earth, if you ask me."

Offended, Raphael turned up his nose. "And we don't want it to stink of cigar as well."

"Stink of cigar?!" Eddie angrily pointed at Raphael with the cigar, and Jonah held him back. "You have any idea what I'm smoking here?"

"A Montecristo Yellow No. 2, and I don't want it on my golf cart."

"If Monty can't come, then neither will I. Haughty little shit. I don't even wanna go on your precious golf cart anymore."

Jonah pushed him back. "Why are you ruining this now?"

"I'm not ruining anything," Eddie whispered with a wink. "I'm getting a free pass to snoop around. Just roll with it."

"I'm genuinely curious about this place. If you ruin this for me--”

“Don’t worry. I need you to keep him busy.”

Eddie pushed Jonah aside and made it to Raphael with one big step. “This is a good cigar. I will fight you over this cigar.” He gave him the universal let’s-fight push. “Put ‘em up, squirt.”

Raphael just shook his head in disappointment. “I will never understand what Helen sees in you humans, and until she sees you for the hopeless bunch you are, I will be relegated to showing you around a facility that is far too good for you. Thankfully, I have the one exception to the rule in my presence today, and I will take Mr. Christ, but for the first time since my creation, I will conveniently forget to pick up a passenger. Enjoy our lounge, Mr. Sterling. This is as far as you go.”

Raphael went back to his golf cart, and Jonah checked with Eddie one more time before following.

“Is this your plan?”

“Yup.”

“Alright then...”

“Enjoy the tour, dude. See you later.”

A little confused, Jonah went on his way with Raphael, and Eddie took a seat at the bar. If he understood Raphael correctly, he lived here now, and it seemed prudent to check if residents were allowed free Macallans before defying the word of an angel.

EIGHTEEN

The empty crystal glass that mere seconds earlier held together a priceless whisky landed carefully on the bar. A thick cloud of cigar smoke followed it, and Eddie got off the stool.

"I'd love to stay for another, but I've some business to tend to."

The barkeeper held up the bottle again. "Are you sure I can't tempt you, sir?"

"No. No... But I have to pick someone up, so... Yeah, pretty sure."

"I would enjoy it rather a lot if you stayed for another drink."

Eddie crossed his arms and examined the barkeeper. His vest and blouse were flawless, and his manners impeccable, but there was something off about him, and it wasn't the hipster beard.

"I know what that whisky costs, mate. Nobody should be that keen on giving it away."

Yet the barkeeper insisted.

"Nah. You're freaking me out. See ya later, hoss."

As Eddie pushed open the door, the barkeeper fell out of character and panicked. "I can't let you leave!"

With his hand on the door, Eddie looked back and grinned evilly. "Why?"

"Because Raphael said so."

"Why?"

"Because... err... you can't?"

Eddie took a big drag of the cigar. "I'll tell you why I *can* leave." He exhaled a thick cloud. "I'm the kind of motherfucker who does things because he doesn't know why they can't be done."

He went over the words in his head. He wasn't sure if he didn't just insult himself, or if he should also try quantum physics, but at least the barkeep was as confused as he was. Eddie didn't feel like waiting for whatever would come next, so he added, "I'll tell Raphael you tried your darndest. Tarah."

And just like that, he found himself on an expertly bricked road into what looked a lot like a theme park's main street.

"I fucking hate theme parks."

Even as a kid, Eddie could never quite match the time spent waiting with the time spent on the actual ride. Back then, the ride was still entertaining enough to keep his mind from thinking any longer on it. Later he realized if he wanted to spend a lot of money on waiting hours to get a 40-second ride, he was better off trying to pick up girls at the bar.

This place, though... It wasn't right. It was clearly built for a large crowd, but there was nobody here. Going by the theme-park logic, that would be glorious, but this was Heaven. There should have been some activity. Above the shops along the wide street were vintage-style apartments that looked like there were actual souls living here, but nobody so much as looked out the window.

Eddie didn't have to go far to meet someone, however. Barely a few steps into his quest to break all of Heaven's laws, the flapping of wings stopped him in his tracks. He looked up to see where it came from, but before he could get a bead on it, a man landed in front of him with a superhero pose.

At least, it looked like a man in the sense that he was dressed in a fitted uniform complete with impressive-looking decorations, and he had a neck to carry a blue lanyard with a card on the end. In fact, he had all the limbs and appendages one would expect on a human. But he also had wings. As he rose up from his landing, he stood at least seven feet tall. His hand reached for the hilt of a cavalry saber dangling from his hip, and he spoke in a booming voice.

"Halt!"

It wasn't something that impressed Eddie before, and it wasn't suddenly going to now.

"Is this about the cigar?"

The winged man was clearly put off balance. It should have been obvious to the intruder that it was about all the intruding he was doing.

"You shall not pass."

Immediately, Eddie started to sputter. "Hahaha. I'm a fan of a good cliché, man, but you don't have to fly 'em in for me."

"What?"

"Where I'm from, that's a cliché." Eddie stuck the cigar between his lips and went in for a handshake. "Eddie Sterling. Who are you again, big guy?"

Completely put off by Eddie's casual approach, the winged man shook his hand. "Michael, assistant manager to God, and her voice in her absence."

Eddie sucked in air through his teeth. "Started out good there, Mike. But that whole voice-of-God thing sounds just a little cocky."

Michael crossed his arms. "I will not hide the truth for some human."

"Hey, I'm not 'some human,' man."

"And I'm not 'man,' human."

"Oh?" Eddie said, surprised. "You're, like, an angel?"

Michael proudly confirmed.

"Ugh, I expected a little better from Helen than to go with the biblical theme... Hey, is it true that angels don't have genitals?"

"The insolence! Of course I come fully equipped! What kind of a question is that?"

"A strategic one."

Eddie directed all energy to his leg muscle and kneed Michael in the groin so hard that it bordered on epic. A surprised heave expelled the air from his body, and the angel collapsed to his knees like any regular man.

"Never fails," Eddie said. "I'm gonna borrow your keycard too, if you don't mind."

Michael tried to reach for Eddie when the lanyard slipped over his head, but he needed both hands on the ground while his body tried to come to terms with all the new things it was feeling.

While an assault to the groin was always a good move, Eddie had no idea of the recovery times of angels. Judging by that one time Rosalie did it to the Devil, it was about the same. Still, he wasn't going to risk being here when this guy regrouped. That saber would make short work of him, whether he wanted to understand why or not.

He jogged away because he was still confident he hit Michael hard enough to not have to run, and let himself in through the nearest door that had a pass reader. The door opened to a set of metal stairs which led Eddie down into a hub area where several wide industrial hallways met. As with many theme parks, the backstage area was far more interesting. It was surprisingly clean, to start with. Sure, there were clear signs of use. Scuff marks, old stains on the floor. Maybe a few doors could use a new lick of paint, but it was generally maintained as well as possible.

The signage wasn't very helpful, though. The hallways were marked with letters, but nothing to indicate which heaven was in which direction. Just venturing out was probably not the best idea, so Eddie looked around for other options.

Two golf carts were parked by a charging bay next to several dumpsters, which made him feel a little sad because he suddenly thought about Willie, and he cheered himself up by hoping he would meet the crazy old bum here somewhere.

He shuffled up to the dumpsters to check. These were really nice; strangely clean, too. Willie could probably make a good home out of these, but a few knocks later there was no reaction. Of course, there wasn't. Why would Willie settle for living in another dumpster if he could have any Heaven he wanted? He probably upgraded to a pigeon coop.

A man in orange overalls startled Eddie by banging on a nearby door.

"The Vikings are coming!"

The door flung open, and a tall man in armor jumped out. "Shit, shit, shit!"

He flipped his eyepatch back in place and tried to straighten a fake beard onto his face while he walked, but the man in overalls stopped him.

"Cigarette!"

"Fuck!"

Discount Odin pulled the cigarette from his lips and looked around before realizing the nearest ashtray was in the smoke room he'd just come from and threw it on the ground. "Sorry."

"Sure you are," the man in overalls sneered and looked around until he saw Eddie. He snapped his fingers at him. "Hey, you. Clean this up."

Then he took Odin by the arm and led him to one of the golf carts.

"I'll drive you. You're never going to be at the staging area in time if you run, and we don't want that armor stinking of sweat for the next shift."

The golf cart raced off, leaving Eddie to deal with the mess. Apparently, he was the designated broom jockey everywhere he went. Not this time, he decided, and kicked the cigarette butt under the nearest container before calling it a day. He had more important things to do, like figuring out which one of these hallways led to the Fallen Kingdom, and if he could steal a golf cart to get there.

There was something about golf carts. No matter what a man's daily driver is—be it a Volkswagen, a Lambo, or, indeed, a Vindicator—going nuts with a golf cart was always fun.

So Eddie inspected the remaining cart and quickly started thinking about a different plan because it needed keys to start, and there was no sun visor to hide them behind. Hotwiring it would have been cool, but the only thing he knew about that was that he'd probably end up electrocuting himself, and he was dead enough already. Maybe he could find an office that had keys.

Surely there was a less suspicious way of finding out, but Eddie went with the first idea that came to him, which was jiggling the handle of every door he found to see if they were open. Aside from the smoke room, none of them were. Heaven had the backstage area locked up tight, and that didn't bode well for this quest.

When he finally did come about a door with a passreader, things didn't exactly get any better.

Two security guards looked up, and the one closest to Eddie said, "Can I help you?"

But he said it in a way that clearly implied he wasn't going to be very helpful.

"Err, yeah, actually," Eddie said nonetheless. "I need to get to the Fallen Kingdom, but I got turned around somewhere. All these hallways look alike, right? We should do something about those signs."

The guard stood up, revealing him to be bigger than Eddie expected. It didn't really worry him, considering he'd just taken down an actual angel. The only problem he saw was that if things turned violent now, he wouldn't be able to get to the second guard before he sounded an alarm.

"I don't recognize you," the first guard said. "What's your name?"

"Ed-- Wardo... Eduardo. Hi, I'm Eduardo. And you are...?"

"The head of security, who is informed of every new employee and can read the name on your pass, *Eduardo*."

Eddie dumbly grabbed the pass and looked at it. *Michael - Assistant manager.* And in large friendly letters, too.

"Uhm..."

The head of security reached for his nightstick. "I don't know how you managed to get here, sir, but this is as far as you go."

"Whoa, hey!" Eddie raised his hands to stop the guard raising his nightstick, or to defend himself if the need arose. "There's a bit of a misunderstanding here."

The other guard also got up. They weren't just going to accept a general sort of misunderstanding as an excuse, so Eddie worked hard on coming up with a plausible elaboration. Thinking on his feet was kind of his thing, even if the ideas he came up with in a hurry often weren't good ideas, per se.

"I'm Helen's new assistant. Michael, ehm, pulled a groin muscle."

The first guard briefly held back, but didn't believe a word.

"Unless pulling a groin muscle prevents him from talking, he would have made sure I got the memo of him taking a sick day. No dice, Eduardo."

"He pulled it really hard."

"You can hold your hands out so I can cuff you, but if you want to put up a fight, I'm fine with that too."

"No. Nope. Wait! Look. It's a little more complex than that. I didn't want to, but you're forcing my hand, and Helen is not going to appreciate that you did..."

The guard stopped his approach. He still didn't think "Eduardo" was speaking even the slightest bit of truth, but now there was the possible risk of angering God, and that merited pause.

"Explain yourself."

Eddie felt some relief. He had the fish on the hook, now he just needed to reel it in very carefully.

"I'm Helen's *personal* assistant," he said, hushing his voice to drive the point home. "Like, really personal."

The guard's face displayed a large amount of disbelief and the other guard even snickered. Eddie went on.

"I wasn't supposed to say anything because we felt sorry for Michael."

And at that point, the line snapped. The guards didn't buy it, and out came the cuffs.

"Wait!" Eddie put his hands in his pockets. At first to prevent getting cuffed, but in doing so, he found the solution to really selling the argument. Without a thought about the reaction of two tense security guards, he whipped it out.

And the solution was, to everybody but Eddie's surprise, a rather attractive pair of lacy white panties. Incredulously, the guards stared at how Eddie triumphantly waved them around.

"God is replacing tired old Michael with her fresh, new lover, gentlemen. I'm your goddamn boss now, so back. The fuck. Up!"

In a ridiculous display of power, he spread out the panties so they could read the message. The head guard leaned in to check.

"Jesus, man. You wanna smell 'em for authenticity or what?"

"No..." The guard stood up straight. "I recognize her handwriting. It's legit... I guess."

"Yeah, I don't like it when my head of security guesses," Eddie stated like he was an actual boss. He quite enjoyed this little sliver of power. He never was the boss of anyone before and it felt kinda nice. "So instead of guessing, you're gonna give me a ride to the

Fallen Kingdom like I asked when I came in here. And you, other guy, round up a posse and do something about the Vikings. I heard they were coming, and why do I need to tell you this? What kind of security detail are you? Helen will hear of this, and the next time I show you her panties, they're gonna read *you're fired*!"

The guards looked at each other. If it was policy now to let every half-witted loverboy boss people around, they might have to check for an opening in the Underworld. Yet, maybe this was just a miscommunication.

"We know the Vikings are coming," the second guard said. "There's somebody meeting them already."

"If you know they're coming, why aren't you panicking and screaming for your mother? Have you not seen what they did to England? Soon as they figure out that guy isn't the real Odin, there's gonna be some ragnarok 'n' roll."

The head guard nodded. "I think I understand the confusion. Let me explain it on the way."

Eddie shrugged. He was going to be long gone before any Viking came swinging an ax at him. If they wanted to be all lackadaisical about it, they could go right ahead and enjoy the results.

The head guard extended his hand. "Hadraniel. Sorry for the inconvenience. If you'll follow me, please."

Eddie shook his hand. "Can I call you Haddy?"

"No."

"Dranny?"

"Please, no."

"What do your friends call you?"

"Sir."

Eddie took a seat in the golf cart. "I'm not going to call you sir."

Hadraniel was perfectly fine with that and hoped to never be called anything by Eddie on account of never having to deal with him anymore after this.

"One moment, please," Hadraniel said and put his finger to his earpiece.

Eddie didn't like it and looked around. It was never a good sign if people you just bamboozled started getting messages on their earpieces. He got ready to bolt at the first sign of trouble.

"Understood," Hadraniel said, and took place behind the wheel.

"You're not going to tell me what that was about, huh?"

"It's none of your concern, no."

"Right, right. And you're still driving me to the Fallen Kingdom?"

"Yes."

Eddie knew there was definitely something up; he could practically smell it. But at the same time, he was now being zoomed to Rooney, so he let it go for now. He did still do his best to keep track of the turns they made. At the very least, he was going to have to figure out how to get back on his own. As soon as he sprung Rooney, the game would be up, and Hadraniel wouldn't be willing to play along anymore.

"Are we going to run into any Vikings, you think?" Eddie asked.

"Hah. You don't have to worry about the Vikings you think are coming," Hadraniel answered with an air of dismissiveness. "The Old Norse gods still have some following. We call them Vikings for simplicity, but it's just a bunch of regular people heading for Valhalla."

Eddie processed it. This presented an enormous amount of great opportunities. If there was a Jedi Temple here, and an actual Fallen Kingdom, anything could become a heaven. As far as Eddie knew, *Fallen Kingdom* was just a game. Sure, some people played it religiously, but it wasn't an actual religion, and he wasn't sure of Jediism either... His mind started doing its own thing with that information, and, within a matter of seconds, Eddie was wondering if he could make a Church Of The Everlasting Orgy happen.

This was something he'd have to discuss with Rosalie when he got back. He was pretty sure Helen would be open to the idea anyway. In fact...

"Is there an orgy heaven?"

Without so much as blinking, Hadraniel answered, "To the left and down the hall. The other one is two exits back. The architects aren't sure where they're gonna put the third one, but they'll need it."

Eddie grinned from ear to ear. He would definitely need to talk to Rosalie if they were going to spend eternity here at some point in the future.

NINETEEN

Rounding the last corner, Eddie saw what the call from earlier was probably about. Michael waited for them with two others who didn't look like the security guards he was used to. Instead of the standard-issue nightsticks, these guys held spears.

"You drove me right into a trap, didn't you?"

Hadraniel grinned and nodded.

"Goddammit, Dranny! Helen's gonna hear about this unless you turn around now."

"Ms. Helen is going to hear about this regardless because you are just a common intruder."

"If intruders are common around here, you should be used to this."

Eddie braced himself and kicked Hadraniel out of the cart. Before the angel could get back up, Eddie scooted over to the driver's seat and floored it straight at Michael, hoping the plexiglass windshield would protect him from the spears and that the cart would have the power to run over an angel. He didn't have high hopes, considering it took two-and-a-half goes with a muscle car to kill the Devil, but turning tail and running would only make them give chase. If he wanted any chance of finding Rooney, he needed Michael out of commission.

God's assistant manager immediately saw what Eddie's plan was and brandished his saber. Even in the humdrum fluorescent light of the hallway, it shone like it was on fire, and all it took was one cut to end the adventure.

Eddie pushed the pedal down and got more power than he expected from this dinky thing.

Like a bullfighter, Michael stepped elegantly aside and swung at the cart. The saber barely took notice of the pipes holding up the roof, or the plexiglass. Eddie ducked just in time, and it missed him by inches.

"Jesus Christ, you could have killed me!" he yelled.

He wasn't sure why he was angry about this; judging by the damage done to the golf cart, he was fairly sure he wouldn't even have noticed if he was hit. The saber had taken a perfectly straight cut through the windshield as if it wasn't even there. And part of it wasn't there anymore now. It lay on the ground by Michael, together with a piece of support and roof.

Eddie looked back and saw Michael indeed gave chase. It took just a few seconds for him to catch up and fly over, and land several feet in front of Eddie to swing again. Only this time, he was going to swing low. The golf cart could be replaced.

Backing up wasn't an option for Eddie either. Hadraniel and the two guards with spears were catching up and boxing him in. His only chance was to the left or right, where there was mostly a lot of white brick wall going on. And a door with a passreader.

Only braking enough to get out without falling, Eddie lunged for the door. He wasn't praying, per se, because he knew there was nobody listening, but he muttered a long string of curses in the vain hope that this would make the door open faster.

The passreader beeped and flashed a green LED.

The lock of the door clicked and opened.

The saber whistled and came down toward him.

Eddie tugged wildly on the door, and its sudden opening deflected the saber. He dove into newly opened salvation and pulled the door with him until it fell in the lock and the handle came out.

He examined the half in his hand. It was neatly cut off where the outside handle would have been, and he smiled.

"Thanks for locking yourself out, asshole!" Eddie yelled at the door. He couldn't hear a reply, but he wasn't interested in listening for it either. If that saber could cut through golf carts and door handles, it stood to reason that listening for replies would get him stabbed in the ear.

In fact, there wasn't any time to gloat. He was surprised they hadn't already cut a hole in the door.

"Better get a move on."

He looked around and his options were fairly limited. This throughway was only just wide enough for two average-sized people to pass each other in a somewhat intimate way, and he could only go left or right. Currently neither side seemed the better option, so he tried to find something he could base a decision on. Anything would have been acceptable. An oddly shaped brick, a flickering light, whatever was out of the ordinary. Looking up, he found what he was looking for. Cables ran along the ceiling and to one side, where they bunched up with more cables, so Eddie headed in that direction. A Fallen Kingdom probably required a lot of cables for... cable things.

In a nice change of pace, he eventually made it to an already unlocked door and went through. The enclosed corridor made way for a metal platform that looked out over a magnificent room that instantly reminded Eddie of Purgatory. Instead of cells and the stink of despair, it smelled quite neutral, and there were pods neatly lined up as far as the eye could see.

Eddie looked over the railing and the pods extended in both vertical directions as well. Wires came out the tops and he couldn't see where they went, but he assumed some of these were the wires he followed to get here.

A sudden flapping of wings made him duck and scuttle to the darkest corner he could find. The last thing he wanted was to go head-to-head with Michael, so he called upon all the stealth skills he learned from video games and hoped they applied in the real world—as far as this world could be considered real, anyway.

To his relief, he saw that Michael wasn't the only one with wings. A woman dressed in white landed one walkway up and checked a pod. Since she didn't seem armed, Eddie decided he could try and charm her into being helpful. He tucked the stolen access pass under his shirt and leaned over the railing to call her.

"Excuse me, ma'am?"

The woman looked around, surprised, until she saw him.

He waved. "Hi there, hello. I need to ask you something! Can I get up there?"

She spread an impressive pair of equally white wings and took off. For a moment, she disappeared out of sight and then swooped in, landing before him.

"Can I help you?"

Eddie flashed his most charming smile. "I do believe you can, yes."

The brunette looked at him over her glasses like a librarian charging a late fee.

"Ugh... Can I help you with anything *here*?"

"No, err, yeah, that's what I meant. I'm sorry. I was trying to be charming and shit..." He held out his hand. "Hi, I'm Eddie."

She briefly looked at it and decided to give him a second chance. "Suzanne. Are you supposed to be here, Eddie?"

"Yes. I'm picking someone up."

And that was about all the chance Suzanne was willing to give him.

"Right. And you thought you'd go through the firebreak, instead of reception?"

Eddie puckered his lips. He might have dropped by the reception if he had known where it was and Hadraniel hadn't driven him into a trap, but experience taught him that going through official channels hardly ever yielded desirable results.

"I got turned around in the hallways."

Suzanne was willing to accept that. Even she had to pay attention going through the hallways, so this halfwit probably really got lost and stumbled his way in here by accident.

"Still, nobody gets picked up without word from the proper authorities."

"Is Helen the proper authority?"

Suzanne arched an eyebrow. "Technically, yes. The ultimate authority. But you are not Helen."

"Neither are you."

"But I'm not trying to pick someone up."

"I am, because I'm Helen's personal assistant, and she says it's okay."

Suzanne didn't trust it. She knew Michael was Helen's assistant, but if the choice was hers, she would have him replaced as well. That wasn't what bothered her, though, but she couldn't put her finger on what did.

"Look," Eddie said. "Do you think I would have made it all the way here if I wasn't allowed? Surely security would have done something about it, right? I just need to swing by the Fallen Kingdom district, and then I'll be out of your hair. Which is nice and full. Flowy. What products do you use?"

Suzanne sighed. Taking him to the Fallen Kingdom was preferable to having him blow smoke up her ass.

"Come on. I'll show you the way. It's a short hop."

"If you tell me where to go, I'll find it myself, and you can get on with your business."

"Yeah, like I'm leaving you unsupervised around the batteries."

She started walking, and Eddie followed, but he looked at the pods in a new light now. They did kind of look like batteries, and it explained the cables.

"So this is what runs the place, huh?"

"No," Suzanne answered. "Heaven runs on the sinergy provided by the Underworld. The universe itself runs on pure soul power."

"Soul power?" Eddie didn't like what he heard. As he looked around, he realized that walking anywhere would take hours, if not days. Battery after battery ad nauseam, and in all directions. He stopped.

"What's in these batteries?"

Suzanne stopped as well and pulled one of the batteries farther out of the wall. At first sight, the black cylinder resembled a battery, but on the front was an oval porthole. She wiped away the condensation.

Eddie could see the face of a man with electrodes attached to his head and chest in various strategic places.

"Like I said, souls." Suzanne pushed the 'battery' back.

Eddie's head started spinning and he grabbed the railing for support. It didn't do much because he was now looking directly at thousands upon thousands more batteries sticking slightly out of the wall. Here and there, angels like Suzanne pulled one out to check on it and take readings.

"Heaven is supposed to be... What is this place? You're monsters!"

"I'm a monster? You thought Heaven was a bunch of physical places next to each other? How long do you think it would take for all Hell to break loose if Christian heaven and Muslim heaven are within walking distance?"

As soon as she mentioned walking distances, Suzanne started walking again.

"So you build a wall! You don't turn people into batteries!"

"A wall! How narrow-minded are you?"

Eddie stopped and crossed his arms. "If I was any more open-minded my brain would fall out, thank you very much!"

"I think it already did," Suzanne said, still walking, so Eddie had to follow. "Imagine the most beautiful place you can think of, multiply it by... mmm, seven, and then put a wall around it. Your beautiful place just became a prison."

"How is that worse than putting people in a tube?"

Suzanne stopped and leaned over the railing. Across from them and one floor down, she saw a colleague checking a pod.

"Jen! Up here!"

"Hey, Suze!"

"Hey, what's going on in that one?"

Eddie couldn't see clearly, but Jen flipped up a monitor, checked for a brief second, and quickly slapped the monitor back down.

"I'd rather not say," she answered.

"Humor me."

"She's dreaming about... ehm... Well, it involves a large number of very fit men. And women... And I think I saw a night elf, too."

"Thanks." Suzanne turned back to Eddie. "That woman in there is having the time of her life, and she's experiencing it as if she's there."

"But she's in a box."

"With electrodes stimulating every muscle in a natural way. Over in Topside, you're still struggling to get a half-decent VR experience, and it's like an infant trying to figure out which shape goes into which hole, compared to what we do here. She is happier than she has ever been, and we have an entire team of guardian angels to make sure she stays happy."

Eddie still wasn't sure how to feel about this. From where he was standing, there were a whole lot of souls trapped in pods to provide energy to the universe.

"I can see by the look on your face that I didn't quite sell it," Suzanne said. "Nobody is forced to be here. Who did you think you were picking up?"

"Robert James Rooney, Herringwood."

"Why does that not surprise me..." Suzanne sighed. "Come on, raise your arms."

"Huh?"

Suzanne spread her own. "Like this."

Eddie followed her example. Promptly she grabbed him by the armpits and took off.

Standing on the walkways along the walls was vertigo-inducing enough. Dangling in the arms of a woman above the chasm was a whole new level of frightening, no matter how attractive the woman was.

"I knew there would be issues when we got him," Suzanne said without a trace of effort lifting herself and Eddie. "Usually, souls are completely repaired when we get them, but he arrived with the bullets still in his chest. We fixed it, of course."

She plopped Eddie down on another walkway that he would have thought to be the same if he hadn't just been lifted past a bunch of them. Suzanne tapped her lips while she looked around, and finally went, "Ah."

She pulled out a pod. "Here he is. Look at his face. Does that look like someone who's unhappy?"

Eddie didn't care what Rooney's face looked like. He felt a surge of emotion he didn't plan on showing anyone and put his hand on the pod. Only now did he realize how little faith he had in actually finding Rooney. Going to the Underworld was one thing. He'd been there before, it was just a quick trip. Going to Heaven was a new kind of crazy.

Suzanne flipped the monitor on the pod up. It looked a lot

like it did when Rooney played *Fallen Kingdom*, but it was photorealistic now. Or rather, it was real. Trees reacted to the breeze and warthogs fell to the ax of Bogdor the Dwarf, who in this ultra-high definition state was clearly a short Rooney with a long beard.

Though his best friend was now the actual dwarf he used to play as, Eddie wasn't sure what he thought about guardian angels just looking at people's dreams whenever they felt like a laugh.

"We can, yes," Suzanne explained, guessing his thoughts. "But we prefer not to."

"No?"

"No. Pick out any five batteries, and I guarantee you three will have pornography. It's laughable. Give people the ability to be and do anything ever, and eventually it will devolve into base lust."

Eddie shrugged and arched an eyebrow. He got that. Lust was fun. He suddenly had questions about the muscle-stimulating electrodes, but decided he would ask Helen about it at a more convenient time.

"Alright, well, sorry to take the one who isn't having dream-sex, but if you could just unplug him for me, we'll be on our way."

Eddie hoped that would be enough, but he was willing to push it further if he had to. He was fairly confident he could talk her into giving him what he wanted just so he would shut up, but it never came to that.

A shiver shot down his spine when he heard another pair of wings flap. He knew it wasn't Jen, or another friend of Suzanne's. These wings beat differently and he'd heard them before.

Twenty

Before Eddie could figure out where the flapping came from, he was struck in the chest by Michael's foot. It hit him hard enough to send him flying, and when his back hit the metal flooring, it took a foot or two before he came to a full stop.

"Thank you, Suzanne," Michael said. "I'll take it from here."

Gasping for air, Eddie clutched his chest and tried to assess the situation. Before he could even properly focus on Michael, the angel was on him and lifted him clear off the ground. At this point, any snarky adventurer would have a pithy remark before turning the tables in an exciting manner, but Eddie's throat was being squeezed. The moments it wasn't, he was being thrown back toward Suzanne.

Leaning on Rooney's pod, he struggled to his feet and helplessly raised his hand when Michael approached and drew his saber. Eddie knew there wasn't anything he could do to turn this fight in his favor when Michael raised the saber over his head. The only thing left to do now was go down fighting so he wouldn't look like a wimp in front of the girl.

However, it was the girl who gave him a fighting chance.

"Michael, no!" she yelled. "You will not swing that thing around near the batteries."

"Suzanne, stay out of this."

She took a step forward. "You are in my house now, Michael. If you damage the pod, you kill the soul. Put that oversized razorblade back where it came from, or you will have to use it on me."

Even in his rage, Michael knew it would be the end of him if he raised arms at another angel, so he sheathed the saber.

"Fine. I don't need it to exact justice on him anyway."

Eddie nodded at Suzanne and sighed, "Thanks."

"Oh, don't thank me yet."

The moment Eddie turned his head to Michael, he received a fistful of knuckles to the cheekbone and went down like a glass on a table in a house full of cats.

"Motherfucker, you sucker-punched me!" He felt his face and determined that everything was still where it should be, despite the strong sensation that it all moved several inches to the right.

Michael wasn't one for mid-fight banter and pulled Eddie back to his feet. He would have held the upper hand, too, if he didn't feel wholly superior to this half-baked evolutionary mishap. Eddie took full advantage of it by attacking and ran into Michael, dragging him to the ground.

Laughing, Michael allowed him to take a few swings, then ended the brief assault with a gut punch and a push that landed Eddie on his back.

It was painfully clear that a fistfight also wasn't going to end in Eddie's favor, so he looked at Suzanne as he got back to his feet. "A little help here?"

She leaned against the barrier. "Sorry. Code of conduct and

stuff. Can't help. But I can get you a pod next to your friend's if you like."

Eddie would have liked that, but he had no chance to say so because Michael grabbed him where the shoulder met the neck and pinched.

"Now kneel for me."

That's all Eddie's body wanted to do, but he fought it as hard as he could. If he was going to die, he was going to do it standing up. So he wished, anyway, but wishes rarely came true, and his legs buckled under the pain radiating through his body.

Michael drew his sword and gently placed the tip against Eddie's throat.

"I don't know what Helen sees in your kind, but until she sees the fallacy of not wiping you from the Universe, I will have to settle for smiting you one at a time."

In a final act of defiance, Eddie maintained stone-cold eye contact with Michael as the pressure against his skin increased to breaking point. Why Michael didn't just ram it down was a mystery to Eddie, and the only thing he could come up with was that dying always happened in slow motion.

He was happy it did, though. Sometimes salvation needs time, and sometimes that's because salvation finds it hard to walk on metal grating in high heels.

"Michael, stand down!"

The angel's entire demeanor changed on a dime, and like a teenager, he whined, "But, Helen, I'm smiting!"

"I can do my own smiting, thank you." She came into Eddie's field of view and took the blade between two fingers to move it away. "New rule, Michael. Next time, you take your smiting to a smooth surface, because if you make me rush up here one more time, I will become very upset."

Michael checked the shining steel for unsightly stains and then sheathed it again. "Fine."

"Are you okay, hon?" she asked Eddie.

He rubbed his throat and checked his fingers for blood. Finding none, he said, "Almost. Hey, Mike?"

Michael looked at him but didn't feel much like answering. Eddie approached him and kicked him in the groin. Michael's knees hit the floor, and he groaned.

"I don't fucking kneel for assholes."

Helen grabbed him before he could start another fight. "That's enough! Ed, you and I need to talk. Come on."

"I'm not going anywhere without Rooney."

"That's right," Helen snapped. "You're not going anywhere, with or without Rooney."

"Excuse me?"

"What did you think? You broke into Heaven. Honey, I'm sorry, but you're not leaving."

Eddie glanced back at Michael to check his status before saying what he wanted to say. It was better to still have him out of commission if he started an argument with God.

"That's my friend in there." He tapped the glass of the pod. "He was killed because of me, and I'm going to fix it."

"And that's the problem. You're not supposed to fix this. You're an anomaly that I have allowed to keep existing because I like you, and I like Rosalie; I don't want to see either of you without the other..." She sighed. "But that you are here now clearly shows me that I have made a mistake and as much as it pains me, I need to rectify it."

Eddie pressed his lips into a thin line and felt the burst of emotion rising up in him. He swallowed it down, and it hurt his chest. Helen was a good friend. The kind of friend you could not speak to for years, but when you met them again, you could pick up right where you left off. For him, her divinity wasn't a factor, she was just good, so it made it extra painful to be at considerable odds with her now.

"Please, Helen," he tried. "Let me take Rooney home. I will start a fight if I have to, but I really would like it if that wasn't necessary."

Behind him, Michael got up with a groan. One kick in the nuts was bad enough, but a second one really took the wind out of him. If his boss wasn't being threatened with a fight, he would have taken some more time.

Helen gestured for him to take it easy. She didn't want a fight any more than Eddie did and hoped a more positive approach would help.

"Look around. I know you've seen the guardian angels, and I know you well enough that you find them appealing. If you stay, I can assign a few nurses to you specifically."

As much as several nurses, preferably in high heels, sounded good to Eddie, he had no trouble seeing the practical issue.

"Sounds like a great plan when I'm oblivious in a box powering God knows what."

"I do know what, yes."

"Inappropriately timed jokes are my thing."

Helen smiled. "Yes, my bad. But it could still be your heaven. Scantily-clad nurses doting over you in your dreams. And I guarantee it won't be just a dream to you. Hon, I can make one look like Rosalie, if you want." With a wink, she added, "Or all of them. Hm?"

Whether it was the wink or the mention of Rosalie, or just the entire idea, it backfired.

Eddie inspected her and said, "I thought temptation was Lilith's thing."

"Aw. It's cute that you think you had a choice if I tempted you."

"Yeah, I'm a cute motherfucker. My Heaven is back home with the real Rosalie and my best friend, so if you could just pop the top on Rooney's pod, I'll be on my way."

Clearly, Helen wasn't going to convince her favorite stubborn human and her demeanor changed.

"Eddie, if you don't cause problems, I'll make sure you have the ultimate experience here... I would appreciate it if you chose that option because all other choices will end badly."

Eddie looked back at Michael. "Sounds like you're going to get kicked in the nuts again in a few moments."

Helen snapped her fingers. "Michael is the least of your worries."

Eddie checked his surroundings. As per usual, he had a mission he didn't know how to complete. Taking down an angel was straightforward enough: dodge the sword, kick the balls, steal the sword. But a fight with God was something else.

Going up against the previous Devil might have been daunting, but at least pop culture made it look like he could be beaten. Eddie never saw a movie where God got his or her ass kicked.

Then he still had to figure out how to get Rooney out of that pod and find a way to get them both back to the Land of the Living. This seemed like a pretty insurmountable list of objectives, but to him, there was no other option than going for it.

"Son of a bitch, that's a lot of stairs!"

Everybody's attention was drawn to the voice. Puffing, Jonah walked toward them like he'd just come from the shops. Surprised, Helen looked at him.

"Wait, you're--"

"Jonah Craig, we've met. But I won't hold it against you if you don't remember."

"No, I remember," Helen said and looked at her angels. "When were any of you going to tell me Jesus Christ was also here?"

Suzanne wasn't aware and shrugged. "I know who's in the pods, but other than that, nobody tells me anything."

Helen knew this too, so she glowered at Michael.

"I was a little busy chasing down our unwanted visitor here," Michael argued. "Raphael should have informed you."

Eddie just saw his tables turned and greeted Jonah. "How did you know I was here?"

"Fallen Kingdom. Of course you were here. Didn't expect you to start a fight with God while you were at it, but I can't say I'm surprised either."

"You heard that?"

Jonah nodded. "Yeah, sound carries pretty far here, it turns out. Lucky for you, too, because I might have come up with a good solution while I was climbing up here."

He tapped Helen on the arm. "You need an elevator in here."

Helen nodded at Suzanne and her wings. "No, not really."

"What kind of a solution?" Eddie asked. "Because I already kinda hated myself for planning to hit a woman, so teaming up isn't really... cool."

Helen sputtered. "Oh, you were really planning to go through with it?"

Eddie just answered with a surly look.

"Oh! You were. You're serious. I actually sort of admire that. Nobody will ever fault you for your loyalty. So, Mr. Christ, how about that proposed solution? Because it would seem our mutual friend here is open to physical... violence-- haha, I'm sorry, I couldn't keep a straight face through that."

Jonah also smiled a little, which just made Eddie more impatient.

"How about a trade?" Jonah said.

"A trade, Mr. Christ?"

"Yeah. You take me, and you give back Rooney. Kill two birds with one stone."

Though the basic idea was good, Eddie was opposed to the larger picture. "I didn't bring you here to use you as leverage. Bad idea. We're not doing it."

"You're not using me as leverage, *I* am using me as leverage."

Eddie leaned in and whispered, "So I can come save you later?"

"No. I'm going to stay here."

"I don't know what kind of brainwashing went on during your little tour, but you're seeing these pods, right? There's people in there!"

"I know. And none of them are being shot at unless they enjoy that kind of thing. Nobody's getting hanged for their ideas. Do you have any idea of the atrocities I've seen in my time on Earth?"

Eddie shrugged callously. "Pf, I get that force-fed in about a week. Barely even registers anymore."

"Exactly. People here are happy. Dude, *everybody* here is as happy as they wanna be. There's a heaven for dogs, man! *Dogs!* How cute is that?"

"Far cuter than what will happen to me if I explain to your girlfriend that I took you to Heaven and left you there. I don't want Jo to pull my eyes out. I use them to look at things."

Helen decided to put a stop to this, and, barring that, at least figure out why there was an argument in the first place.

"Gentlemen, if you would. Eddie, why are you trying to talk him out of this? Are you really dead set on a fight you can't win?"

Eddie gestured around wildly. "No! I'm surrounded by friends here. Except for that asshat." He thumbed at Michael. "I can't trade one friend for another! Jonah didn't even have to come here, for fuck's sake! Now I'm supposed to stab him in the back by jumping on the first half-assed plan that pops up? No. Fuck no."

"Bullshit, Ed," Jonah said. "The first half-assed plan was apparently picking a fight with God. This is the second half-assed plan, and it's a definite step up."

Eddie looked at Helen. "Do you think it's a step up?"

"From a fight? Yes. Is this what you want, Mr. Christ?"

Jonah looked around at all the pods. To the casual observer, it may have looked gruesome, but Jonah knew that every single soul here was at peace.

"I'm tired, ma'am. The hate, the fighting... the utter ignorant idiocy, and no signs of improvement. Two millennia of that is quite enough for me. I don't think I can go back to that."

Helen took one look into Jonah's eyes and knew enough.

"Alright. Suzanne, would you kindly prepare Rob Rooney for travel and have him meet us at the station?"

"Ma'am!" Michael exclaimed before Suzanne could say anything. "You're not actually considering this?"

"Michael, meet Eddie Sterling. The only human to trespass in Heaven and disable you *twice*."

"Second one doesn't count."

"I'm sure the dull pressure lingering in your abdomen suggests differently. My point is, this is a solution that satisfies all parties and therefore, the best solution."

Michael's hand rested on the hilt of his saber as he tried to swallow his disgust. His eyes took in the situation, and he estimated he could at least run Eddie through before being struck down. Then his eyes met Helen's. She didn't say anything to change his mind; the look on her face was enough, and Michael took his hand off the hilt.

"Well then," Helen said and turned away, "would you care to join us, Mr. Christ?"

"Err, sure, but didn't we just make a deal?"

"And I will hold you to it, but I expect you'd like to say goodbye to Robbie, which will have to be at the station. I'll have somebody pick you up there."

"Oh, okay. Sure."

It began to dawn on Jonah what he had done, and it felt strange. It wasn't regret, but he'd spent almost two thousand years hiding, and he simply couldn't remember why. He hoped he wouldn't suddenly remember either.

Twenty-one

After an emotional but still very manly backslapping hug with Jonah, Eddie cleared his throat. He wasn't sure what to do now. He had already thanked Jonah profusely, goodbyes had been said, hugs had been made, but the train wasn't leaving yet. So he was an extra little bit happier to see a golf cart ride directly onto the platform to drop Rooney off. More hugs needed to be done.

Still confused about being pulled from a very convincing Fallen Kingdom, Rooney tried to piece everything together. At no point after his death did he wonder why he was a mighty dwarf, or where that glorious beard came from. It all felt just like before he died, it made sense, and he enjoyed it quite a lot.

But it was all fake, apparently.

"Jesus, Ed. You came all the way here to get me?"

"Sort of, yeah. But actual Jesus did the important work."

Eddie nodded at Jonah, but Rooney didn't make the link. "Hey, man. Sorry I missed the Night Elf raid."

Jonah shrugged. "You were a bit dead. I understand."

Rooney squinted at Jonah, then at Eddie, and back to Jonah again. "Wait. Did he mean *you're* the actual Jesus? Christ?"

"Anderson. Jesus Anderson. Sorry."

"Oh."

"No, of course it's Christ, dipshit," Jonah laughed. "But it's not that impressive, really. Didn't do any resurrections. Mostly tables, chairs, and oaken chests."

Rooney was confused. Of course, he knew Jonah was a carpenter, which made all the more sense now, but somebody had to have resurrected him.

"If you didn't, how am I here? Am I still dead? Can I get on the train?"

Helen popped out of her private compartment to hurry the conversation along.

"For ease of conversation, we call everybody in the Afterlife dead. The reason you're going Topside is because Mr. Christ offered to trade places with you."

Wide-eyed, Rooney stared at Jonah and didn't know what to say. He had some idea, but calling him stupid for doing so didn't seem appropriate at this time.

"You're not coming?" he asked Jonah.

"No, I'm staying. And don't give me that look because it wasn't as selfless as it sounds."

"No, I got that far. But you're really leaving me hanging here. We were supposed to take on the Ice Troll Queen next week, man."

Jonah laughed. "You'll just have to take whatsername, the elf."

Rooney shook his head and argued like they weren't trading places in Heaven. "You know Laura's a frost-based rogue. We need a fire mage."

Helen thought it was time to wrap things up. "Gentlemen, as... weird as this is, the Number 9 always leaves on time, and if you're not on it, I'm keeping all three of you here."

Jonah took a scrap of paper from his pocket with measurements for a pigeon coop on it, but he flipped it over and scribbled something on it with a stumpy pencil. He handed it over.

"Here's an alternative solution."

Rooney looked at it.

"Who's John1919? Looks like a password."

"It is. It'll get you into my *Fallen Kingdom* account so you can get my sword. I think you should be able to wield it and the fire damage is off the charts."

Rooney's lip trembled, and he threw his arms around Jonah. To the casual observer, this just seemed like a dumb little thing. To the veteran *Fallen Kingdom* player, it was akin to inheriting a million dollars. Now with the password in hand, Rooney ensured Jonah that he would keep the mage alive. People would see the burning silhouette of a lone fire mage on their horizons; at night, they would hear the distant flapping of a fiery cape--

"Yeah, I just liked clicking on enemies and watching the numbers go down," Jonah said. "I don't really mind what happens to my character, just make sure you get the sword before my sub runs out."

Rooney nodded. That subscription wasn't going to run out, he'd make sure of that.

Jonah looked at Helen. "Look after these two morons for me."

Helen nodded with a smile. "I'm afraid that's indeed going to take up most of my time. Mr. Christ... Jonah, it's been interesting meeting you again, and I hope we get a chance to catch up soon."

"So do I. Oh! Could you please drop by Jolene to explain all of this?"

"I will," Helen said. "Now, come on, boys. Train's leaving."

The Number 9 pulled out of the station and picked up speed fast until it barreled on relentlessly, though it was barely noticeable. Helen's private compartment was quiet enough to dampen the chugging of the steam engine and the rhythmic beating of the wheels on the tracks. Outside, no landscapes rushed by. Not long after departure, the train became enveloped by thick mist, and now the only thing they could see was a billowing gray soup rushing by.

"It's weird," Eddie said. "When we came here, the train was full."

Helen looked up from her phone. "Not a lot of souls leave Heaven. It's the final stop. Except for a few tour groups, or us, the Number 9 returns empty."

"How does that even work? The tour groups, I mean."

"Over time, we found that power outputs are far better when souls get to go out for exercise every once in a while. We've managed to stretch dreamtime as far as we could without it becoming detrimental, but we wake them up periodically. There are facilities to keep them entertained in the meantime, and Underworld Tours is one of them."

Up until now, Rooney had been staring out into featureless mist. This casual talk of taking souls out for exercise bothered him for some reason.

"And then you stick everybody back in the box anyway," he said, still staring out the window.

"Yes, I need power," Helen answered matter-of-factly. "And it turns out that dreams generate an enormous amount of power. It's quite amazing, really. Dr. Ignacio figured it all out; even I will admit that I wouldn't know where we'd be without him."

"Good for Dr. Ignacio," Rooney snapped, "but I've now had two lives taken from me. Just so you could have a battery. What was I even powering? Because it better not be your phone charger."

This happened sometimes, Helen knew. People could be cranky when waking up from the dream. A lot of care was taken not to disturb souls in the middle of something, but the guardian angels were a busy bunch, and once in a blue moon, it happened.

Clearly, Rooney had it bad, and it was understandable. He had to go back to a life he had already given up on after settling comfortably into a new dream life. Souls weren't meant to go back, and at this point, Rooney was as much an experiment as a goodwill gesture toward Eddie.

"No, we use sinergy for everything local," Helen calmly explained. "The energy your creative little brains put out is, quite oddly, so powerful it would blow our network. I use it to create stars."

Eddie and Rooney looked at each other. The latter couldn't quite wrap his head around it, but the former thought he had it figured out and didn't like it one bit.

"Like, talent show stars? And I use two of those words very loosely."

Helen laughed heartily. "Oh, that's precious. No, dear. Talent shows and their unfortunate results are an entirely human creation. You severely overestimate our cruelty."

So that left only one other option, but Rooney needed to know for sure. "So, like, other solar systems? I thought you said you didn't want to risk more life in the universe."

"Oh, I periodically check if nothing's infected."

"Then, why even make more stars?" Eddie posed. "That's like juggling guns and complaining you got shot."

"Tsk-tsk," Helen said theatrically. "Bit of an inappropriate analogy right now, don't you think?"

"Just answer the question."

Helen shrugged, and Eddie wasn't sure he'd ever seen her do that. It looked wrong, and her answer wasn't much better either.

"I like the twinkly lights, okay?"

Eddie chuckled. And then laughed.

Helen frowned and crossed her arms. "Don't laugh! I'm allowed nice things. I work hard."

Which didn't help the situation. God pouting like a neglected girlfriend just made it funnier for Eddie. However, the real kicker was the reason for the universe he lived in.

"You mean we live in an expanding universe because God

Almighty likes twinkly lights?"

"No, you live in an expanding universe because I accidentally made an explosion when I was a kid. The stars keep it from becoming an imploding universe."

"Sure. I think you regret admitting you just like them."

"One does not preclude the other, and if you want to tease me about it, you should be aware that I can and will turn this train around."

While Eddie worked hard to keep his trap shut, it all sounded rather acceptable to Rooney. Not so much that Helen just enjoyed twinkly lights, but that his energy was used to make actual stars. Somewhere out there was a piece of him shining down on every living thing. This was something he could cope with, and he smiled to himself while the Number 9 just chugged along, unconcerned with faraway lights.

The platform was very clean. Peter could see this very well because he stared at the floor intensely to avoid eye contact with Lilith. That didn't keep her from berating him, though.

"I was on the fence about whether we needed a stationmaster, but I didn't want to make the function obsolete just after you got it."

"I appreciate that, ma'am."

"I'm sure you do, but in the meantime you have shown your appreciation by allowing an unauthorized soul to get on the train, go to Heaven, and assault God's assistant manager. While that last part is actually a little amusing, I very much doubt that you are fit for the job. I would advise you--"

The rest of her words were drowned out by the whistle of a grand steam locomotive pulling into the station, and she didn't take the time to repeat them because she needed to catch up to the front where Aunt Helen was.

"I am so sorry," she said when the door opened and Helen stepped out. "Dr. Ignacio still seems to be under the impression that Eddie does the things he's told."

"Is he here?" Eddie asked, getting out behind Helen. "I like that gullible little guy."

Lilith scowled at him. "No. And where's your friend?"

With nice dramatic timing, Rooney hopped onto the platform. "Right here."

Lilith's mouth fell open. "No, I mean the other one-- What? What are you doing here? Aunt Helen, what's he doing here? There was another guy. Where is the other guy?"

"Calm down, hon," Helen said and motioned Peter over. "The 'other guy' was Jesus Christ, and he offered to trade with Rooney."

Peter nervously came before Helen. "Yes, ma'am?"

"You don't have any more friends that are coming to blackmail you, do you?"

"No, ma'am. All the apostles are accounted for."

"So I can count on you not letting this happen again?"

"Yes, ma'am. Absolutely. I sincerely apologize."

As casually as she made him come all the way here, she waved him off again. "Get back to work. One more screw-up like this and I will let my niece decide what to do with you, understand?"

Peter nodded submissively and trotted away.

Lilith was barely even paying attention to it. She was trying to deal with what was apparently a monumental fuckup of her own.

"The actual Jesus Christ? Like, with the cross, and the fanclub?"

"That's the one."

"And I let him walk?"

"Yeah, but right into Heaven, so don't beat yourself up about it."

"You're not mad?"

Helen smiled. "Let me introduce you to Eddie Sterling, Shit-stirrer General."

Eddie saluted Lilith. "Ma'am."

"There's really not just one person I can be upset with," Helen said. "And if that many things were screwed up, a good leader needs to look at themselves. After all, was it not us who gave Eddie the ability to do what he keeps on doing?"

Lilith looked at him. She personally told him how to contact her father. She could try to dance around it as much as she liked, but she was partly responsible for this. Might as well own up to it like Aunt Helen.

"You're right," she sighed. "You always are."

Then she turned to Eddie. "This has been the last time. The next time you come here, you are not leaving."

Eddie nodded. That was fair enough, until the next time he needed to go to the Underworld. He really did hope it would never come to that, but the barrier between life and death didn't stop him before, and he didn't see why it was going to any other time.

"I mean it, Sterling," Lilith hissed. "I can see that look on your face."

Helen started walking. "Eddie, dear. I'm on Lilith's side here. Your stunts are dangerous and put the entire universe at risk. No more of this nonsense."

"That's a setup for a sequel if I ever heard one," Eddie grumbled. "But fine. It's a hassle anyway."

"Good. Lillie, I know of something you can do to make up for your little faux pas."

Lilith caught up to Helen.

"I thought you weren't mad."

"I'm not, but next to looking at myself, I'm also looking at you. Jesus walked right into Heaven, but he could have walked anywhere."

"How was I supposed to know who that was? I never met him!"

"That's why it's just a simple thing I want you to do for me."

Lilith put her hands in her pockets and pouted. Things were rarely simple around here.

"You'll see to it that Rob's body is dealt with."

"Hey, whoa," Rooney exclaimed. "You just got me out of the pod!"

"I mean the body in the morgue. I would like to spare people the confusion of dealing with two Rob Rooneys."

"That's a good idea," Lilith confirmed. "I'll fix that, but out of curiosity, why don't you just do your rapture thing?"

"Because I need all my miracles when I explain what happened to Jolene."

Lilith sucked in a breath through her teeth. Compared to that, stealing a body from a morgue was child's play. It was common knowledge that Jolene was a lovely woman, unless you got on her bad side. Aunt Helen would have to put in a considerable effort to smooth this over.

In the garage, Eddie immediately noticed that his car wasn't where he left it. This annoyed him because if he wanted transportation that wouldn't necessarily be where he left it, he would have sold his soul for a boat.

He found the car nicely parked by the other cars.

"Janick!" he yelled, and the orange demon emerged from his office shack.

"Who is yelling?" He looked around, saw Helen, and determined she didn't sound like a man. This severely diminished the urgency of answering the call, and he felt especially un-urged when he saw Eddie by the Vindicator. "Why do you yell?"

"What did you do to my car?"

"I parked it. It was in the way."

That much they could agree on. Eddie definitely left it in the way, and it was now definitely parked.

"How?"

"I pushed."

That was less believable, considering it required Janick to turn the car roughly 90 degrees to park it, and Eddie was sure he left the parking brake on.

"No, you didn't," he concluded.

Janick didn't have time for arguments about who did what to cars. This was his garage, and he did whatever he wanted to whichever car he decided. As he proved by grabbing the Vindicator somewhere under the bumper and pulling it out of its spot.

"I pulled."

Eddie thought the explanation was unnecessary, and Helen decided this whole shtick was going on for too long.

"Thank you, Janick," she said. "We'll be on our way."

"Yes."

Janick hobbled back to his office, and Eddie unlocked the car. He opened the door and flipped the seat forward, but Helen's attention was elsewhere.

"Lillie, can we give you a ride?"

"No, thank you," she answered and opened the door to a pale blue Suzuki Liana. "Last thing we want is him having to drive me back."

Even Eddie thought that was a good point.

"I'll swing by the church after the morgue and say hi to the goths," she added and got in the car. With more zeal than the Suzuki badge suggested, Lilith drove off.

Eddie waited for Helen to finally get in the car so they could go as well. They looked at each other until Helen figured out what he expected from her, so she smirked at the backseat and then at Eddie, but the latter remained stone-faced.

"Oh, you're serious," she said with genuine surprise.

"Uhuh."

"No."

"Yes."

"No, hon. Unless you're putting on a driver's cap and telling me this is a tiny limousine, I'm not riding in the back."

Now Eddie looked at the backseat, then at Rooney, and finally back to Helen. "It's my car."

"That's debatable to begin with," Helen said plainly. "But if we accept that as fact, it is also your backseat, and you can ride in it. "

She punctuated her words by gallantly gesturing him to get in.

"But--"

"Ed, get in the backseat," Rooney said.

"You get in the back!"

"Fuck no. I'm riding shotgun with God."

Outnumbered and grumbling, he got in. "Next time you die and go to Heaven, you're on your own, dickhead."

Helen pushed the seat back and took place behind the wheel. Her elegant fingers pressed on the comparatively crude starter button, and the car roared to life. She grabbed the steering wheel and let the vibrations of the 426 Hemi big block flow through her body.

To even her own surprise, she chuckled with a hint of arousal, and purred, "Ooh, I haven't had this much power in my hands since my fling with Genghis."

"I... uh, you know what? Sure," Eddie moped. "Just don't fuck with the stereo."

Immediately, Helen's finger reached for the stereo.

"I said--"

"Oh, shut up. You'll love this."

At the press of a button, the opening guitar and piano duel from "Bat Out Of Hell" filled the car up to the roof, and Helen revved the engine.

"Alright, let's roll!"

It was strange, seeing the way home light up without having George in the car. Helen's eyes were a bright blue, but those were her regular eyes. Then again, how much light did she really need to follow an onramp onto a highway of fire?

Eddie braced himself for the wild ride that was coming, but again Helen surprised him. He thought he knew his car, that he and it were as one. Yet here he was with Helen behind the wheel, making him feel like he barely made it through his first driving lesson.

As if the road and the flames knew who was driving, the ride was smooth, and Helen had no issues pushing the pedal down.

"It's not exactly my Cadillac," she said, barely audible over the dulcet tones of Meat Loaf, "but I understand why you like this thing so much."

"Orpheus isn't a thing!"

Helen glanced at him in the rearview mirror. Eddie could only see her eyes, but they smiled at him. They made such an impression on him that he couldn't understand they didn't spark any sort of memory of an affair.

TWENTY-TWO

Herringwood wasn't just a quiet town, Yaeger realized. It was dead quiet. At face value, that sounded like it would be quite conducive to observing a morgue, but not even the hospital the morgue was in showed many signs of life. Following Yaeger's logic, that would be a bad thing.

In reality, it was entirely mundane. A doctor went in, a nurse came out, the sick lay in their beds, and the deceased lay on their slabs. Neither were doing much of anything. Unfortunately, that was exactly why they were still sitting here: to see a corpse walk out the door.

Yaeger experienced bouts of anxiety during the past few days. There was a lot riding on this for him. But as the hour of judgment drew near, he felt surprisingly calm. Disturbingly calm, perhaps. So calm, he didn't care what kind of calm it was. He just let it come over him because it was nice to not feel stressed for once.

He sighed and reflexively looked at Rigby. The sigh-police didn't react at all, and when Yaeger took a better look, he noticed that Rigby wasn't even looking at the hospital. He had his knuckles against his lips and an earnest look on his face. The look just wasn't directed at anything.

"Are you having a stroke?"

Rigby waited long enough to answer for Yaeger to start worrying, but then his hand moved away, and he inhaled deeply. Calmly and controlled, he let the breath back out and, without turning his head, said, "Old people don't have strokes all the time."

"But they do sometimes, and you're just staring, so I figured I'd check."

"Rest assured, it is not a stroke."

"Then what is it? Because you don't seem like yourself."

Rigby showed a wry smile when he finally looked at Yaeger.

"Mr. Hall is on his way," he said. "We've got nothing."

Yaeger's mouth prepared to argue but his brain put a stop to it. He didn't believe in any miracles anymore. Their experiment was over.

"I propose we head to that diner you had your eye on," Rigby said. "For a last supper."

"What if we don't turn ourselves in?"

Rigby turned the key in the ignition, and the rusty machine coughed. Then it gargled and backfired. A spurt of soot-black smoke dissipated behind them, and the half-dead engine idled irregularly.

"We pay for our sins," Rigby said, clutching the vibrating steering wheel. "We conspired to take an innocent life, and jail time is the least of our worries, my friend."

Yaeger saw it all clearly now. Deep inside, he felt that Sam Hall should be going to jail with them, but without the Old Man, the Current Day Saints would have no chance of finding Jesus Christ at all. Logically, Yaeger and Rigby needed to take the fall to protect the organization.

He didn't consciously consider this when he approached Rooney, but, in hindsight, it turned out he was at peace with it. The judgment any man could pass on them was nothing compared to the Lord's. Paying for their sins beforehand would probably be a smart choice.

Yaeger nodded. Rigby drove off.

Now, a lot of things could be said of the car Rigby and Yaeger drove. That it wasn't roadworthy, for example. Or that it smelled like something somewhere inside it was on fire. One thing that couldn't be said was that it was subtle. The engine struggled to keep the unimpressive vehicle moving, or to remain inside the vehicle in the first place, if the irregular vibrations were any indication.

"Feels like we're not going to make it," Yaeger said, considering his previous successes in trying to visit the Rising Wind Diner.

"Not if we keep taking wrong turns," Rigby answered.

Yaeger smirked. He sincerely thought this was the fastest route and managed to convince Rigby of it. Surprisingly easy, too. To the point that the lack of pushback worried Yaeger. Now that they turned left at a dilapidated tunnel after a long country road, the frustration finally seemed to make its way out.

"Okay, my bad," Yaeger admitted. "But this shaking is its own separate problem."

"I don't think it's the car..."

Rigby slowed down to check, and the vibrations remained. As they seemed to grow worse, Yaeger reached for the oh-shit handle and settled on the door handle when he found his first choice missing.

"Is it an earthquake?"

Rigby had experienced several earthquakes on an especially protracted investigation in Alaska—this didn't feel the same. He never saw tunnels erupt with flames in Alaska either, but that could have been due to the cold.

Rigby slammed the brakes and nearly hit his head against Yaeger's as they both looked back to get a good view of what was happening.

"Busted gas pipe?" Yaeger tried. He knew full well that it wasn't, but it was the least troubling explanation he could think of.

Rigby didn't help his concerns at all. "How many tunnels have a gas connection, do you think?"

From the unnaturally swirling flames, a blue economy sedan burst forth. Smoke trailed behind it when it landed and kept tearing on in the direction of town.

"What on Earth was that?!" Yeager exclaimed.

Rigby looked at him like he was stupid. "A reasonably priced car racing out of a tunnel in a torrent of fire."

"Oh. Okay."

A shockwave hit them and shook the car. Rigby pulled over to get out and take a better look. The fire seemed to retreat, only to burst out a second time like a drunk experiencing the drawbacks of that second bottle of vodka. From the violent expulsion of flame, another car burst forth.

"Yaeger!"

Yaeger was already on his way out of the car and saw what Rigby saw.

The Vindicator's tires screeched on the asphalt as it briefly came to a halt. For a moment, the blonde woman driving turned around, and then the car took off again.

"Did you see who was in the passenger seat?"

Yaeger nodded almost hard enough to give himself a concussion. "The guy!"

"Yes! The guy you shot!" Rigby grabbed Yaeger. "Alive and well!"

Yaeger was at a loss for words. He'd spent the past days hoping for this, and now he couldn't believe he actually saw it. For lack of anything more profound to say, he went with, "The Lord works in mysterious ways."

As did their boss, so Rigby grabbed his phone, but Yaeger stopped him.

"What are you doing?"

"Calling Mr. Hall to let him know we'll meet at the church instead."

"Why?"

"Because he's going to wonder where we are when he arrives at the diner."

Yeager, now closer than he ever was to the mythical diner, wasn't ready to let go of the dream of a decent meal.

"What if," he said, "and hear me out..."

"I don't really want to."

"No, wait. What if we went to the diner anyway?"

"We'll lose the car."

"We know where it'll be. And that we're losing it either way." Yeager gestured at their own car. "I say we floor it to the diner now, get there early and we can get the best of both worlds."

Rigby rubbed his chin. "Which worlds?"

"We get those Chicken Legs the whole town raves about, and we get Sterling after that. We know where to find him. We get our cake, and we can eat it, too."

"You mean chicken legs."

"And eat those."

Rigby thought about it. If he was honest with himself, he was getting tired of the energy bars in the trunk as well. Besides, they knew where Rooney was, so a quick stop for a meal didn't seem like a problem to him.

"Get in the car. We'll make it quick."

Happy as a child in a toy store, Yaeger practically jumped into the car.

As always, between taking orders, Gina was wiping down the counter. It was more a reflex than anything, since her counter was spotless; mainly because she already wiped it just a minute ago.

Her attention was drawn by a car pulling into a parking spot, and while several people looked up to see if it was really as depressing as it sounded, it didn't last. At current inflation rates, people neglecting their vehicles in favor of food were becoming more common.

Gina didn't judge because it was her food they were neglecting their vehicle for, and aside from cars with political bumper stickers, one couldn't judge a driver by their car, as was the case with the occupants of this vehicle.

She guessed Rigby and Yaeger were traveling salesmen, but it didn't matter. In the end, they were all simply customers.

"What can I do for you fine gentlemen?"

"Two portions of your Famous Chicken Legs, ma'am," Yaeger said without asking his colleague.

Rigby didn't mind. He'd heard of Gina's Famous Chicken Legs before he even set foot in Herringwood and was sure he wouldn't be disappointed.

"And a table with some privacy, if possible."

"Y'all aren't planning to do some kinky OnlyFans stuff in my diner, are you?"

Shocked, Yaeger exclaimed, "We're not--"

Rigby shut him up by putting a hand on his shoulder.

"Well, you might wanna tell him that, hon," Gina said and winked.

Charmed, Rigby explained himself. "We're meeting our boss to discuss business."

"This is a diner, sugar. Privacy isn't high on our list, but you can grab a seat in the back. Most folk don't make it that far," she said, and almost at the same time, passed their order on to the cook. "I'll bring it over for you."

"Thank you, ma'am."

Yaeger held his tongue until they sat down. He had things to say but didn't want the diner lady to hear it. According to him, someone who just assumed people were gay probably wouldn't have a problem spitting on customers' food.

"Are you just going to let her think we do... ehm..."

Rigby looked at him indignantly.

"You know," Yaeger tried.

"No, I don't know," Rigby derided him. "Please, explain. I'm very curious to find out how that sentence ends."

"We don't do... *butt stuff*."

Rigby tried to keep down a snicker, but that only made it come out harder.

"I'm glad you find this amusing," Yaeger snapped.

"Please, my easily riled up comrade. Relax."

"How do you expect me to relax when that woman thinks we are sinners?"

"We *are* sinners!"

"But not butt sinners."

Rigby calmly laid his fist on the table and unfurled his index finger, aiming it menacingly at Yaeger.

"Let it go," he said. "We have more important things on our minds than squabbling over who sinned on who."

Yaeger pulled up his nose. Rigby ignored it for the sake of their conversation.

"We just witnessed a person we knew to be verifiably dead emerge from a torrent of fire. Not only that--"

Rigby paused when Gina brought them their orders.

"Thank you, ma'am."

"You're welcome, hon."

Rigby waited for her to walk away and continued where he left off. "Not only that, but he was in the car of the person we already suspected to be our Lord and Savior."

Yaeger picked up an unassuming Chicken Leg, unprepared for what he was about to experience. If he knew what was coming, he wouldn't have delayed putting it in his mouth.

"Yeah, and as relieved as I am to see him alive, we didn't see Sterling anywhere. That blonde woman was driving."

Rigby shrugged. "Doesn't matter. If she's the one who resurrected him, then she's the new incarnation of our Lord Jesus Christ."

"Jesuette," Yaeger snickered and took a bite. His eyes widened as the taste spread through his mouth, and it didn't stop there. An explosion of sensations expanded through his face, and when it reached his eyes, tears welled. After lukewarm water and energy bars at irregular intervals, Yaeger's brain had no idea how to process this Chicken Leg, and he wept.

"Sweet mother of the Sacred Heart..."

"What's gotten into you?"

"Eat," Yaeger managed to answer.

With Rigby's first bite, the time for talking was over. Eating was now top priority, and all through it, Rigby was thinking how he should at least heap a modicum of praise on Yaeger for making them come here anyway. Unfortunately, it came out as, "Want another round?"

Yaeger nodded appreciatively, and Gina knew it was coming even before she put their first order on the table.

Smiling, she went to put the second batch on their table and then went back to wiping the counter, checking if everybody was happy on her way back. The diner wasn't that big and she only ever needed a waitress on weekends. Often Christa would take the shift, considering window washing in a town like Herringwood was a finite pool of work. Still, most of the time, Gina was still able to manage on her own and just kept Christa around for the company.

Today was a quiet day, though, until a bordeaux '78 Continental rolled in and took up a parking spot and a half. An old man dressed in all white exited. He certainly knew how to make an impression, and Gina kept a close eye on him because people who made impressions usually weren't strangers to causing problems.

When he entered, Gina saw his suit was more like a preacher's clerical, complete with collar, except that the collar was black. As were his pocket square and the band around his cattleman's hat. A bold fashion statement, especially in a place where 'sauce fingers' was the unofficial slogan, but still not what really caught her eye.

Subtly, she moved a hand under the counter to rest it on the 12-gauge she kept for 'special occasions.'

"You got a permit for that big iron on your hip, fella?" she inquired.

"Fully licensed to carry, ma'am," he answered in a Southern drawl that almost matched Gina's. "East Texas, ma'am?"

"Texarkana, born and raised."

"Then what on Earth brings you to a town like Herringwood?"

Gina winked. "Folks needed Chicken Legs. I'd say you do, too, but with a suit that white, even I'd think twice."

"That's quite alright, ma'am. I'm just here to meet two friends of mine."

"I'm guessing it's them two fellas in the back."

As the old man started to walk away, Gina tapped the counter to get his attention one more time. "From one Texan to another, if I see that piece come out of the holster even a little, your ass is grass."

At first, the man answered with a smile, until he saw she was dead serious. He wasn't one to fear another human being, but he knew when to be cautious. "Yes, ma'am."

He wasn't here to make trouble. He was here for an update on the quest for Jesus, and those two chicken-eating fools were going to give it to him. He stopped at Rigby and Yaeger's table and looked down on them like an oil baron staring at an empty well.

"Mr. Hall!" Rigby gasped.

The most of a greeting they got was a brief look they had to share between them.

"Y'all enjoying your meal?" Sam Hall asked.

Rigby knew the only correct answer to this question was fearful silence, but Yaeger never got that memo.

"It's divine!"

Mr. Hall looked at Yaeger, and Yaeger looked back, far too preoccupied with the taste of Gina's Famous Chicken Legs to see how little his boss cared for that particular brand of divinity.

Mr. Hall cleared his throat, straightened his suit, and maneuvered himself to sit down next to Yaeger.

"Scooch over, son."

So Yaeger did, even wiping the seat. Mr. Hall sat down and moved far enough to the middle of the seat to squish Yaeger up against the window. He looked down at Yaeger's half-empty plate, spat on it, and then looked at Yaeger.

"The charming lady at the counter has kindly made it clear she'd take umbrage if I remove my revolver from its holster, but she didn't say anything about taking you out back, so if y'all don't wanna end up like Ol' Yeller, start talking about actual divinity."

Yaeger's heart was pounding in his chest hard enough to make him forget how to speak, and he looked at Rigby for help. So did Mr. Hall, though it was less of a cry for help than a menacing stare.

Rigby was relieved he didn't have the bad news they initially thought, and explained what they saw to Mr. Hall. By the time he was done explaining, he expected a healthy amount of disbelief even from the man who started the Great Mission, but all he got was a scowl.

"If I understood you right, and I'm quite sure I did, you saw a supernatural event occur where a car emerged from fire in which were sat a resurrected man and the person who resurrected him."

Rigby tried to nod and shake his head at the same time. "Yeah, no. We assume Sterling was there because it was his car. We didn't actually see him. But we know where we can find them, so--"

"You had a possible resolution to an almost seventy-year mission within your reach, and you chose to stop for dinner?"

"They'll be at the church, sir."

"And you are not at the church... why?"

Confidently, Rigby pushed his plate toward Mr. Hall. "Taste."

Sam Hall occasionally had to deal with a disgruntled employee and he always fixed whatever problem they had by resting his hand on the grip of his revolver. Hardly ever was he disobeyed in a calm and polite fashion as Rigby did now. That, and the fact that he couldn't draw his weapon, made him take a chicken leg and have a taste, as suggested.

He looked Rigby in the eyes while he took the bite and magically managed to get nothing in his gray horseshoe mustache.

Confident in the power of Gina's Famous Chicken Legs, Rigby grabbed a napkin and held it up for Mr. Hall, who took another bite, put the Chicken Leg down, and wiped his fingers while he chewed.

"If they're not at the church, y'all gonna regret it." He snapped his fingers at Gina. "Ma'am, three portions please."

TWENTY-THREE

Now that he was so close, Eddie was getting anxious about going home to Rosalie, so when Helen turned *his* car in the wrong direction, he needed to make a stink about it.

"Hey! Where are you going? Church is the other way!"

"I know," Helen said without giving any indication she was going to turn around. "I lived there."

"And now I live there. With a girlfriend so out of my league that I really want to check if she's still there."

Helen smiled. For all the trouble he could cause, at least Eddie was self-aware.

"She'll be there. And you can see for yourself as soon as I get to Palm Springs."

"Florida?!" Eddie exclaimed.

Rooney turned around and shook his head. "She means the trailer park, moron."

"Then she should say 'trailer park,' *ingrate*."

"Boys!" Helen said, like a mother driving unruly kids to school. "I can turn this car right around and let Lilith put you in a cell."

Eddie crossed his arms. "You should have taken Jonah's bike like I said when we stopped at the crossroads."

Helen turned onto the last stretch of road for the Palm Springs trailer park. "And like I said, I am wearing a skirt and high heels. I am not riding a motorcycle. I promised Jonah I would talk to Jolene and I don't break promises. I'm just dropping myself off, and then you can go wherever you want in your precious car."

She let the car roll and came to a full stop exactly in front of the entrance. She got out and flipped the seat for Eddie. Rooney stepped out and leaned on the roof.

"So, do we wait? Pick you up later?" he asked.

"There's more than one way to travel for me, hon."

Eddie threw his hands up. "Then why did we drive--"

"Because this is a fine automobile," Helen said and brushed her fingers along the hood as she walked away. For a brief second, it seemed as if the car got goosebumps.

"I'll see you when I've spoken to Jolene."

Eddie and Rooney both watched her walk. There was something special about her radiance in this end-of-the-road trailer park. And how her hips swayed. There was probably more in that for Eddie.

"Dude," Rooney said.

"What?"

"You're looking at her like she's a porn site."

Eddie chuckled. "Yeah, I know, I just... Can you believe I slept with her?"

"No. Get in the car. Jesus Christ."

"Damn, dude," Eddie said and drove off. "You've been cranky the whole trip, man. What's up?"

"I had the perfect life! I was doing my thing and mooching off your Wi-Fi, and it was okay because you let me..."

"Of course. You're my best friend."

"Thanks, but then I died, and I got another perfect life. I was happy being Bogdor, sitting on the porch of a house I built myself, killing frost wyrms when I felt like it."

Eddie wasn't sure what to do with this info. *Fallen Kingdom* came at a time when he'd already more or less moved on from video games. His idea of Heaven was clearly different from Rooney's.

"But then that life gets taken away from me, too, because you can't live without me. A guy is gonna get cranky after getting two lives taken away."

Eddie slowed down so he could manage driving and a serious conversation at the same time.

"What are you saying? You wanna go back?"

Rooney seemed to consider it for a moment but ultimately decided against it.

"No... No, I don't. I got a do-over, and I know what's waiting when my time here is up." He stared out the window for a moment before turning to Eddie and going on. "I've got a third life now, and it has the potential to be the best one yet."

Eddie nodded, and thought hard about what to say now. His eventual choice was off-kilter, but at least he was honest. "I don't know how to deal with this kind of sincerity, so I'm gonna push the pedal down and pretend it's just because I wanna go fast."

Rooney had an answer, but the sudden high-revving roar of the engine drowned it out.

Not much later, that same engine caused Rosalie to swing open the church door before Eddie even was all the way out of the car, but she waited in the doorway. Eddie couldn't determine if she was happy, worried, or sad.

In truth, Rosalie wasn't sure if she was imagining it. When she began to realize that it was really Eddie, she cried.

He hurried to hug her, but when he came within arm's length, Rosalie hit him on the chest.

"Four days!" she sobbed and hit him again. "Goddamn you."

Eddie knew she had to get it out of her system, but she packed quite a punch, so after the third hit, he wrapped his arms around her and held her close. This calmed her, and it had the added benefit of locking her arms between them.

"It only felt like a day, tops."

Rosalie got out of his grip and wiped away her tears. "It was four. I know, because I counted every damn minute. You left me alone for four days!"

"I offered to take you with me."

"I should have, but..."

Rooney cleared his throat. "It all worked out, didn't it?"

Rosalie jumped at him and threw her arms around his neck for a hug that went on just a little too long for Eddie's taste.

"He's the whole reason I was away, and he gets all the huggings?"

Rosalie ignored him but still let go and put her hands all over Rooney's chest. "Are you okay? Does it hurt?"

Rooney took her hands. "I'm fine. Now, anyway. It's good to be back."

Rosalie gave him another hug and looked at the car over his shoulder. Then at Eddie. He knew what she was going to ask, and he preemptively shook his head.

"Where's Jonah?" she asked anyway.

"We traded places," Rooney answered. "Maybe we should go inside."

"Is it go-inside bad?"

Despite not having an answer yet, Rosalie went inside. Rooney followed and started to explain, but Eddie interrupted him. "You were in a box for most of this, remember?"

"Fine."

"It's not *that* bad," Eddie assured Rosalie as he sat down with her. "Turns out that Jonah was Jesus, and he offered to stay in Rooney's place."

Rosalie wasn't sure how to interpret his words. She really didn't have enough context to know if Eddie wasn't just saying something that only made sense in his head. But then she remembered who her boyfriend was and how they got together.

"Jesus Christ? With the cross and stuff? Our carpenter?"

Eddie nodded.

"Guess that makes sense. Why not." She shrugged and pointed over her shoulder. "And the goths? Are they secretly demons or something? You know, just checking."

He thought about it and looked at Rooney just in case he knew something, but neither of them could recall anything that suggested any kind of divinity or supernatural behavior.

"Pretty sure they're just weird humans," Eddie concluded. "Hey, wanna hear how I kicked an angel in the nuts?"

Rosalie batted nary an eye. Eddie said stuff like this even when he was just talking about earthly things. Right now, it just made sense.

"Curious segue, but sure, I'll take it."

Eddie barely started the epic tale of running amok in Heaven when there was a knock at the door. He didn't get up and finally looked at Rooney when the knocker pounded on the door again.

"Could you get that, please? It's probably Lilith."

"Dude, I've just been brought to life. I would like to sit down for a bit."

"You were lying on your back for what I just learned amounts to four days. So before you resume mooching, open the fucking door for me, please."

Rooney snickered. Fair enough. Opening the occasional door in exchange for free Wi-Fi seemed like a reasonable trade.

"Lilith's coming?" Rosalie asked, somewhat concerned.

"Yeah, but don't worry. I didn't piss her off *that* much. I think. Helen had her pick up Rooney's body from the morgue, and she'd stop by to say hi to the goths."

"Wait, what do you mean 'Rooney's body'?"

"Oh, yeah!" Eddie exclaimed. "Turns out we're probably still in the ground here. I don't get how it works exactly, but we're copies. I dunno if it works differently if you're buried, but apparently, Rooney's body needed to be picked up to avoid confusion."

While disappearing Rooney's body would indeed deal with some confusion, entirely different confusion entered the church. Rooney returned and his face was pale, trying hard to remain in a neutral state.

"There are three guys at the door."

"What do they want?"

"To talk to the Lord."

"That's gonna be a problem."

"They seem to think otherwise. And, Ed..."

Eddie got up. "And they seemed to have let themselves in."

He immediately spotted the revolver on Sam Hall's hip, but it didn't deter him. Nor did Rigby and Yaeger coming up behind the man. Eddie was usually very welcoming, but only to people who were invited.

"If you gentlemen follow me, I'm gonna let you right out again."

Sam raised his hands to show he had no evil intent. "My Lord, if you'll allow us ten minutes of your time..."

Eddie looked him over. The ridiculous white preacher suit, dumb cowboy hat. "Nope. Let's start fucking off right now, shall we? You've got until we reach the door."

He took a step, but Sam didn't. "Lord, please. It is of great importance that I plead my case with you."

"Man, I don't know who you think *you're* talking to, but I'm talking to a trespasser-- Hold on." He turned to Rooney who was tapping him on the shoulder. "What?"

Rooney whispered something in his ear and turned away. When Eddie focused a very angry gaze on Yaeger, he told Sam without looking, "I'll get you to you in a minute."

Yaeger tried to dodge but it was too late. Eddie dove at him like a cheetah hunting gazelle. Unfortunately for Yaeger, the gazelle generally got off easier. A crushed windpipe and then the sweet embrace of death would be far more preferred to the relentless pummeling Eddie let loose on Yaeger.

Cursing like a sailor, and occasionally reminding Yaeger shooting Rooneys wasn't cool, Eddie beat the young man's face into a bloody mess. By the time Yaeger's body went into standby, Eddie still wasn't done, and the cocking of a gun didn't stop him either. Without stopping the beating, Eddie looked at Rigby pointing a gun at him with a trembling hand. He growled, and Rigby stepped back in fear of what far more resembled a demon than the Lord Jesus Christ.

Finally, it was the victim of the actual shooting who felt he needed to put an end to this.

"Ed, enough!"

Eddie stopped and looked back. "You sure? I can hurt him more for you."

"I'm sure."

"Alright." Eddie got up and scoffed at Rigby. "Put that thing away before you hurt yourself."

Sam took his pocket square and flapped it open. "Please, let me clean your hands."

"The fuck?"

Sam gently took Eddie's hand and started wiping off the blood. Confused, Eddie looked back at Rooney and Rosalie. They didn't have a clue either.

Suddenly, Sam stopped. His grip tightened as he looked at Eddie's palm, and his face turned into a grimace.

"No stigmata..." he mumbled. "Where is your stigmata?"

Eddie shrugged. "I drive a Vindicator."

"Scars!" Sam yelled. "Where are your scars?"

Angrily he turned and approached Rigby. "You didn't check for stigmata?" He almost tripped over Yaeger.

"Fuck," he exclaimed, then kicked him.

Eddie, Rosalie, and Rooney stared in shock at what was unfolding before them.

"You incompetent fucks didn't check for stigmata?" Sam kicked Yaeger again. "The Lord was nailed to a cross, crowned with thorns, stabbed with a spear, and you didn't stop for one fucking moment to check if the target had at least one shitty scar?"

He kicked Yaeger one more time for good measure.

"Oh, *that* Lord," Eddie chuckled. "You thought I was Jesus Christ?"

Sam didn't find it funny and scowled at him.

"Goddamn, old man, you were close, though." Eddie could see his fist ball up and tremble but found this too amusing to let it go. "Jesus actually did all the woodwork you see here. We listened to music together too, and I think my girlfriend kinda liked him..."

Eddie turned to check with Rosalie, and she nodded. "He wasn't hard to look at, no."

"See? So I had to deal with him. He's in Heaven now. I can fast-track you there if you really wanna talk to him."

Sam's hand twitched, but it didn't do any more because the front door swung open, and Lilith barged in.

"Ed! Where do you keep your goths-- Oh. Hey, uh, are you aware there's an unconscious guy on your floor?"

"How do you know he's not dead?" Eddie joked though he wasn't entirely sure it was only a joke.

Lilith scoffed. "Death is my core business, and I've got a corpse in my trunk. I know what death smells like."

Rooney turned to her as if there wasn't a potentially violent situation going on in the living room. "Oh, you managed?"

Lilith nodded.

"Weird... I wanna see!"

"Oh, you really don't," Lilith said with an accompanying

gesture. "Trunk isn't that big. I had to, like, Tetris you in there. It's not pretty."

"Excuse me!" Sam burst. "What in God's holy name is goin' on here?"

Instead of a balled fist, he now had his fingers clenched around his revolver. So far, he wasn't pointing it at anyone yet, but that it was out and ready to go was problematic enough for Rosalie. Though living with Eddie and regular visits from deities made her react in an atypical fashion. She stepped within arm's reach of Sam and bitch-slapped him with all the frustration of the last four days.

"What's happening here is a man walking uninvited into my home and drawing a weapon. Now, you put that thing back where it came from, or so help me, I will find a place for it, and it's not going to be the damn holster! You got me, old timer?"

The sheer confusion made Sam put the Navy Colt away. "Who are you people?"

Taking another page from Eddie's playbook, as that seemed to work, Rosalie smirked. "We are not the kind of people you want to start pointing guns at."

"Yeah, please don't," Lilith agreed emphatically. "If you kill one of them, it's somehow suddenly my fault, and I really don't have time for that shit again."

"Even the Devil doesn't wanna deal with us," Eddie piled on. "But if I were you, I'd worry about my girlfriend first because I know her tired-of-this-shit face, and this is it. I get it a lot."

Sam barely heard the rest of Eddie's sentence and squinted at Lilith, who was paying little to no attention to him. She was just dropping by for a visit and still needed to figure out where the people she wanted to visit were.

"So, Ed-head. Goths?"

"Oh, they live in the basement--"

"You're not the Devil," Sam barked.

Lilith looked at him, smirked, and took a step. "And what makes you so sure?”

"I've met him…"

Twenty-four

For a brief moment, no more than a second or two, the waters seemed calm. For those two seconds, it felt like they were just going for a nice walk on the beach this June morning in 1944. A splash of water over the side of the landing craft brought Sam back to reality. He couldn't see the beach from where he was sitting, and he didn't mind because he knew what was waiting for them. These boys were his responsibility, but he knew half of them weren't coming home. He didn't know which half, so for his own sanity, he focused on one of them.

A wide-eyed kid from Shitstick, Wherever, who had no business playing war. Eli Blueberry, but with Sam's thick drawl, it sounded like "Bloobry." Blueberry insisted that he had no right being comfortable at home if he didn't save the world from "them natsies." It didn't look like he was going to do a lot of saving now, though. He leaned over the side to throw up.

"Hey, back in the boat! Unless you want your head shot off."

"We're still out of range, lieutenant," Blueberry answered after wiping his lips. A mortar shell exploded in the water next to them and changed his mind.

Closing in on the beach, Sam could see the tops of the cliffside casemates looming. They didn't look very bombed. In fact, as far as bunker roofs went, these were of exceptional quality. Almost like the shelling from the ships had been just for show. And if the casemates were intact, the 42s inside them would be as well.

The coxswain yelled a thirty-second warning.

"This is it, boys!" Sam yelled. "When that ramp goes down, y'all fan out! Groups are targets; one guy might stand a chance. Our job is to run up a beach, just like when we were kids, but with more bullets this time. Those of y'all need prayin', do it now."

Among those who said a prayer was Sam himself. He asked God to do what He could to help them across the sand and hoped that would be good enough.

Then the bow ramp went down, and no prayer could help them. As soon as line of sight was established with the casemates, the bone saws did their job. Without mercy, salvos sounding like tearing fabric tore through the prayers of the first rows of men in the LCI. Struggling to hurdle their comrades, the next few boys were cut to ribbons, and a pile of bodies was blocking the most direct way out.

"Over the sides!" somebody yelled. It might have been Sam, but even he wasn't sure anymore. He expected Death to welcome them on the beach, but they hadn't even touched sand yet. He was overwhelmed by the unmitigated wave of chaos that poured into their formerly safe space.

Eli raised himself up on the side, and Sam saw two puffs of red mist erupt from his shoulder and neck, ending his quest to save the world then and there. The boy drooped back into the boat, and his empty eyes stared up at Sam, accusing him of leading them into Hell.

An explosion to the right rocked the boat. The remaining men started fleeing back from the ramp as if it made a difference. Where could they go? They were in a drawer with one open end, and staying in it meant being ground into a red paste. Sam did his best to herd them out, and he looked around to find his sergeant. The boys looked up to that man, he would do a much better job of getting them somewhere. Sam gagged when he noticed he was now standing on his sergeant, and the pressure caused blood to squirt out of the hole below his eye.

"Go, go, go! Stay in here and you will definitely die!"

Going out there didn't increase chances much. Especially not for the ones who were dragged down to the bottom by their waterlogged gear. Sam hated himself for being pleased to see the Germans turn their guns to the next boat, but he wasn't too proud to make use of this brief respite. The remains of his platoon that did make it out of the water were pitiful to say the least. They were ten now, but that wouldn't last. Private Lazscowicz made a move to take cover behind the first thing he saw, which was a mined log ramp. Sam yelled to stop him but it made no difference. Even if Lazscowicz had heard him over the explosions and pained screams, his own terror would have driven him to cover anyway. The moment his body touched the wood, the mine next to his head exploded. His helmet and part of his skull landed next to Sam. Catatonic, he struggled a few feet on and managed to find cover behind a hedgehog. The steel beams offered very little in the way of protection, but just enough for the Germans to focus their bullet-storms elsewhere.

Black smoke from explosions mingled with the lighter smoke from the nearby grassfires the bombers had set off, covering him from direct gunfire, and he saw the face of one of his final eight appear before him. The boy really was a boy. Sam couldn't remember his name, only that he had always questioned if this kid was old enough to sign up at all. The lad's lips moved, but Sam couldn't make out what he said. Then the kid grabbed him and shook him.

"What do we do, sir?"

"Err, ehm..."

"Sir!"

"The shingles. Get to the shingles!"

It took a great effort for Sam to make himself move. This hedgehog seemed much safer than crossing more beach to get even closer to those machine guns. Yet he managed. He was their leader; it was his job to get them to safety, and even though he had failed miserably at that so far, he would bring these boys home. He rolled out of cover and started going after them, just in time to see how an errant mortar shell blew the group apart. In his path, Sam saw the kid covered in soot and blood, but he was still alive. He grabbed a strap of the kid's pack and dragged most of him along, though his left leg came off below the knee.

The cries of pain and pleas for his mother pierced Sam's ears, and for the last stretch, that was all he heard. When he reached the relative cover of the shingles, he pulled the kid close and caressed him like it was his own son.

"We're safe here," Sam lied. "You lost a leg, but you'll live, alright? Be tough, and we'll get you outta here."

The kid tried to nod, but a spurt of blood gushed from his mouth, and Sam noticed the hole in his stomach.

"Medic..." he whimpered as if he already knew that shouting wouldn't get a medic here either. The kid died in his arms, and with him went Sam's strength to fight on.

"You fucking kraut bastards!" he shouted and stood up. "You couldn't even let me save one!"

He grabbed his Colt and fired a few pointless shots at the casemate. "Take me! I'm right here!"

Likely they simply didn't hear him down there, but it might as well have been because they didn't think one shell-shocked Yankee was much of a threat. The worst he could do down there was tangle up their neatly placed barbed wire.

Sam turned and looked at the beach. It was littered end to end with the torn-up bodies of men who had barely seen battle at all. They were simply food for the guns, sent because an angry little man thought he needed *lebensraum*. All this senseless death and destruction, boys fresh out of their mothers' laps, cut down before they could see the newer, better world they thought they were fighting for.

He was struck in the back by a German bullet, cracking his rib and puncturing his lung. Sam didn't pay attention to the vicious pain. He sank to his knees and slumped. It was okay, he thought. Even if they won this war, there would be more, and more again. He folded his hands because he had some time to kill before life would leave him completely.

"God, where are you?" His head felt heavier than usual when he lifted it to look at the sky, even when he took his helmet off. "We needed you, and you abandoned us."

His efforts to look up were pointless. Dark smoke blotted out the sky, and gray mist that smelled like it came from nearby fires enveloped him. He wasn't sure if this was how it ended, or that it was actual smoke, and he didn't care.

"I'd give anything for this to end. If you are listening at all, please grant me that."

A strong hand grabbed him and pulled him back to cover.

"Get your head down, lieutenant!"

Pain shot through his body when he was forced down, and through his blurry vision, he saw a five-star general with a black goatee. Sam grinned and would have laughed out loud if it didn't hurt like hell.

"What's so funny, soldier?"

"You are, sir. I might be dying, but I'm still lucid enough to know a five-star general has no place on this beach."

"Well, you asked for help, and here I am. General Tobias, nice to meet you."

The smile ran away from Sam's face, and he looked again. "Are you God?"

The general laughed. "Not quite, no. I'm the guy that usually gets blamed for shitshows like this."

Sam puffed from the pain in his chest. Just his luck. Going to church every Sunday, thanking Jesus and all his buddies for every meal, dying in the arms of the Devil.

"Hurts like a motherfucker, doesn't it?" the general said.

Sam nodded slowly.

"I can make you a pretty good deal. You give me your soul, and a stray explosion is gonna create a hole in that concertina wire. Bet your buddies would love that."

The whole problem in dealing with dying men was exactly that. They didn't have a lot to lose. Neither did Sam, so he guessed it wouldn't hurt to get a better deal out of this.

"I'll shake on that," he said, not even sure if he was physically still able to shake anything. "If we can sweeten the deal."

General Tobias looked around. He wasn't happy about it, but he had a quota to make, so he decided to hear Sam out.

"I get to speak to God before I die."

"Dude, what?" The general seemed confused. "You're minutes away from talking to--"

"I'm minutes away from being at God's mercy." Sam paused to take a few labored breaths. "I want... a level playing field when we speak."

"Dammit, alright," the general sighed. "Deal."

Sam tried to take his hand but didn't have the strength to raise it anymore and passed out.

"Yeah, alright. You take a fucking nap while I figure out how to drag your limp ass out of here."

He grabbed a nearby radio kit and dialed in. It always took a while with these old radios to get a connection, but finally, there was an answer. "Ignacio! It's me! Send a couple of demons to my location. Have them bring wire cutters. I promised a guy a hole in barbed wire... Yes, I'm being serious... Hm-hm. Yeah, they'll have to carry him to safety, so make them look like-- Huh? ...No, the Americans, actually... Alright, make it snappy. I'm under fire."

He hung up and sighed at the thought of having to carry Sam to a field hospital, but a deal's a deal.

TWENTY-FIVE

Eddie looked at Sam in utter disbelief. "I call bullshit. You're not old enough to have been a lieutenant on Omaha Beach."

Then he looked at Lilith, assuming the Devil would sooner tell the truth than somebody who was actually there. But she was preoccupied with checking her phone, and he wasn't surprised. This seemed to be a common theme for deities during pressing situations.

"I'll take that as a compliment, boy," Sam said. "I'll be a hundred next month."

Eddie studied him. Sam Hall was old for sure, but the way he carried himself took years off him. His eyes, though a dark hazel, were bright. Not as bloodshot as you'd expect from a geriatric man. Nothing about him said century-old, but Rigby suddenly made all of that moot, and Eddie took a step back.

"You sure about that?"

Sam turned to Rigby and found himself at the business end

of the .38 that started this. Sam was hardly impressed by it, and neither was anybody else. In fact, the only one who had an opinion about the new situation was also the only one with some common sense in her head.

"What's with you guys and all the damn gun swinging?" Rosalie exclaimed, though more with genuine wonder in her voice than worry. "Edward Sterling, I am not cleaning up bits of brain if he shoots!"

"You don't need to worry, little lady," Sam said, keeping his eyes fixed on Rigby and lining up with the gun. "Even if Mr. Rigby here took a moment to load his weapon and had the actual grit to pull the trigger, I have my deal. I ain't worried."

"Yeah, checks out," Lilith said, finally putting away her phone. "Took a bit of effort to pull up his files, but my father took that deal. This guy's not dying any time soon."

Rigby's hand trembled, as well as his lips, but neither were from nerves. He never intended to shoot Sam. Murder was a sin, after all, but his anger had to go somewhere, and pistol-whipping was a good alternative. He clocked Sam across the face with the butt of the revolver.

"Deceiver!" he yelled with a trembling voice. "Years I've spent in the driver's seat of cars with broken ACs, unwittingly feeding your lies to misguided kids like Yaeger. Weeks, months at a time, I've spent away from my wife and child! For what? For a pawn of the Devil!"

He swung again, but Sam caught his wrist and drew his own weapon, pressing the barrel against Rigby's stomach.

"Was there even a plan to fly those that came after me to Kolob?" Rigby asked. "Were you really trying to find the Lord Jesus?"

Sam pushed him away and trained his sights on Rigby's head.

"Kolob was just an excuse to get you and others like you on my side, Brother Rigby. It's frighteningly easy to sway simple-minded individuals to your cause if you tell them exactly what they want to hear."

Rigby yelled from the pain of his world falling apart and pulled the trigger on an empty gun. Weeping, he fell to his knees.

"I *am* looking for Jesus," Sam said. "I will live forever but I still age, and time will catch up to me. I need the Great Redeemer to get out of this deal before I become an incontinent wreck."

Eddie started laughing. "Oh man, are you barking up the wrong tree! You should be looking for a lawyer."

Sam turned and aimed the gun at Eddie, who wasn't very concerned with it. In fact, he pushed his forehead against the barrel and taunted Sam.

"Go on, Wild Bill. Pull the trigger and see what happens. I'm walking right back out of Hell to--"

"No, you're not," Lilith corrected him. "Blacklisted, remember?"

Eddie pursed his lips. He kept forgetting, and being reminded of it now was just shitty timing. "Lil? Can you fix that deal? Because I may have made an error in judgment."

"The way I see it, Aunt Helen needs to fix this, but she's not answering her phone."

"Oh," Eddie said. "She's actually--"

The lights flickered briefly, and a second later, the bedroom door opened. Everybody, including Sam, looked to see who was coming out. When they did, Rosalie gave Eddie an angry push.

"Hey, ow!"

"You've had worse!" she hissed. "And you'll get worse if you don't explain to me why Helen is walking out of *our bedroom!*"

Up until now, Eddie had no idea Helen was in their bedroom, but he immediately saw Rosalie's point. The last place he wanted to see Helen now was the place where his girlfriend found God's panties. This did not paint a very positive picture for him, nor did the implication that Helen could have been in their bedroom whenever she felt like it. Eddie had heard about God being omniscient, or all-seeing, but he never gave it much thought. And if it meant that Helen sat at the foot of their bed to look at them in their sleep, or... when they were *awake*, that was just cheating, voyeurism, or both.

"Hey," Eddie said and met her halfway as she approached. "What were you doing, ehm... in there? You hang out in our bedroom a lot?"

"Technically, it's still my bedroom and I can appear in it whenever I feel like it."

Eddie cringed. He really didn't want Rosalie to feel watched in her own private chambers, and after all the work he had put into overhauling the church, Eddie didn't much feel like moving somewhere God couldn't simply appear.

"Oh, don't make that face," Helen said. "I don't pop in whenever. Anymore."

"Scuse me?"

"Alright, it happened once. But I got out of there before you knew I was there."

Eddie squinted. "But I was there, hm?"

"Both of you, actually," Helen added a superfluous wink. "You need to work on your technique, Ed."

Eddie blushed and glanced at Rosalie, who shook her head.

"Relax," Helen said and slapped him on the back, "just kidding. I know her happy face when I see it. So, what's this? What's going on here with the cowboys and the guns?"

"You arrived exactly on cue, actually."

"Of course. Let's pretend that was on purpose."

"I'm actually not entirely sure what's going on here," Eddie confessed, but he tried to explain it as best he could with his limited comprehension. "This clown with the gun—which he could put down now, by the way!—is looking for Jonah... I think Lilith should explain this."

"Aha." Helen hardly paid Sam Hall any heed and even brushed

his gun aside as she elegantly stepped to Lilith to give her a hug and a kiss on the cheek. "Fill me in, sweetie."

Lilith nodded. "Yeah, hi, by the way. So. The hat's Sam Hall, and he made a deal with my father, which he's trying to get out of by finding Jesus because he thinks that'll help for some reason."

Helen looked at Sam, and slowly some seventy-year-old memories came back to her. "What was the deal, exactly?"

Lilith thought for a moment. She knew, but this seemed like a time to have her facts absolutely straight. "Ehm, a hole in a barbed wire fence and, err... Hold on." She took out her phone and looked up the particulars. "Yes, the hole, and immortality until he has a chance to meet God."

"Oooh!" Helen snapped her fingers. "That's why Toby started calling me again after so long. Learn from your father's mistakes, dear. Never take the immortality deals, quota or not."

Helen positioned herself in front of Sam.

"If you wouldn't mind lowering your gun for a moment. I find talking at gunpoint rather distracting."

Nodding dumbly, Sam relaxed his arm, and Helen extended her hand.

"Nice to meet you, Mr. Hall. I am Helen. My niece informs me I'm late for our appointment, and I would like to apologize for that."

Baffled, Sam shook her hand. "You... You are--"

"God, sure, if you want to put a label on it."

Helen's nonchalance bothered Sam, as well as the idea that God was a woman, *and* related to the Devil and his spawn. His confusion quickly turned to anger.

"I asked to speak to the one true God. Not some woman with delusions of grandeur, let alone one with ties to the Prince of Darkness."

Helen scoffed. "When did I imply I was related to Ozzy Osbourne? We've met briefly, but I doubt he remembers it."

Sam's hand raised his revolver again. "That you choose to make light of this tells me you ain't no one. Git gone, woman. Everybody knows God is a man."

Eddie leaned in. "You really don't wanna do that."

"Hush up, boy!"

Suddenly, Helen seemed to become larger, and angrier. She might not have cared for all the reverence that came with being God, but she cared even less for being dismissed as a nobody. Her voice, though still her own, became godlike indeed.

"Your god may be a man, Mr. Hall, but *the* god is standing before you. I created your universe, and were it not for the friends I made, I would have unmade it long before you ever came around. I am the Almighty; I am the creator of all you know and all you see before you. Mr. Hall, *I simply am.*"

And that should have been it. More often than not, the few people Helen deemed acceptable to know that she was who she was just accepted it with a deep look in her blue eyes. Maybe they'd make her guess numbers first, or make a little joke out of disbelief, and she was fine with that. Meeting God and finding out that everything you thought you knew about it was wrong merited a joke. Sam clearly needed more than a look to be convinced, and going Old Testament like that did the trick, but it still didn't seem to please him very much.

"You could have ended that slaughter!" he yelled. "All those boys, fighting for a good cause, dead in the sand, rotting in the water. Where were you? I prayed for you to help us."

Helen turned around, hands behind her back, and her classy high heels clicked as she took a few steps. Then she turned back, her head cocked slightly.

"Prayer is for you, Mr. Hall. I do not care. Do you think you were the only one praying? Even the atheists in your boat said a prayer. The Germans also said a prayer."

"So you went to them!"

"I went nowhere, Mr. Hall!" Helen rebutted. "My brother listened to your prayers because there is no easier way to cut a deal than on the battlefield. I do not concern myself with war."

Sam cocked the hammer. "We were created in your image. You should concern yourself with our wars."

Helen righted herself and crossed her arms. "You crawled out of the mud, grew yourself a pair of legs, and you went straight to killing each other. It's a miracle you got around to forming a civilization at all, but I had nothing to do with it. Your wars are just that: *your* wars. Argue against it all you want, but in the end, you're the one brandishing a weapon."

Sam looked at the gun in his hand and nodded slowly, as if he understood her point.

"You're right," he admitted. "But I'm holding this gun to rid the world of a great evil."

Eddie got ready to lunge toward Lilith, should Sam try something. A second later, he pounced, pushing off on the couch, and knocking Lilith down with his jump at the sound of a shot filling the church. Surprised, she pushed him off her.

"Goddammit, Eddie!" she called out, entirely unharmed. "I don't know whether to be flattered or offended that you just assumed he was talking about me."

"Then who--"

"Eddie," Rosalie said. Worried confusion rang in her voice as she kneeled next to Helen, lying motionless and face-down on the floor. "I think she's dead."

Rosalie tried feeling for a pulse, but she wasn't sure if Helen ever had one. Pulses were human things, and Helen just looked like one. A dead one, at this point, because apparently bullets worked perfectly fine on gods.

"You shot God, motherfucker!" Without a thought for his own safety, Eddie now pounced from Lilith to Sam and took him down instead, fully intent on starting a fistfight with a man who had five bullets left. Something he realized when Sam smacked him across the face with the gun and took aim.

Eddie got back on his feet. "Rosie, the Mormon-stick, please."

"No!" she said and grabbed him. "Enough with the killing!"

"Almost," Eddie hissed. "Just him, and then we're done. Promise. Let me go!"

While Rosalie struggled to keep him from doing something stupid, again, a crackle sounded. Like distant lightning tearing the horizon in half, but no thunder followed. What did follow was a blinding light. Eddie turned to the source. While he and Rosalie were arguing over attacking a man with a gun, Helen rose up, and a ray of light pierced out from where the bullet entered her chest. She did not look amused at all and covered the wound—for lack of a better word—with her hand until the light seeping through the cracks of her fingers disappeared, and she was whole again. The blouse wasn't, though, and that angered her the most.

"I liked this blouse," she said. Her voice was calm in the most frightening way. Sam raised his gun in a reflex but without any real intent to fire again. He was too terrified to remember how the trigger worked.

Helen put her hand on the barrel and took the gun from him without resistance. She handed it to Rosalie, even though Eddie reached for it, and focused icy blue eyes back on Sam.

"Up until now," she continued, "I've been a benevolent God. Uncaring perhaps, but never malicious. If it's Old Testament you want, Mr. Hall, I'm more than willing to provide it now." Helen reached out to him. "You've met God, whether it was what you hoped for or not. The deal is done. This is only going to be fun for one of us."

Her hand landed on his shoulder, from where burning light started to consume him. Sam screamed. If Helen had a way to do whatever this was painlessly, she purposely wasn't doing it. When the light enveloped Sam completely, his scream stopped abruptly, and he disappeared in a flash.

"Whoa!" Eddie exclaimed. "What was that?"

Helen checked her watch. "Rapture."

"That's a real thing?"

"Sort of. It's really not all it's cracked up to be."

"No, I got that." Eddie scratched his head, looking around. Yaeger still lying there, Rigby confused and shocked on the floor next to him, the empty spot where Sam was.

Rooney suddenly perked up because he thought Helen's trick looked a lot like *Star Trek*. If Scotty screwed up the transporter controls, anyway.

"Did you, uh, rapture him into oblivion, or is he... somewhere else?" he asked.

"Mars."

"The planet?"

"Yeah. Red, lots of sand and rocks. Arnold Schwarzenegger went there once, that one." Helen checked her watch. "Oh, you'll get a kick out of this: there's life on Mars, right about... now."

She kept an eye on her watch while Rooney tried to wrap his head around the idea of life on other planets. He was kind of happy to be alive in a time where that was possible, however brief it had left to live. It gave him some kind of peace to know that there was actual life on--

"Aaaand it's gone," Helen said.

"Aunt Helen!" Lilith sighed. "You know how much of a hassle it is to get souls off Mars."

"I do, hon, but look!" Helen stuck her finger through the hole in her blouse.

"Wait, you've done this before?" Rooney asked incredulously.

Helen nodded and chuckled like a child pranking its parents. "In a couple of hundred years, interplanetary archeologists are going to have a real conundrum on their hands."

She walked to Rigby and offered him her hand. Pulling him onto his feet, she said, "I'm sorry you had to see that, Mr. Rigby, but I did you a favor."

Rigby could barely comprehend what was happening, let alone that he was face to face with God. Tearfully, he looked at her, and without fully realizing he was doing it, he said, "I'm sorry."

"What for?"

"I wanted to shoot him. I didn't care it's a sin."

"Don't worry," Helen said, patting him on the shoulder. "We judge on a case-by-case basis. Takes a little longer, but it nets far better results. Now, your man needs medical attention. Anyone out cold for that long is going to have complications."

With a shaking hand, Rigby took his phone from his pocket and tried to dial 911, but Helen gently pushed his hand down. "Let's not bother anyone else with our domestic problems."

She kneeled beside Yaeger and put her hand on his forehead. She kept it there for a minute or so and finally wiped it on his shirt to get the blood off.

"There. He'll be fine. He's still gonna hurt, though."

"Can you do--"

"I could, but I won't. He doesn't have to die, but he still shot my friend."

Rigby nodded. Seemed like a pretty lenient deal. He gave Yaeger a few moments to regain control of his faculties and then helped him up.

"What happened?" Yaeger slurred. He looked around with blurry vision, but even like this, he was able to recognize Rooney. The sudden burst of endorphins from seeing him pushed the blur back, and then he saw Eddie. In a single gasp, everything came back to him. The hellish, angry face over him, the flurry of fists hitting him everywhere. He took an unstable step backward in a reflex, and Rigby had to catch him.

Helen gave him a nod. "Perhaps your friend needs some fresh air. Try Canada."

Rigby got the hint and helped Yaeger out the door.

TWENTY-SIX

With Rigby and Yeager gone, and relative peace and quiet back in the church, Lilith sighed. This all seemed like a happy end, at least for some people, but she actually had a big pile of excrement on her hands now.

"Aunt Helen? A moment, please?"

Lilith walked as far out of earshot as the church allowed, and Helen followed.

"What's up, dear?"

"What are you doing?" Lilith whispered angrily.

"I'm not sure what you're referring to."

"This!" Lilith gestured at the church, at Rooney, at Eddie and Rosalie. "All I ever hear is how the universe needs balance, and now we're just leaving three Fateless to live out their lives?"

"Yes."

"But... That's bad! My father just had to deal with one Fateless--"

"Which we have now."

"Sure. But it was cause enough for concern, and now you expect me to run an entire Underworld with three people walking the earth that we can't direct to balance the scales. Are you purposely trying to make it hard for me?"

Helen put a hand on her shoulder.

"Lillie, listen to me--"

Lilith pushed it away and didn't even try to whisper anymore.

"No, you know what? You listen to me for a change. I'm already getting enough stink-eye at the office because I'm the girl who got the job because of her daddy. I already work twice as hard to prove I'm not just a nepo-baby, I don't need you going around making things harder for me because you think it'll help me toughen up, or build character, or whatever bullshit reason you're going to come up with. Even after I ran away from my father, I knew Fate was the most important law, and now we're just pissing all over it?"

With a hint of amusement, Helen let her finish. Then she crossed her arms and looked her niece in the eyes.

"Are you done with your little tantrum?"

"There's more where that came from."

"I'm sure there is, and feel free to demonstrate that another time," Helen said calmly. "Sweetie, I've been God for fourteen billion-ish years. I know how far something can bend before it breaks, and in time you will, too. If this turns out to cause issues for you after all, you send whoever is causing them my way."

Lilith crossed her arms like a surly teen and was clearly fuming. Helen rubbed her arm for some kind of response, and she got it.

"Fuck this, I quit."

"Is that what you really want?"

"If I'm only an effective boss because Auntie God is looking over my shoulder, what's the point? I'm not fit for this. I was fine in the cemetery with my friends... Ugh!" Lilith rubbed her nose and flapped her hand at Eddie. "All I had to do was ignore that jackass, and I wouldn't be working my ass off now trying to keep a whole goddamn universe balanced."

Helen put an arm around her niece.

"You've been doing a good job so far, and I know you'll only get better. But if you really want to quit, you can tell me now, and I won't make a fuss. I'll figure something out for a replacement."

Lilith pressed her lips together and looked around. Rooney was sitting on the couch, not doing anything specific. Eddie and Rosalie moved to the kitchen and were discussing something of their own. They seemed happy, and that was the flipside of the coin. If she never helped Eddie get her father's number, he wouldn't have gone down the path that eventually put him here in his own kitchen, next to the girl he had always dreamed of. Lilith wasn't going to take all the credit for it, but the ghost of a smile briefly wafted over her lips.

"I'm just nervous, Aunt Helen. If I fail, the Afterlife fails."

"The fact that you are nervous about failing tells me you're the right soul for the job."

Lilith leaned into Helen and allowed herself to enjoy the closeness for just a moment.

"You think?" she asked.

Helen chuckled. "I'm God, hon. I don't think, I know."

Lilith snickered. That certainly didn't fly when they played Trivial Pursuit. Helen was aware of this and navigated them both back to the living room.

"Did you know your father spent an hour throwing up when he realized the magnitude of his task?"

That was indeed news to Lilith. Taking and often holding human, or humanoid, form was a relatively recent development. Throwing up didn't seem like something they could do before that.

"Oh, it's true. Wasn't pretty either. Ever hear of the Gimpy-Gimpy tree?"

Lilith nodded. Dr. Ignacio had used it in one or two experiments before her time, but she had seen it described in a report as "inhumane." Not a word often used to describe anything in the Underworld.

"Exactly, that's what happens when the Devil throws up, hon. Might wanna keep that in mind next time you go binge drinking."

"Trust me, after last time, I'm good for a while." Lilith gave Helen one more hug. "I'm finally gonna go say hi to the friends I barely see anymore. Eddie! Goths?"

"Basement!"

Lilith walked off, and Helen turned her attention to the loving couple. "Why are you so pale, Eddie?"

"Recovering from a heart attack."

Minutes earlier, Rosalie had brought Eddie into the kitchen so they could discuss a private thing of their own. Because she didn't know exactly how to start this conversation, she opened with a classic, which Eddie interpreted entirely wrong.

"I need to tell you something."

Eddie never once feared that Rosalie would have something to hide from him. There was always a small part of him that took into account she would one day have enough of his shit and leave him for someone better, or at least sane. But he could always depend on her to say so. Having affairs was just not her thing. So the feeling that washed over him, crawling up his spine, draping over his shoulder, and compressing his chest, almost made him lose his balance. For someone who was having something frighteningly close to a heart attack, he did a pretty good job of keeping a straight face.

"Are you okay?" Rosalie asked.

Clearly not a good enough job.

"Yeah, no, sure, I'm fine. Low... blood sugar? What-- what did you wanna tell me?"

She looked at him and smiled. "Nothing as bad as you clearly seem to think."

Eddie nodded, urgently.

"I talked to Dad, who is a little upset you left me hanging, by the way..."

"You're right, that might be worse than what I was thinking."

"What *were* you thinking?"

Eddie shrugged. "I think of the weirdest shit, but not getting shot in the head by my father-in-law."

"You're going to have to talk to him and probably spin the Boston story again, but that's not where I was going with this."

"Then please get to where you're going. I've already been to Heaven, and you're killing me with the suspense."

"I'm gonna be a cop."

Eddie stood up straight. "That's it?"

Rosalie nodded.

"That's kinda cool. Weird, but cool."

"Why is that weird?"

"Because I'm me. I'm the guy in the drunk tank. I'm the guy who breaks into places because the Devil's daughter asked him to. I'm the guy who gets arrested by... well, you."

Rosalie winked. "And now we have a good idea for roleplay, hm?"

Eddie had a lot of things to say about that, but couldn't because he had to explain to Helen why he looked pale. The heart attack seemed like a better excuse than the truth, which was that the blood was rushing from his face because it was urgently needed in different parts of his body.

"I just told him I'm going to the police academy," Rosalie explained.

"No, you didn't," Eddie countered. "You said you were gonna be a cop."

"And a police academy is generally the way to go about that. Dad is getting me into his old academy, but you'll have to manage without me for a few months while I'm there, so..."

"Are you sure you want to do that?" Helen joked.

Rooney dove right on the opportunity to take the piss out of Eddie as well. "I'll make sure he doesn't summon any demons in the meantime."

Eddie threw his hands up. "Ack! You never let me do anything fun!"

"Yeah, your kind of fun tends to knock the universe out of balance," Helen said. "Somebody needs to keep an eye on you."

"And would that be you, huh?" Eddie flirted.

Helen planned to flirt back but was surprised to get an evil scowl from Rosalie, so she stopped herself before she could do any damage.

"I've still got a thing going on in Vegas, hon. I'm sure Rob will keep you in line for the sake of all of us."

Rooney snorted. "Oh sure, put the fate of the universe on my shoulders right after I've been resurrected. Can I get one day off, please?"

"Okay, I'm a dumb ogre," Eddie said. "Let's change the subject. What did Jolene say?"

"She didn't mention your intelligence or ogre-ness," Helen answered. "She's actually going to pick up Jonah's bike. Oh, and I'd give it a while before you visit with her again."

"Not pleased, huh?"

"Turns out she kinda put two and two together when she saw Jonah's scars. Didn't take a lot of convincing from me, but she had some issues with your bringing him along at all. She mentioned something about turning you into a coat. I don't think she was serious."

"I do. And if I still had a carpenter worth his salt, I'd put extra locks on the door."

"Yes, well..." Helen hugged Rosalie, and then Rooney. "The sooner she turns you into a coat, the sooner we have you, so I shall take my leave now."

She winked at Eddie as he saw her out.

"Can I give you a ride to the tunnel?"

"That would be nice, thank you."

"Hold on." Eddie trotted back to Rosalie. "I'm gonna give Helen a ride--"

"Why?" she snapped.

"Because... it's a nice thing to do?"

Rosalie had her opinions about it but kept them to herself.

"Look, I'm gonna give her the ride and then swing by the police station to smooth things over with your dad."

"Want me to come along?"

Eddie wanted to say yes. Dealing with Chief Watson was intimidating in the best of circumstances, let alone trying to explain where he'd been for the last couple of days.

But he didn't say yes. "No, I should be able to talk to my father-in-law without backup, right?"

"Okay..."

Eddie grabbed his coat and headed out the door with Helen, where she headed straight for the driver's side of the Vindicator.

"Uh, no way, lady," Eddie said. "If you like the car so much, get Janick to build you one."

"Even though I just got shot because of you?"

"Really? Emotional blackmail?" Eddie gestured her away from his side. "You're fine. Show me even a hint of a scar, and I might consider it."

Pouting comically, Helen got in the passenger side. "You just want me to take my shirt off."

"Yeah, and I still wouldn't let you drive."

The Vindicator tore away loudly, and after a while of Eddie glancing at the hole in her blouse, Helen had to say something about it. "I'm not actually going to take it off, hon."

"Yeah, I figured that much. I'm just wondering about the light. That was some bright shit. What was that?"

"Oh, not much different from what happens if you get shot."

Eddie frowned. "I'm pretty sure Rooney didn't emit any kind of light."

"No, he emitted blood, because you're full of that," Helen laughed. "I'm made of pure light. We take on these human forms so you don't go blind looking at us."

"Sure, that's the reason."

"Well, not the only reason." Helen winked.

"You say 'us,' but your brother just kinda oozed black shit."

"He used to be of light. But resentment and, I think, jealousy turned him putrid."

She stared out at the road, and Eddie let her for a while, but he couldn't stop thinking about it.

"Is that why he had to die?"

"No, he had to die because he broke the laws," Helen answered immediately. "Left to his own devices, he would have broken everything."

Eddie pulled up to the payphone, and they got out.

"You good here?"

Helen nodded and gave him a goodbye hug. "No more Afterlife shenanigans, alright?"

This time Eddie nodded, but halfheartedly.

"I'm serious, Sterling," Helen said. "We'll make sure the next time you come is the last time."

"Sounds like a threesome I had once."

Helen sighed. "Alright. I'm going to pretend you said, 'Yes, I won't do it again,' and leave."

Eddie lit a cigarette and watched her walk into the tunnel until she disappeared into the darkness.

Meanwhile, at the church, Rosalie put a beer in front of Rooney and popped the cap on her own.

"So," she started, after taking a sip, "Heaven is like *The Matrix*?"

Rooney took the beer and stared at it. Being dead made you

thirsty, and this was the first drink he had since he returned.

"Only in the sense that you're sort of a battery, but they take pretty good care of you. It's not bad, to be honest." He realized this wasn't what he wanted to talk about. "Are you and Ed alright?"

"Yeah, why?"

"I could see you weren't happy with him, just now."

Rosalie sighed and leaned on her knees, one of only a few poses that didn't really become her.

"I'm not so much mad at him as I am at Helen. She knows what she did, and she pretends it's normal to just appear in our bedroom, acting like everything's peachy."

"I'm sorry, what did she do, exactly?"

"She slept with Eddie even though she knew he and I were a couple."

Rooney nearly jumped off the couch. "He actually had an affair with her? I thought it was a bad joke!"

"At the going away party. We don't know what actually happened, but I found Helen's panties in a drawer. I thought I was okay with it because we were so blackout drunk it might as well not have happened, but seeing her just now, acting like nothing happened..." She took another sip and shook her head. "Didn't go down well."

Her phone rang.

"Eddie?" She leaned back and crossed her legs. "Hm-hm... You don't say... Yes. So instead of taking me with you in the comfort of a car, I now have to grab my bike and paddle over... Yes, you should have brought me along... Okay, I'll be right over."

She ended the call, put her phone back, and got comfortable.

"What was that about?" Rooney asked.

"Dad locked Eddie in a cell and refuses to let him out because he thinks Eddie cheated on me when he was away."

"He did cheat on you, didn't he?"

"Technically, yeah. But Dad doesn't know that."

Rooney looked at her, calmly enjoying her beer.

"Shouldn't you, ehm... go?"

Rosalie chuckled. "In a minute. Let me just enjoy my beer first."

"Admit it," Rooney chuckled back, "this is a little bit about Helen, isn't it?"

"He didn't need to offer her a ride, no."

Rosalie winked and took her time enjoying her beer before getting up and leaving for the police station to convince her father to let her boyfriend out of jail.

Epilogue

A month later, Rosalie told Eddie to leave. Mind you, not because of anything he did, but the local gas station was not in the direction Rosalie would be going for the police academy. Eddie had left to go fill the tank up while she finished packing. They had a two-hour drive ahead of them and with mileage that was generally measured in feet, it meant Eddie preferred to start any trip with a full tank. Rosalie thought it was a good idea, in this case especially. Obviously, Eddie was on a first-name basis with the station owner, so she didn't feel like waiting in the car for fifteen minutes while the two did primal grunts and apelike vocalizations about muscle cars.

Not today. She was nervous enough about starting police academy, and it didn't help that Eddie made her sit through four movies that were only related to police academies because of the title. Rosalie mainly just rode them out to humor him; it wasn't her brand of funny.

She stared at the bag for a moment. It seemed like she should have packed more. It didn't feel right that she could fit everything in one bag. A big one, sure, but still. She didn't get a lot of time to think about it, as her deep logistic ponderings were canceled by a knock at the door.

"Come in, I'm decent."

"Oh... Never mind, then."

Though Asphyxia might not have been joking entirely, she came in anyway and promptly realized this was the very first time that she set foot in the bedroom. Brash as she might sometimes be, she did understand the concept of privacy very well. So well, in fact, that she now stood uncomfortably by the door and scratched the palm of her hand as she was wont to do when she was nervous.

"You were invited in," Rosalie said. "It's okay."

"Hm-hm, yeah, but it's weird. I kinda think about being in here sometimes, you know..."

"Yes. You were never subtle."

"I'm sorry, it's the hormones. Putting on make-up was one thing, taking it all the way is... bigger." Asphyxia puffed her cheeks and nodded to confirm to herself these were the words she wanted to use.

Rosalie smiled and put one of Eddie's Judas Priest shirts in her bag. Just in case she wanted to have him with her when he couldn't be there.

"I knew you before," Rosalie said. "Being a girl suits you better."

That made Asphyxia lunge forward and hug her like a baby monkey hugged its mother.

"Alright, alright." Rosalie tried to get free, and even though her father had shown her enough techniques to break free from most assailants, none of them covered vice-grip hugs. Eventually, before Rosalie lost consciousness, the problem solved itself, and Asphyxia let go to sit on the bed.

"So, you've no problem leaving me alone with Eddie?"

Rosalie stopped what she was doing and closely examined the girl. She tried to keep a big grin from popping onto her face, but eventually lost that battle and snorted when it did. "You and him would actually make a good couple. You're the same kind of crazy, which is why I have no problem leaving you two alone because you're also the same kind of reliable."

"Thank you for the vote of confidence!" Asphyxia seemed to appreciate that as if she wasn't expecting it.

"Of course--"

"So you won't mind if I sleep on your side of the bed while you're gone?"

Rosalie sighed. "See, same kind of crazy."

"Really, I promise it's just sleeping."

"Get out."

"Getting out."

Asphyxia got up and gave her a quick wink before heading out the door. Rosalie laughed and focused on her bag again. Even though she felt she packed too little, she took out a pair of casual-smart ankle boots. She didn't need to impress anyone but her instructors, and if they were the kind who needed to get impressed by her appearance, the training probably wasn't what Dad said it was. An extra pair of running shoes would come in far more handy, so she grabbed those, and when she turned to put them in the bag, Helen appeared before her in a flash of light. Rosalie jumped back and flung the shoes away, nearly hitting her.

"Jesus!"

"Oh, come on. You know I look nothing like him."

Rosalie shook off the shock and inhaled deeply to get her heart back into a normal rhythm. Someone just appearing right in front of you out of thin air and a flash of light that suggested something was very wrong with the closest socket tended to increase a person's heart rate.

"This is our bedroom!"

Helen waved Rosalie's words away. "Don't worry, I called ahead. Eddie said it was okay--"

"It isn't!" Rosalie snapped.

"Whoa there, sweetie. What's got your panties in a bunch all of a sudden?"

"*Your* panties!"

"Err... what?"

Rosalie picked up her shoes and angrily threw them in the bag. "I don't need the woman who fucked my boyfriend materializing in my bedroom!"

"Oh, those panties." A subtle curl of Helen's lip made Rosalie angrier.

"Don't you smile at me! If you were anybody else, I would slap you."

"You already did," Helen purred.

"That just sounded gross."

God or not, Rosalie wasn't going to stand for this downright arrogant behavior and got up in Helen's personal space.

"What kind of person leaves a message on used panties? Are you proud of yourself?"

"You really don't remember a thing from the party, do you?"

Rosalie started getting nervous. Helen meant *the* party, now seven months ago, when Rosalie and Eddie had just returned from the Underworld. Apparently, there were things in the moonshine-induced black hole that she needed to know about.

"What happened at the party?"

"I should be offended," Helen said, theatrically offended. "Am I that easily forgotten?"

Rosalie shrugged. "You're giving off the impression I was there watching, but even Eddie doesn't remember a thing, so--"

"Sweetie, Eddie wasn't here."

Rosalie pursed her lips, looked at Helen, and then felt her eyes drift slowly to the underwear drawer. As it started to dawn on her, she closed her eyes and rubbed the bridge of her nose.

"Ooow." She leaned on her knees and Helen saw it fit to support her.

"Are you alright, hon?"

"Yeah... Yup. I'm just..." She stood up straight and worriedly asked, "You didn't leave those panties for Eddie, did you?"

"There you go." Helen patted her on the back. "I left them for you. *Lover.*"

"Oh, god!"

"Yes, there was a lot of that."

"Oh, go-- uhh... Please stop talking."

Helen laughed out loud. Rosalie plopped down on the bed and genuinely looked troubled, so Helen sat down with her and carefully put an arm around her to gauge her physical response. Rosalie didn't shake it off, but so far, she was starting to feel worse.

"Hey, don't worry," Helen softly spoke. "I knew what we were getting into. I may have been a little drunk myself, or I would have stopped you. Maybe. But I don't expect you to be my girlfriend now."

Rosalie shot her an indignant look. "That didn't even once cross my mind!"

"Then tell me what's wrong, and we'll see how we can fix it. I owe you that much since I should have been the responsible one."

"We're not fixing anything! Fixing it means telling Eddie, and I've been giving him a hard time about having an affair with God!"

Helen tried not to laugh. That sounded ridiculous even in her ears.

"I can see you're trying not to laugh! Thanks for all the help. Have you ever seen how he looks at me? I can do no wrong as far as he's concerned, and now I'm gonna have to stomp all over this nonsensical angel-like image he has of me because I did not only have an affair, I've had it with someone he would've loved to have it with, *and* it turns out I'm the one who initiated it!"

Helen rubbed her back. "I wouldn't call it an affair. A one-time fling, at best."

"We're not calling it anything! I don't want to look him in the eyes and see him break when he finds out I'm not perfect. He doesn't need to know."

Helen got up and slowly walked through the room. Rosalie tried to remember seeing her do it back then, but apart from what her mind conjured up on the spot, there really was nothing.

"I know Eddie," Helen said. "I'm willing to bet this doesn't harm his opinion of you. After all, he already knows you don't like Judas Priest. How perfect are you really?"

Rosalie frowned at her, and Helen winked.

"Besides..." She put her hand on the door and gave it a short but firm push. It didn't swing open; instead, it stopped dead and sounded like it hit wood.

"Ow!"

Helen looked at Rosalie. "I think he already knows."

Eddie came into the room, rubbing his head.

"Eddie, hon. You should know by now not to eavesdrop behind heavy oak doors."

He looked at Helen, squinting his eye on the side where he'd been hit. "And you should know by now that learning from past mistakes is an alien concept to me."

Rosalie got up, worried about what would come next. The timing couldn't have been worse. The last thing she wanted on the day she left for the academy was an extra flood of emotions. Best case scenario, she was going to start her new career in the midst of a fight. Worst case, she'd start it single. And all because of a few too many drinks at a party that wouldn't have happened if she hadn't died and Eddie went to get her back. She wished she'd never been to the Underworld, now more than ever. That whole drama was the shitty gift that kept on giving shitty little pellets of more shit, culminating in the steaming pile right here in her bedroom now.

She felt so bad about blaming him for something she did that her lip started to quiver. Rosalie looked at the floor and muttered, "I'm sorry..."

Eddie went over and put an arm around her, though it was hardly as loving as it seemed. That's not to say there was no love, but the shit-eating grin on his face really didn't help.

"For what?" he asked.

"For sleeping with Helen and blaming you."

Helen gave Eddie a corrective slap on the head. "Stop torturing the only woman who will put up with you, shithead. You just want to hear her say it."

"Hm-hm," Eddie answered with a mile-wide smile. "I do."

"Well, you've seen what I do to people who piss me off, and you're pushing the limit."

"Alright, alright," Eddie turned so he faced Rosalie directly. "Babe, you could punt puppies into a meat grinder, and I would still have a high opinion of you. Also, somewhere during our time together, you might have noticed I'm a man. This," he pointed back and forth between her and Helen, "is not quite the issue for me that you think it is. I would sooner say that... how shall I put it? That this opens up a cornucopia of new possibilities, and if you really feel that bad about it, we've got a two-hour drive coming up we can use to discuss how you want to make up for it."

Helen poked him in the neck. She only used one finger, but when God's finger pokes you, your body does weird shit. As did Eddie's. The jolt he felt made his legs go "fuck it!" and he tumbled to his knees.

"There you go, dear," she said to Rosalie. "He's back on his knees for you. That's what Yoda was talking about. Me. I bring balance to the goddamn Force."

Still, being a benevolent deity, Helen helped Eddie up. "Try to guilt her into a three-way with me again, see what happens."

Eddie made no such attempts. He didn't want to spend the last two minutes of his life on Mars. Not that he was never going to try the threesome angle ever, but he'd discuss it with Rosalie like two grown adults. However hard acting like an adult was for him.

Rosalie did have a smile on her face again, and Eddie assured her a few more times that she really needn't worry. Still, she decided to change the subject. The upcoming drive would be filled with ample opportunity to talk this over.

"Why did you materialize in our bedroom anyway?" she asked Helen.

"I just came to wish you good luck. I know I'm partly the reason you've had an unconventional time, and I feel a little bit responsible for the whole bunch of you."

"God really is our co-pilot," Eddie mumbled.

Helen smirked at the idea. "I wouldn't even get in a plane with you if Rosalie was naked in the back."

Rosalie sighed. She expected more than one callback to this, but not from Helen's corner.

"If that was the case," Eddie rebutted, "I wouldn't have time to take off anyway."

"Right." Rosalie zipped the bag shut. "I'm gonna put the bag in the car. Fuck both of you. Bye."

Eddie grinned at Helen.

"What?"

"No? Fuck both of us-- Nothing?"

Helen smiled politely. "Juvenile. Eddie, you've got a good woman there. Look after her like she looks after you."

"Naturally. But we both know she doesn't need my help with anything."

"No, she doesn't," Helen grinned. "But it's always nice to know someone's got your back. See you around, Ed."

Eddie nodded. After Helen disappeared again, he stared at the door through which Rosalie had left just a few moments ago.

"Lucky bastard," he said to himself and left the room as well. On his way to the front, he beat his fist on Rooney's door.

"I'm going out for a long one. Don't open the door for strangers!"

"Only if they offer me candy! Wait…"

Eddie sighed. He didn't want to wait anymore. He had to be without Rosalie for a while, and the sooner he saw her off, the sooner she'd be back.

Rooney yelled through the closed door again. "Jonah says wish Rosie good luck."

"Will do."

Eddie left, and Rooney finally had peace and quiet in the usually lively church. This was definitely the best way to go on a quick dungeon raid with a friend.

He moved the headset mic back in front of his mouth. "I think technically you're an NPC."

Jonah laughed. "I'm literally in the game, yes, but I don't think I count as an NPC. Helen is making sure I'm comfortable, so she had IT connect me. It's quite amazing what they did, really."

"Playing a videogame beyond the barriers of life and death? Yeah, awesome. So you wanna talk tech or fuck up some ice trolls?"

"I'll take option B."

Between technology and ice trolls, ice trolls always won.

For more fun and nonsense visit
bakkerbaard.nl

ACKNOWLEDGEMENTS

Dunja Duys and Wendel de Haan
The original alpha readers, who soldiered on through the
unpolished first versions

The beta readers
Cal Laborde, Chris Chinchilla, Lucija Dupljak, Matt, Matthew,
Sarah Mae W

Lucy of the Latter Day Saints Helpdesk
Who patiently answered all my questions, even though I told her
what this book was about. The LDS are not affiliated with the
Current Day Saints, mainly because the CDS doesn't exist, but I'm
sure there's at least one asshole out there somewhere who thinks it
was a good idea.

The good people of WritingForums.org
Who also patiently keep answering my questions, whether
incoherent or inane.
It should be stated that they are not affiliated or endorse this book.